AFTER THE BEES

A REVELATION NOVEL

ALLISON PAIGE

Published in the United States by Finnegan Publishing Group
Printed in the United States of America

First printing edition 2019
Second printing edition 2022

ISBN: 979-8-9865593-0-8 (Paperback)
ISBN: 979-8-9865593-3-9 (ebook)

Cover art by India-Lee Crews

www.finneganpublishinggroup.com
www.authorallisonpaige.com

I

We shouldn't let our guard down. Anything can go wrong at a moment's notice, but it has been too long since I've held James this close. I run my fingers through his hair and pull him down to me. The broad span of his hand slides down my side to the curve of my hip. His hands are everywhere, followed by his lips.

I push his face back to catch his bright green eyes. "I love you," I say.

Something flickers across his gaze and his mouth quirks. He kisses me in response, hard and fast.

His hands harden, fingers encircling the entirety of my biceps. Squeezing. I bite his lip in my discomfort and flex, trying to get him to release me. The responsive bite is sharp. Razorblades cut into my mouth until I taste the warm flow of copper.

"James," I gasp. I push against him.

James is strong, but this is different. It hurts when he touches me. I can feel the bruises spreading under his touch. His nails dig into me. Even the slopes of his back are more defined, more powerful. They ripple as he presses against me.

He shoves his face next to mine and runs a lashing red tongue across my ear. "It's Leyak," he says. My heart slams against my chest and the thing above me chuckles. "Say it. Say *my* name."

We've been careful. They couldn't have taken James. I shut my eyes and twist to try and look at him. James' beautiful green eyes are so dark they're completely void of color or emotion. The bones in his face shift, narrowing his wide eyes into slits. His features sharpen into the face of a beautiful monster. The cool feel of his tan skin is like fire. I cry out as the smell of burnt flesh tinges my nostrils, but the only sound that escapes me is a strangled croak.

A taloned hand wraps around my neck. Another clamps to the inside of my thigh and shoves it to the side. "Scream for me," the monsters hisses.

I lurch forward, the scream lodged painfully in the back of my throat. I shove the invisible weight off and pull at my sweat-dampened clothes. It's just a nightmare.

A whoosh of air escapes my lungs. I can still feel Leyak's hands searching for new places to hurt me.

It takes a moment for my eyes to adjust to the slate-colored walls and realize I'm no longer in Michigan. Instead of a bed, I am laying on the stone-cold floor of a cave somewhere in the mountains. Leyak is only a memory. He can't hurt me anymore. I rest a shaking hand to my chest to steady my racing heart.

It has been three years since Leyak, and still he torments me.

I grab my journal from the bag I keep next to me. Writing has never kept the nightmares away, but it helps. I keep hoping that one day I will write the entry that finally makes all the bad disappear. I turn to the entry I wrote last week.

Fall 2031 - It started when the bees died. At first, no one worried because it was only out west in California, but then they started to die in the East. One by one they flew on the wind across the Atlantic. One by one they fell from the sky. It was as if they were running from something. Those who lived made it to the gardens people had prepared for them, but they only lasted a few months.

We were warned we couldn't survive without the bees. We had four years to live, they said, once they vanished. Within two months of the last sighting, we lost everything.

The harvests... well, there were no harvests. Grocery prices skyrocketed. I specifically remember apples shot up to $20 each. Livestock grew skinny and withered away. Scientists did everything they could to regenerate all we had lost but, before they could succeed, a plague swept the world.

It came like a swarm. It was so dark and deadly that the only thing we knew to call it was Sin. The Christians laughed at us. Sin was not a physical thing; it was something you did, not something you could grasp. They were wrong. Sin polluted the world, taking the form of many things: storms, boils, and darkness. Absolute darkness that filled the brightest day with dread. No one believed sin was palpable until they held their dead children. After that, they just screamed. We all did.

Some of us survived, immune to the black pollution. I prayed to God we hadn't. I prayed to anyone who would listen. If anyone did hear me, they turned a deaf ear.

Bodies piled up in the streets like mountains. The smell of rot was more overpowering than the thick smog of the plague that still hung in the air. If it was hard to breathe before, it was impossible then. There were no scavengers to eat the dead, but I once saw a woman picking at her lifeless infant.

James and I had a hard time finding food; animals were scarce and edible plants almost as hard to find, but we never stooped to picking over bodies. We weren't religious, but something about desecrating a human body unnerved us.

It wasn't long before they came. Or, others said "they woke". It's hard to say what actually happened.

It wasn't the apocalypse promised to us. It was so much worse.

These beings who overtook us, who still devour our minds and flesh, are not aliens. They are not zombies or vampires. They're demons. Worse than the ones they speak of in the Bible. They plague us more than any horror movie or novel could have prepared us for.

I snap the book closed. I'm pretty sure writing everything out is the reason for my nightmare. I should have let the memory be forgotten, but a part of me wanted my version of this horror story to be remembered. If I allow myself to forget what happened, I'll become complacent.

It's hard to remember everyone I've lost. More than anything, I miss James. I miss companionship. So much has happened since Leyak and the other demons overtook us. Sin is the only thing we can breathe and very few are able to withstand it. Those of us who can breathe the air are in hiding. The rest belong to Hell. I don't know why I even keep a journal. It's useless but a way to pass the time when I'm not running.

I haven't seen another human in three years. My journal has become my only companion, as there are no animals to befriend. I came across a dog once. I hated how it wagged its tail at me, but I was hungry and hadn't eaten in weeks.

I'm the minority who can survive this rotten world. I'm one of the immune. I do my best to stay hidden from man and monster alike. As long as I don't exist, I can't be hurt. Only on my own am I strong and able to live. I never believed in God. I never prayed to God before the Possession, but I do now. I beg Him to save us. Still, He doesn't answer.

What has happened in Heaven that we could be left like this?

Presently, I'm somewhere in Montana. I think. Between the mountains and plains, I found a place where no one can find me. No humans or demons live here. It's off the map, one might say. It hasn't been the best decision, I must confess. One day it snows and the next is blistering hot. This weather is maddening. Currently, there is a downpour obscuring my vision outside the little cave I've made home.

I shift to relieve the tension building in my lower back. Today would have been mine and James' six-year anniversary. It's the same day Leyak stole him from me. Maybe that is why the memory came back, why Leyak haunts me after so long. Even after all this time, I can't let go of the past. I can't escape the nightmares that drove me to the wilderness.

I tuck my journal beneath my arm and look out at the haze. I stand, stretching my legs one heel at a time. I should have stretched after working out. My joints protest as I pad to the back of the cave where I've let a fire burn down to the coals. I'm never too careful. I don't burn when it's dark unless it's freezing. If it's necessary that I do, I make sure my flames can't be seen.

I toss dried leaves over the coals and blow gently. My makeshift pit is around the corner, so even if anyone does see the cave, they won't be able to see the fire until they are inside. The flames bring precious heat to my cold hands.

I reach for my satchel and pause. Before my fingers touch the first piece of jerky, my stomach sinks. I'll have to go hunting soon. I'd been lucky to find the nest of rabbits, skinny little things. I thought I had better rations. I have enough to last me through the week. Beyond that, I only have five sweet-roots left. It's the one plant I've relied on for a constant meal, but lately it has gone scarce. I curse.

I toss my journal across the dirt and glare at it. I'd be lucky if anyone human found the damn thing. If they ever did, it means I was either dead or caught. I would never part with my journal willingly. I drum my bitten nails over the dirt for a moment, looking at it. I should get it. It's not fair to take out my frustration on the one thing I cherish most.

My bed is nothing more than a smooth part of the cave floor. I touch the back of my waistband, my thigh, and my boot to make sure my blades are accounted for. I learned a few survival tricks before leaving home. One of them was you can never have too many knives.

I've acquired quite the collection. Some are made for pockets while others are better suited for hunting. I always keep two hunting knives and one karambit on me. I've stashed others in various hideaways in and outside the cave because you never know.

Eventually, I fall asleep. The sound of something sniffing wakes me. Their warm breath huffs out over my face and neck and then gradually moves down the rest of my body. I open my eyes a slit, looking between my lashes to see it. It's too dark to tell. The fire has burned down to the coals. The face swings back up to mine and breathes in again.

Deft fingers pull the collar of my jacket away from my neck. It's a demon.

Most demons mark their territory on the neck, though I've known them to bite elsewhere.

Some humans who are taken are spared, though it's hardly salvation. They're used as tools to run Hell's bidding where a demon can't. I don't know all the details, but I heard if you are left unmarked, you're one of the lucky ones. A single bite from the damned will do it. They inject venom into us that not only overpowers us but binds us to whichever monster inflicted the bite. I think it might be better to be possessed by one, totally lost, than to be used as a game piece.

The monster above me purrs with satisfaction when it finds no mark. It presses its gritty lips against the side of my neck. I let my hand fall to the ground and touch the hilt of one of my knives. The beast either doesn't notice the movement or doesn't care, but still I wait. I can't strike when its mouth is hovering or on me. I'm not just afraid of the venom but of losing a part of my body I'd very much like to keep intact.

Its dirty hands pull at my clothes, lacing sharp teeth and claws through the fabrics so they will tear. I pull the knife from its hiding spot as the demon moves lower. Its breath blows across the flat of my stomach, followed by a coarse tongue.

As soon as the tongue retracts, I strike. I thrust the blade up into its neck. The demon stiffens, but I'm already prepared for it. I grab it by the hair and thrust again, sliding the blade into a softer part of its neck.

The demon stumbles back, digging its claws into my chest, and screams as wetness spurts from its throat onto my face. I lunge forward and push and pull the blade again and again. Hands cling to my shoulders, and sharp nails tear into my flesh as I fall on top of it, but the unnatural strength I expected quickly fades. The fingers fumble to push me away, no longer fighting. It curses me with garbled words, lashing out with a long, red tongue. I've done a good job of severing most of the neck so it can't speak or scream. I thrust the blade into the sternum and up, pushing with all my strength and with a grunt.

The demon convulses and the flailing ceases. I push off from the body and slam back into the wall. The air smells of decay and sulfur. It fastens to me, stains my skin and clothes. My stomach rolls in protest. I swallow the bile that rises into the back of my throat, coughing to keep it down.

The rush of adrenaline coursing through my blood fades and reality sets in, along with pain. Deep puncture wounds run from the top of my shoulders down to my collarbones. I fumble in the darkness for my bag. I've got to stop the bleeding.

How did it find me? I have been careful not to leave evidence of not only my whereabouts but my very existence. I groan inwardly. It could have been anything now that I think about it. Even losing a strand of my hair in the woods could have led the monster right to me. I always keep it twisted in a knot, but two days ago I took it down when I went for a swim. I touch over it now, my fingers skimming over the brown locks that touch my shoulders. I never put it back up.

I'd thought, *What harm could leaving it down for a little while do?*

I wince as I press a piece of cloth to each of the wounds. I've nothing to hold the dressing in place.

Fuck, that's not the worst of it. The wounds are bad enough that it will be difficult to climb or do any strenuous work until they heal. I slip on my leather jacket in hopes that the added pressure will secure the poor bandages.

Such a careless mistake nearly killed me. I wind my hair into a bun with shaking hands. Strands of hair stick to the blood that covers them.

I slide down the wall, not once taking my eyes from the dark mass in the corner of the cave. I should run, but what if it has companions? My vision has improved, but I still can't see well at night. If there are others, they'll be sure to catch me before I even know I'm being hunted. If I run, I'm at risk. If I stay, my fate is the same.

Hours tick by. My eyes play tricks on me as the shadows of the night move. I think I hear things, but I convince myself it's all in my head. The foul stink of decay thickens the air the longer the night drags on. The tremors in my hands grow worse.

At first light, I gather my belongings and stuff them in a single rolled bag. I haven't taken my eyes off the body all night, in case it somehow heals and wakes with a vengeance. Once I thought it had, but when I stabbed it nothing happened. I can't wait around any longer, though. I've got to move.

I'd been lucky to find this place. Now it's ruined. If one demon could find it, so could others. I can only hope luck will be on my side as I leave the cave I've called home for the last three months. I'll have to move away from the river. If the demon does have a friend, it's the first place they will look. I always keep an extra supply of water on hand, but I don't like moving away from the source.

I toss my pack over my shoulder.

"Leaving so soon?"

I spin around. Not to the demon lying dead on the cave floor but to another who stands at the entrance. I wasn't the only one waiting for morning, it seems.

He is heavily shadowed in front of the dusky forest. He *tsk*s and wags his finger at me when I reach for the knife at my back. The blood drains from my face down to my feet as the monster approaches. He smirks and, reflexively, I tighten my hold over the hilt. It's hard to see where he is looking when his eyes are so black, but I can feel him give me a once over before he turns his head to the demon in the back of the cave. I turn with him, unbuttoning the snap holding my knife, as he walks by.

"You will not have as much luck with me as you did with my friend," he says without looking at me. "I will let you keep your knives, but if you try to use them on me, I will break every bone in your body and use them against you." He crouches low, his hand skimming over the demon but not touching it.

He looks back at me. I push the snap back into place and remove my hand, folding it with the other in front. His power is overwhelming, like a dark storm full of hail and lightning. The power in his gaze stills me. How do I get out of this? It's a stupid question that brings my heart to the back of my throat. I can't escape, not without a bite or this new creature inserting one of his other friends inside of me. I should have taken my chances under the cover of darkness.

"What is your name?" He stands, his shadow swallowing the light across the cave floor. He looks back at the mangled body and frowns. The fallen demon could not have been older than sixteen. I've killed younger.

"Leah," I answer softly.

"Leah, you have killed someone very close to me."

"It was going to bite me."

He nods as he approaches me. "What gave you the right to defy him? Hm?" He grabs my chin roughly and turns it up. His full lips turn back in disgust as I recoil. "Perhaps I should give you one of my own. Ah, ah, you will keep your hands where they are or I will rip your jaw from your pretty little face." I pull back my hand as soon as he catches me reaching for my karambit.

I swallow. I've seen humans with missing parts. They looked like zombies as they ran around doing Hell's business. It was grotesque. The demons didn't even find amusement in it. They did it because they could.

"Are you the only one?" he asks, lifting his face to sniff.

"Yes," I say through gritted teeth.

"I thought so," he says, letting me go. "Surprising. How long have you been here?" He looks around the cave, searching for something.

I wonder who he is and who the body belonged to before he inhabited it. The demon has an unnatural beauty, but I wonder how much of it is human and how much is fallen. He towers over my average build by at least seven or eight inches. His black hair brushes his shoulders in faint waves. Like the rest of him, it's well-kept and clean. His skin is a dark gold; it shines too much to be tan. And his face is perfectly chiseled with a high brow and wide-set cheek bones that would be best suited for someone indigenous.

"Who are you?" I ask. Fear makes my voice tremble, so I try to sound brave when I say, "I should know who is going to take me." I was a coward the last time a demon robbed me. I am not the same woman I was three years ago.

Amusement then greed flashes across his bottom-less eyes. This is a monster who likes to play with his food. The realization makes my legs weak and the lump in my throat tighten.

"Raum," he says with a smirk.

"And the man?"

The smirk stretches into a sneer. "The man is no more." His pitless eyes flit over me and he nods towards the entrance. "Come, you have a pyre to build." He brushes past me with intent and stops a few feet outside of the cave to see if I'm following.

II

It's late into the evening by the time we finish building the pyre. By we, I mean me. Raum makes me cut down the branches, handing me a much bigger blade to do the chopping. It's one of my own, a kukuri I kept hidden in the forest. The long, curved blade is not made for cutting wood, but who I am to tell a demon otherwise?

My shoulders scream in protest, begging that I stop the hacking, but I don't dare. Though he seems unfazed that I might try something, the constant weight of his gaze keeps me in line. I won't strike while he watches me so carefully. Not yet.

Once I've completed the hard work, Raum extends his hand to me. I tighten my grip on the kukuri before handing it over. The smooth wood of the handle slides from my grasp into his.

I listen halfheartedly when he tells me how to arrange the branches so a body can lie across the top. Honestly, the idea of burning the demon in ceremony is ridiculous. It deserves to rot. I'd say it could burn in Hell, but those gates weren't hot enough to hold them to begin with.

Raum carries the body out and lays it over the assortment of wooden arms. He makes me light the fire, which proves to be the most difficult part of the ordeal.

The wood is saturated from the rain. It takes me two hours to get it to smoke. I have to do a lot of digging around the cave to find anything remotely dry.

Raum watches me with an expression that cools my blood whenever I get the idea of running. When the idea first came to me, I turned around to flee only to find him waiting behind me. He tilts his face up and sniffs, no doubt smelling the blood that has oozed through the cloth across my shoulders. The more I work, the harder it is for me to move. My wounds scream, but I know better than to complain to a demon. This is nothing compared to the suffering he can inflict.

We stand beside the orange glow, the only sound between us being the water popping free of the wood. I pull a bandanna from my bag to tie over my face as the smell of burnt flesh fills the air. Raum is unperturbed by the stench. He hums a song that instantly fills me with dread and solace. I grow despondent as I listen.

"Leah, you look troubled."

"Your song," I start to say, but I don't know how to finish. I shake my head. It's more than the song that bothers me. I understand building the pyre might be punishment for killing the demon, but that can't be the only thing this monster intends for me to do. The way he looks at me suggests he has bigger plans.

Leyak left me unmarked because it was more fun. That's what he told me, at least. Leyak didn't have a good sense of control. He preferred to feed off my fear over me falling under his influence by mistake. I'd seen it before, humans who did things according to a demon's desire without realizing it.

It's clear Raum has similar tastes, though his reasoning seems different. He is intimidating but not spiteful. Still, the question taunts me.

"Why haven't you bitten me?" I ask.

Raum takes his time before turning his attention towards me. "Would you like me to do it now? I can lay you out beneath the flames. I do not think I could bite you just once, though," he adds suggestively, the fire reflecting in his eyes.

My nose curls and my lips draw back. Heat pools down my face, into my neck. Demons are vulgar, disgusting creatures. I'm grateful he can't see either response behind my bandanna. I don't want him to take the red stain on my face as a blush of invitation. The idea of him touching me makes my skin crawl, and a visible chill runs through me.

Raum chuckles and moves closer to me. "Is that fear or anticipation?" he hisses.

"Neither," I snap. My feet are rooted to the ground. I can't bring myself to move as he reaches for me.

He tugs the bandanna down. His eyes skim my face before he tucks a stray piece of hair behind my ear. I see my reflection in his eyes, standing small beneath him as he lowers his face. My narrow face is pale despite how tan my skin is. Dirt and dried blood hide the few freckles on my cheeks.

Raum presses his lips against my skin. Warm air caresses the slope of my neck as his lips part to make way for blunt human teeth. I stiffen. The pressure hardens and I'm torn between being afraid that his teeth will turn into fangs and poison me and whether he will break my skin with his dull bite.

I should try to kill him now, but his teeth on my skin hold me in suspense. I'm scared. This is actually going to happen and I'm not even brave enough to fight back. All the strength from last night has been sapped by my fear, or some power Raum has over me. His teeth don't sharpen, so I don't reach for my knife. We wait to see what the other will do first.

Raum growls softly, bringing more chills to my skin. He replaces his teeth with his tongue, running over the indention he has made as if he means to repair any damage done. His breath trails up to my ear and he gives it a nip, chuckling whenever I jump.

"Have you ever been with one of us?" he asks.

I push him away abruptly and instinctively touch my neck. He hasn't poisoned me. Not yet.

Raum grins wickedly. He reaches for me again, snaking a strong arm around my waist. His fingers dig into my hip and mine dig into the hilt of my knife. I draw the blade on him, slashing my karambit through the air towards his throat. Quicker than lightning, he grabs my wrist and twists so sharply that I cry out, dropping the knife. Raum's grip tightens until I yell mercy.

He shoves me to the ground, pressing the weight of his chest into my back until my legs slip out from under me. I crawl forward, throwing an elbow back when his face swoops next to mine. Raum hauls me back by the waistband. He deflects my sharp kicks and pushes me on my stomach. Cold fear grips me as I struggle to pry myself out from under his weight. He tugs at my waistband again and I twist, trying to buck him off me.

"Stop moving," he hisses. He wrenches the knife from my belt and then takes the one from my boot. "Do you have any others?"

It takes me a moment to realize that he isn't about to force himself on me. I turn my head to the side to get a look at him as he runs his hands across my back. They move up to my shoulders and I stifle a sound of pain as he presses into the wounds left by his companion. Raum pushes me over, his eyes making another quick inspection over my front.

"That's it," I whisper.

His glare hardens and he unzips my jacket where he finds yet another knife and two wire cords. He pockets the cords and discards the knives into my bag before throwing it out of my reach. "And now?"

I nod. "Yes. I promise."

"Perhaps I should be more thorough," he says, slipping his hand under my shirt.

"Stop," I hiss whenever his fingers brush my stomach. "I swear that was the last one." My voice breaks, which leaves a satisfied smirk on his face.

To my surprise, Raum removes his hand and sits back on his heels. We sit in silence, me watching the fire and he watching me. I tuck my hands between my thighs so he can't see how bad they shake. I should have run. He might have killed me, but at least I wouldn't be waiting in suspense for his intentions. It doesn't make sense that he hasn't tried anything yet. He doesn't even seem angry that I killed another demon. Didn't he mention it was his friend, or brother?

As if picking up on my thoughts, Raum speaks. "How did you manage to kill Culsu?"

I notice how close he is to me before saying any-thing. This could be the time he chooses to strike, de-pending on how he reacts to what I'm about to say. I shouldn't tell him it was easy. I've fought with demons before, but I've never been fortunate enough to kill one so easily.

"I took it by surprise." I glance at him then turn away quickly. "I don't know." I'm not lying, if Raum can even pick up on lies. Complying with him will bide me more time.

"You took *him* by surprise," he corrects me. I had assumed the demon was male before but couldn't be certain. As far as I know, they jump into whatever body is available. Demons are not particular when it comes to wearing our skin.

Now that we are discussing Raum's friend, the de-mon had been very skinny, weak. I imagine if Raum had found me first, last night's events would have played out differently. Culsu had been slow and frail. Meanwhile, Raum is healthy and made of rippling muscle. He is, without a doubt, the biggest demon I have ever seen.

"We were passing through when he wandered off. Culsu was young, and when he was hungry he could not be contained until he was satisfied." Raum's eyes seem to glow red as he looks back at me. A new energy surrounds him like a dark cloud, and I tense, waiting for him to make a move. My flight senses kick in, but it's as if he has me under some spell, as if I'm rooted to the ground. "I suppose you were lucky. For a woman, I am surprised you marked him at all."

"He wasn't that strong." I don't know what makes me say it, the fact that he is being condescending because of my gender or my mortality. Either way, it bothers me. I feel the need to defend myself.

"He was stronger than you, little girl," he purrs.

I disagree. I notice the worry line between his brows. "Why haven't you bit me? Honestly."

"I think it's more fun if you're willing," Raum says.

I suck my teeth. "You'll be waiting a long time."

Laughter fills the air around us. It's a beautiful sound I have always hated to love. When demons laugh it is the sound of wooden drums, iron bells, a choir singing in perfect harmony. It is the sound of perfection.

He cocks his head. "I don't think so. How long have you been on your own?"

"That doesn't mean anything."

"Answer the question," he says smoothly.

Raum is the strangest creature. I never imagined that coming face to face with another demon would turn out like this. I heard they liked to play with their victims, but having a conversation with them is unheard of. Perhaps Raum is playing some game with me, lulling me into a state of comfort. Although it's hard to be anything but terrified of him.

"Three years," I finally say.

Raum's eyes widen. "You have been out here for three years?" His lips remain parted even after he asks the question.

I shrug. "I've only been in the cave for a few months." He continues to look at me, as if he is waiting patiently for the finer details. I humor him. It's been a long time since I have spoken to anyone, be it friend or foe. What harm could it do? "Before then, I picked up pretty frequently and moved around. I never stay in one place for too long. I don't want to get caught." I say the last part with a little laugh.

"What made you stay here?" he asks, tilting his head.

"My whole time in this part of the country, I haven't seen any signs of humans or demons. I thought it must be remote enough that no one else had thought to come here. This place was perfect. What little edible plants grow flourish, and there is a river about two miles away. Animals are scarce, but I've been lucky." And now my little sanctuary is ruined. I knew better. If I had kept moving, like all those other times, I wouldn't be in this situation.

"Why are you out here?" Demons tend to keep to larger cities. Humans are their main source of food when they do not inhabit us. Not everyone had the opportunity to run like I did. It took me a year to escape Leyak.

"We were going to Babel. It is a place where you can speak to the gods freely," he says, still staring. Has he even blinked? His eyes are burrowing through my clothes, through my skin.

"I've heard of it." By gods he means God and the devil and any other deities who believe they are entitled to the power of the universe. I don't know how true any of this is, but it's what I heard before I went into hiding. After all, I believe that if the demons can rule the Earth, God must not care about us anymore.

"You look tired, Leah."

Now that he mentions it, I'm very tired. I didn't sleep at all last night and hardly slept the night before. The smell of rot still pollutes the air and makes my stomach churn. "I have your friend to thank for that."

"Let us go back to the cave," he says, rising to his feet. "You need to rest before the sun comes up." He tosses my bag over his shoulder and starts to trek up the incline.

Once again, I follow him. Mostly because I'm curious and partially because I'm not going anywhere without my knives. I could look for the others I have hidden away, but I doubt Raum will let me get very far. His threat of breaking my bones and leaving me to die comes back as a whisper through my head. I pause as the voice strokes a quiet part of my mind. Can demons read minds? I'd never considered it before, but Raum might be different than the others. Everything must be possible when it comes to demons.

There is no way I'm going to fall asleep tonight. Last night, I was afraid a dead monster would rise and attack me. Now there is a live one intending to stay the night with me. I don't believe for a second that Raum won't try something while I'm asleep.

The blood has long dried; the ground drank what it could. Only a light whiff of sulfur tickles my nose as I stop at the edge of the cave. I know Raum is somewhere inside, but I can't see where he has gone.

"Afraid of the dark?" His voice reaches out through the darkness, taunting me.

"I don't trust you," I call, but take a hesitant step forward.

"I won't bite you tonight. I promise." The smile creeps at the edge of his voice.

I'm sure he is a fine liar.

I take a couple more steps until I'm completely enveloped by the blackness. I can't see him, but I can feel him. There's an overwhelming dread that thickens the air.

He comes from behind. His touch is so soft that I don't even jump. He runs his hands along my arms and pulls my back against his chest. His breath deepens against my ear and he gives it a little nip. "Your fear is delicious," he hisses.

Instinctively, I reach for the blade I keep at my back. He laughs behind closed lips and slides around me like a snake. He takes my hand, leading me farther into the cave where, though I could not see before, it seems even darker. Fear's affliction takes hold of me and I breathe harder. My chest constricts, tight as a fist.

"Lie down, Leah. For tonight, you're safe," he says.

It's hard to breathe. I have to hold onto him while I find my knees, and then my stomach. It's cold tonight. I won't have to worry about him hurting me if I freeze first.

I have never been more afraid to fall asleep. Raum wraps around me as he lies at my back. His limbs are like shackles that pin me down, holding me firmly to him. While his heat soothes my chills, I can't control the fear that grows stronger with each breath. Blind, afraid, and at the mercy of a demon, it will be a miracle if I wake up again.

III

Raum's lips brush across my neck. I open my eyes and let them adjust to the dim light. Morning has found me. Sweet heaven above, how is this possible? I turn over, away from the wall the demon so cleverly wedged me near, and look at him.

His face hovers over mine as he looks down at my neck. Those hungry black eyes envelope me. Though he doesn't touch me, I can feel him roving over every inch of my body. I swallow.

"Are you having second thoughts?" I ask. I pull my collar up against my ear.

"I'm tempted," he says. "Your wounds make it difficult to resist." He rolls away from me. "Get up. We are leaving."

I squint, my face betraying my confusion. He picks up my bag and slings it over his shoulder. I watch him walk to the mouth of the cave before I jump to my feet.

"Where are *we* going?" I ask.

"To Babel," he says matter-of-factly.

"Why the hell should I go with you?" I brush the dust from my clothing and follow him down the hill, past the pyre. It's nothing but a pile of smoking ash. My canteen is strapped to the side of the bag. I suspect the rest of my food is still somewhere underneath the flap. I want to rip the bag from him.

"Because you belong to me now. I decide your fate. I will bite or kill you when the time comes. Be careful what you say," he says quickly as I open my mouth for a retort. "You don't want me to make that decision sooner. Do you?" He flashes a satisfied smirk.

"I'm not a piece of property! I'll come with you because the first chance I get, I am going to take *my* bag off your back and I'm out of here. If you wanted to kill me, you would have done it already. I know you eat us when you're desperate enough." I grab his arm and give it a hard squeeze. "You're healthy. You probably ate a day or so before you found me. How many people did you eat to get so strong?"

Raum snatches my hand before I can pull it away and jerks me toward him. "Not enough to satisfy my hunger. It is a long way to Babel. Across the mountains, an entire ocean, and more land in between. Perhaps I'm saving you for a snack." He leans forward, his eyes sweeping down my front. He bites the air in front of my face.

I punch him. He doesn't flinch, but my throw was hard enough to redden his cheeks and then twist it into a mask of fury. Raum bends my fingers back and I scream. He presses them a hair from breaking.

"Stop! Please! Raum. Please. Don't break them. Don't break them!"

I try not to move in his grasp in fear that anything I do will finish the job for him. I'm nothing without my hands. Without my knives, I feel naked, but if he breaks my fingers I'll be useless. It would be worse than if he killed me.

He slings my hand away. I cradle it to my chest, curling my aching fingers against my shirt. The world blurs around me as I tremble. Raum's throaty laugh taunts me. How could he do this? That's a stupid question. The fact he is showing me any mercy is a miracle.

"Look at me."

What is he going to do with me?

"Leah," he snaps.

I swallow and turn my brimmed eyes to him.

"For the rest of our time together, you are going to be a good little girl. Hm? This bag and what is in it belongs to me now, just like you. You may have none of it unless I give it to you. You will not steal from me. If you run, I will hunt you down and drag you back screaming. If you attack me, I will break your hands. If you do anything to displease me, I will hurt you. Do you understand?" Raum's voice is cold, violent. Any kindness he might have shown me before is gone. His eyes are full of controlled fury as he looms over me.

I nod. "Yes," I choke. I look down as he stares. I shuffle forward, following him without protest.

Raum's anger continues to poke and prod me, keeping me in a constant state of fear and numbness. He projects it from time to time, culling me into submission. During our hike, I fall behind. I'm careful not to drift too far away, though, in case he should release his wrath. Not once does he look back to see if I'm following. He knows his threat was cruel enough to keep me in line.

We follow the river I mentioned to him for hours before he stops. I come up short and look around, wondering if he has seen or heard something my ears can't detect. My fear has turned to anger and I plot against him. All I need is one knife.

The sun will set in a few hours. I've been so wrapped up in my mind that I haven't noticed we've been walking most of the day. I lick my lips and smooth my tongue over the roof of my mouth to try and get moisture flowing. Raum let me drink twice from the canteen, but neither sips were enough to sate me.

I've never been this far down the river. The water hasn't receded, but the shore is devoid of ferns and moss. Everything is brown and dead orange. The only plants holding onto their green are the pines and a few others I'm unfamiliar with. It's chilly out but not freezing. It's as if even the plants don't know what season it is.

"We will rest here. You should clean yourself up." He nods to the water and looks at the trees. I follow his gaze through the bare branches, but I can't see anything.

"Are we staying the night?" I look at the wide set trees and shallow bank. Even though I don't have to worry about anyone finding me, I'm not comfortable with the idea of sleeping in the open. I like to feel protected and there is nothing this forest can offer me. It feels sick, barren. The trees grow tall and skinny, the undergrowth limited. There is nowhere to hide.

"No. We will keep going into the night, but away from the river. Clean up and drink." He passes me the canteen and moves farther down the bank. I bring my hand up. Culsu's blood has crusted over my face and clothes. It would be nice to wash it off.

Raum slings the bag over a branch and slips his shirt off. I can't help but stare. His physique is definitely superhuman, taut with muscles no normal mortal has. It's like someone has cut into him, chiseled him into the perfect killing machine. He undoes the buckle of his belt and pauses. His hands have stopped moving so I work my eyes up his stomach and chest and face...

"See something you like?" he asks when I meet his eyes. I blush, embarrassed and angry at myself because not only did he catch me staring, I had been looking in the first place.

"I see a thief and feel sorry for the man you stole from," I say.

"I assure you, Leah, that this body is all mine. I have inhabited it long enough that it is identical to my likeness." He pulls his belt apart and looks at me suggestively. "You can touch me if you like."

I scrunch my face. "You're disgusting," I say, walking in the opposite direction.

"Don't go where I can't see you."

"I won't run." I glance back at him and away quickly as he shoves the denim over his hips. I stalk off with a sense of urgency and am relieved when he doesn't call or chase after me. I won't run. Not yet.

I grumble to myself as I rip my clothes off and drape them over a tree. Of all the demons to find me, it had to be Raum. Any other would have done their business by now. Either I'd cease to exist or I'd happily serve under his mark. Either would be better than suffering like this.

I wade into the chilled water. My breath hitches as the water curls over my hips and stomach, pulling me down into a breathtaking embrace. Beneath the water, I find a moment of peace. I stay there, listening to the rippling above me, the smaller stones moving in its current.

I scrub the blood from my body, both Culsu's and my own. The water stings my wounds, but it feels better once they're clean. The shallow slices over my collarbone have already started to mend, but on my shoulders, where Culsu's talons punctured me, are nasty divots.

I crawl up the face of a stone where there is a broad band of sunlight. I wring out my hair, combing the tree line for any signs of Raum. I ease down on my back. It's foolish of me to let my guard down so easily, but Raum already has me. There is nothing else for me to fear.

A restless feeling that I'm being watched keeps me on edge. I sit up. As soon as I do, every hair on the back of my neck stands up. Across the river, Raum is turning away. He doesn't make a sound as he moves through the forest, and my heart hammers. I *never* heard him. How long had he been standing there watching me?

I wait until he is out of sight before I hurry to my clothes and quickly slip them on. I glance around the bank for a weapon, deciding on a jagged rock not much bigger than my palm. I slip it into my pocket and pull my shirt down to hide the bulge.

Raum is waiting for me at the top of the bank when I make it back. Demons, with their dark eyes, always look hungry, but unless I'm imagining things, he looks starved as he takes me in. I zip my jacket up to my neck.

Once the sun sets, it's dark. *Dark*, dark. There is no moon to light our way and I'm forced to hold onto Raum, lest I trip or run into something. At first, I hold onto his arm, but then he slides his hand into mine and laces our fingers together. A completely unnecessary move that makes him chuckle whenever he notices my discomfort.

We don't stop walking until it's night again. I've made long journeys before, but never without sleep. My feet drag and my eyes grow heavy. He lets me rest from time to time, but it's not enough. I can hardly stand.

I stumble into Raum, jerking awake, looking around wildly to try and figure out where we are. There's only darkness, shadows upon shadows. He turns to me and takes my face in his hands. His touch is a whisper and then, suddenly, I'm floating. My legs are swept out from under me and my head falls back. I give in to the darkness and fall into a pit of dreams full of fiery storms.

When I wake, it's to a fire burning in front of my face at midday. I listen. Raum's deep breath comes from behind me, but I can't tell if he is asleep. Do demons sleep? I roll onto my back and crane my head. His back is to me and it expands slowly with the yawning inhale of dreams. My bag is tucked beneath his head.

I bite my lip and sit up slowly, assessing the situation. The fire looks new, at least an hour old. There is fresh wood between the flames that hasn't yet been burned. Raum could very well be asleep, or he could be pretending. If he is asleep, he might be a light sleeper. Demons have acute senses and, if he doesn't wake up immediately, I don't doubt it would only take a few minutes for him to realize I've run off. I could leave without my weapons, but that would be stupid. Raum would catch me, and I'd feel more confident if I had at least one knife on me.

I stand and walk a few feet. Still, he doesn't move. I touch my thigh. The rock is gone, removed while I was unconscious. I bite my lip to stop the curse from slipping out.

Before I decide to run, I need to figure out where we are. This forest is hillier than the one by the river and I don't know how long I've been asleep, or if he has changed directions on me. We should be heading west.

I pull myself between the trees as I work my way up a slope. I slip on a dry patch of leaves and it sends a wave of them down below. Raum still sleeps. I allow myself to smile with relief as I watch him. When he doesn't move after I've counted to one hundred, I continue my climb.

Once I reach the top, my heart sinks. There is nothing but an open forest littered with skinny white trees.

I make my way back down to the makeshift camp. The fire still burns but Raum is gone. I brush my palms over the thighs of my pants. Please don't let him think I've run off. My heart beats faster and I pick up the pace, trying not to run. Running will make me look guilty.

My bag has been left unattended. As tempting as it is to pilfer through it, I don't take the bait and sit down on the opposite side of it. I know he is somewhere watching, waiting patiently so he can hurt me. If he does, it won't be because I gave him a reason.

I don't have to wait long before he reappears. He makes no sound as he comes up behind me, but I can feel his presence towering over me. I slowly stand, not wanting to be on the ground if he does strike, and face him.

"Back already?" he asks.

"I just wanted to see where we were," I say evenly.

"To run away."

"You've made it clear what will happen if I do. You know I didn't even touch my bag."

Raum smirks. "Take what food you need out of it. When you've eaten, you may choose one knife." I give him a dumbfounded look as he brushes past me. "There is a small herd of deer close by. I will allow you to hunt with me for your good behavior."

I scowl as I catch the tossed bag. "How kind of you," I mock. I fish out a large strip of jerky. My mouth waters as the flavor washes across my tongue.

In addition to the knives he found on my person, I kept two others in my bag. I lay them out in a line and, though I already know which one I'm going to choose, I give him a little show before making my selection. Raum never takes his eyes off me as I run my finger over each blade and hilt until I come to the hunting knife I generally keep at my waist. The handle is made of bone and the blade is made of Damascus steel. I like it for its appearance, but it has also been my most effective and trustworthy tool.

"Why do you choose that one?" Raum asks as I reattach the sheath to the back of my belt.

"It's good for gutting and skinning after we've caught something. Plus," I say as I tuck my shirt in, "it's the best weapon I have for defense if anything should happen." I say the last part evenly. As if he will take my threat seriously. He should.

I watched Leyak use the same knife on James time and again. I know it can cut flesh like paper, dice intestines like vegetables, and cut into me so gracefully it wasn't until I saw the blood that I realized I was bleeding. One of Leyak's torments was to let James out so he could torture him in front of me. I know exactly what this knife is capable of and how to wield it. I stole it from Leyak so I could use it to kill demons like him. I wish I had used it on him before I fled.

Raum's eyes sweep over my body and he brushes against me, moving me in the direction he chooses. "Don't worry. I won't let anything happen to you." He runs his hands over my waist. "I have a request."

I swallow and turn carefully. His face is too close to mine and I don't want to accidentally brush my nose and lips across his. My hesitation makes him smile and he leans closer. I take a step back.

"Yes?"

"Not now," he says. "Just know I will ask you later and that I hope you will consider it." He gives one side of my hip a little squeeze and then moves away. I watch him go for a few yards before following, not sure whether to be curious or frightened by his future inquiry.

IV

The herd is nothing more than three small does. All are too scrawny, their ribs and spines sticking out beneath their mangy coats. If we are both going to eat, we will have to kill them all. Two for Raum, one for me. He will likely eat most of the third one too. There's no breeze, so it's no trouble to approach them without them noticing. I worry that when the wind does come through, we will be on the wrong side of it.

"How would you catch them?" Raum asks.

I scan the ground between us and them. "I'd set a snare, or if there was more time dig a pit. I'm not quick enough to tackle one." This is one of those moments I wish I kept a gun or bow. Knives seemed like the smartest weapon at the time. They are manageable and easy to disguise, but they're useless when it comes to hunting larger prey. Besides, this is the first sign of deer I've seen in two years. I'd thought for sure they had died out.

I hate the way Raum looks at me, as if he genuinely appreciates me. I'd like to go back to him being cruel. I can't believe that thought even enters my mind. I shift under his eyes as I go over various plans. None of them will work.

I bite the inside of my lip and concede. "After you," I say thinly.

The corner of his mouth twitches and he gives me a curt nod. He moves down the slope like an apparition, slinking soundlessly, nearly fading in and out of the surrounding shadows. Is he crazy? I open my mouth to scold him but know my voice will startle the deer. He takes slow steps, breaking leaves, but he might as well be floating over them because they make no sound under his weight.

One of the deer notices. Her head and tail come up in unison, but instead of bolting she tosses her head. Her nostrils flare. The snort alarms the other two to stand erect. All three sets of eyes widen; the stark white rings stand out even from where I stand. I glance at Raum.

He walks right up to them. The lead doe tosses her head with a threatening stamp of her cloven hoof. It's bizarre, the way they stand there instead of running.

Chills sweep across my skin as they lower themselves. All three buckle a front leg and bow to Raum. One at a time, their noses brush against the dirt. Their flanks quiver. They come up in unison and focus on the demon as if in a trance.

Raum motions to me and I head down. Unlike him, I make a ruckus. Branches snap and leaves crunch under my boots. Not once do the deer take their eyes off him.

"What is this?" I whisper as I step behind him. He turns his hand out at his side. I wrap my hands around his arm and peer around him. I don't need to hold onto Raum, but I must. This is too eerie. Something isn't right.

"They think I am a god," he muses.

I look between them. They are not entranced by power. I don't know how, but the animals are hypnotized. I let him go and brush my hands off to keep the same glamour from my skin.

"What have you done to them?"

"Nothing," he says, opening his arms. "I have the same effect on all mortals." His black eyes swallow me whole. "Except you, Leah. You're too wise to accept anything I could offer you."

Before I have the chance to ask what he means, he touches my arm and tells me to take my kill. I look between them. They're rigid like soldiers at attention, ears perked forward.

It's a sacrifice. The notion chills me. Even so, I touch my blade and pull it out slowly. Still, the deer do nothing.

I approach the first one and touch its shoulder. Her nostrils flare as she snorts. I can feel her fear trembling under my palm. This isn't a way to die, but we need to eat and food, especially meat, is scarce.

I slice her throat.

The others falls at the same time.

"My gosh," I choke. I step away as their blood soaks into the earth. Their hollow stares look too much alive as they finally see me.

Raum drags the smallest to the side and nods to me. "Take what you need. Don't worry about cleaning the bones. I will eat those."

I touch the face of the deer and look over the body half-heartedly. I should be grateful for the food, but I know I only have it because of dark magic, because of Raum.

I cut out the stomach and lay the entrails to the side. I can feel his eyes on me. There's nothing special with what I do, so I don't know why he looks at me like I'm a curiosity. I turn my back to him once I separate the skin from the meat. I wonder if he will let us stay in the area long enough for me to tan the hide or dry the meat.

A crunch leaks through the air and I look back. The sight is so horrific that I can't tear my eyes away. Raum's jaw has come unhinged, his throat and chest swollen, expanded by the deer he has swallowed half-way down. The deer seems to shrink the more he takes in. All the while, I can't bring myself to blink. It's humanly impossible for him to consume an animal in such a way. Instead of his belly expanding with fullness, his muscles bulge and his limbs elongate. Raum said the body was his, but what else has he changed? What else can he do?

I heard the devil had been turned into a snake after he tempted Eve. I never believed that. I never believed in anything until the Possession. Now, as I watch the thin legs slide down Raum's throat, I wonder if he is part snake.

I turn away before he starts on the second deer and cut the meat furiously. I don't believe Raum has any real intention to eat me, but that's all I can think about. I cut haphazardly, my shaking hands making it harder to be precise. What if he changes his mind? What if the deer aren't enough? Another crunch leaks through the air. I jump; my blade slides forward and nicks my palm. I get a clear vision of my head falling down his throat.

The knife falls from my hand as I bolt. Raum's swift presence pursues me, driving me into a panic. I press the wound to my chest when suddenly the ground rushes up too quickly when my feet slip. I fall into the dirt with flailing hands.

"Don't!" I throw my hands up to shield myself. "Please, don't!"

Raum grabs me by the wrist and hauls me to my feet. A thin frown is set between the laugh lines of his face. I press my weight back when he grabs my opposite shoulder to hold me still. He runs his tongue across my wrist, cleaning the blood that runs down. Like the deer, I am either too stunned or too stupid to move as his tongue moves to my palm. I hiss as his lips fasten to my broken flesh and a burning heat erupts under his probing tongue. He is going to eat me!

Before my mind can register what is about to happen, he releases my wrist. There is a black line where open flesh should be, a scorch mark. I pull my hand back to my chest. I'm torn between crying and laughing with relief.

"Did you get enough?" We both know I didn't. I only managed to cut off a steak before cutting my hand. He pulls me back to the deer, picks up the knife, and cuts away. He slices off more meat than I can eat. At least a month's worth if it's turned into jerky. He pulls a scarf from my pack and wraps the meat.

"We will walk a few more miles, then you can eat again."

I nod and take the load from him without meeting his eye.

Raum passes me the knife before lifting the remains and unhinging his jaw once more. I swipe the blade across my thigh and sheath it, turning away quickly. By the time he has finished eating, he is as broad as a linebacker and more intimidating. Before, my head reached his chin. Now I am at the cusp of his collarbone.

Our camp is small like the last, but the fire is a little bigger. Raum cuts two medium-sized steaks for me. He holds them in the flames, igniting his hands. The smell of burning flesh overpowers the smell of cooked venison, but it doesn't stop my stomach from grumbling. I haven't allowed myself cooked meat in forever. I've always been worried about the shortage of food, and cooking it only makes it spoil faster.

He tosses the steaks at me like I'm a stray. Like one, I bring it to my mouth greedily. I'm not shy with the way I shove it into my mouth. The meat is nearly rare. Blood dribbles down my chin as I sigh. Delicious. I have half a mind to comment on the way he treats me until he slices the rest of the meat and dries them between his hands. Instant jerky is another, yet peculiar, thing I add to the list of things Raum can do.

At least for now I know he means to keep me alive.

"How is your hand?" he asks.

I look at him across the fire. I wonder if he's giving me space because he scared me. It's ridiculous. He'd been close to breaking my fingers not too long ago. I turn the same hand he nearly snapped beneath the flames. "It's already scarring. What else can you do, Raum?" I tear off a piece of meat and shove it into my mouth.

His eyes glow red across the flames. There is a curve in his lip, but he doesn't allow a full smile to surface. "Anything," he says with a mild pause, "except walk on water."

"You're a humble creature," I scoff.

"Humility does not suit me."

I suddenly find myself staring into the flames and thinking about Leyak. Raum is wicked, but in a way I find him to be kinder than Leyak. He keeps me warm at night and he has healed and fed me. The most Leyak did was let James slip through before he was completely lost. That had been his cruelest trick of all. The weight of the knife at my waist feels heavier.

"You asked if I have ever been with one of you before," I say, and he looks up at me slowly. Raum cocks his head to the side, a sign I recognize as interest. "It wasn't by choice. One of you possessed my boyfriend while we were kissing."

He leans forward. "You didn't notice?" I try not to take offense that my torment intrigues him. I'm sure it's natural for a demon.

"Not at first. It wasn't until he started biting me that I realized it and then I noticed he felt stronger and—" I stop and shake my head. I don't want to think about the details. I certainly don't want to share them with Raum. I'm not even sure why I've mentioned it.

"Did he give you his name?"

"Leyak," I whisper.

Raum is thoughtful for a moment, and then his mouth presses together. "He didn't try to mark you?"

"No. I don't know why. I guess he got some sort of amusement dangling my freedom in front of me." I smirk. Raum is doing the exact same thing, except, unlike Leyak, he has promised his mark, or death, if I try to escape. "He let me run, actually."

Again, Raum goes quiet. He looks me over and muses to himself. "How does a runner become a hunter?"

"Leyak took the only person who meant something to me. In the beginning, James was still present. Leyak let him out and he just kept screaming for me to kill him." I close my eyes as if to wipe away the memory, but I can't. I'll never forget. His face had morphed into an expression of agony, tears ran down his face. I'd never heard anyone scream like that. "I swore never to be a coward again. I was too afraid of what would happen to me if I tried to hurt James, to hurt Leyak's host."

"What happened to this *thief*?"

I smirk at his choice of words and the bitter tone he uses for them. "He took over my city, played a big role in consuming Michigan." I finish off the last steak by licking my fingers clean. I quench my thirst from the canteen Raum graciously hands me. "I don't know anything else." I shrug. "Like I said, I ran."

Raum smirks, shaking his head. "You are unique, Leah. I must say I am impressed, even if you are a coward."

I grit my teeth and scrunch my nose in disagreement. I'd like to argue, but he's right. I'm more afraid of him than I have been of anything in my life. And Leyak had done far worse to me than Raum. I must remind myself that I'm stronger than my fear.

"That request I mentioned to you before, I'd like to ask it," he says.

A weight drops in my stomach. I clear my throat and nod. "Go on."

"The meat and animal blood are not enough for me. I need your blood to keep my strength. A few swallows to sustain me."

Beside the fire, I grow cold. He might not eat me, but he wasn't kidding when he said he was keeping me for a snack. "Do I have a choice?"

"You do. If you refuse, it will be painful, but if you are willing, I promise it will feel good. You won't even notice that my teeth are in you." He says it matter-of-factly. There's nothing suggestive in his voice, but a blush still manages to creep to my face. I imagine he could make the experience quite sufferable if he wanted to.

"Will you poison me?" Some choice. I'd rather the experience be as painless as possible, though.

"No."

I swallow and nod at once. He rises and I follow suit, noticing that he walks to me slowly as if he is afraid I'll startle. I let out a shaky breath as he closes the space between us. His lids lower as he looks down at my neck which is covered by the upturned collar of my jacket.

"Take this off," he says. His voice, normally so cruel, is smooth and sultry.

"Are you trying to woo me?" I ask nervously. I pull the jacket off and cling to it. I don't want to let it go when he takes it from me and tosses it to the ground.

I wonder if this is it. If he will actually slip his venom into my veins, and then God knows what I'll do for him.

His gaze touches over the claw marks engraved into my skin before sweeping up to my eyes. He tips my chin up. "You have been good, Leah. You have nothing to be afraid of." He runs his hands over the wounds in my shoulders, singeing them closed with a bitter sting. I bite my lip to stifle a moan of pain as the heat delves into my tender flesh.

"Ok," I whisper, though I don't think he hears me. I turn my face away so I don't have to watch. He moves behind me, sliding one hand up to cradle my face while his other presses to the front of my waist. My chest heaves as I feel his lips hover over my skin. I tense, my knees lock into place.

"Relax," he says against the shell of my ear, taking the lobe between his lips. "Close your eyes if you must, but let me see your face." His tongue trails down the length of my neck. I tip my head into his hand as his lips come to rest at the nape of my neck and his teeth pierce my skin.

As promised, the bite is not painful but red hot like an iron that sets my blood on fire. I moan and grab his arm around my waist as it tightens. His tongue strokes the blood from my vein and his lips suck hungrily. A streak of pleasure shoots through me.

My legs buckle and, as I fall, Raum bends with me. I come down on my knees and hand. I hold onto him with my other as he tries to keep me lifted. Then, suddenly, his hands no longer hold me but move over my body. One moves across my shoulder and hip while the other untucks my shirt from the front and snakes across my stomach to my breast. He squeezes and bites harder, sending another thrill of desire between my legs that leaves me gasping.

He positions himself over the top of me. His hands are on my breasts now, and I lean forward and arch into him. I catch a glimpse of his face beside mine. His eyes are the dark shade of my blood.

The button on my pants pops and the zipper pulls down. I feel his hand slip inside and the other works the denim over my hips. I reach back and push it down, giving his hand that's wrapped around my front easier access, and his fingers slip inside of me.

I come to as I realize his mouth is no longer fastened to me but moving over my back. The world snaps in front of me and I feel his need pressed behind me. I feel his fingers moving in and out, stroking me and how wet I am. How did I get here? I grab his hands and try to pry them off me, but he is much stronger than I am.

"Raum."

"Yes?" he hisses, removing his fingers only to grab my hips with both hands. My own wetness against my skin shames me. How could I still feel this way when he no longer bites me? What has he done to make me lose consciousness?

I don't know when he had time to remove his pants, but suddenly I feel him sliding between my thighs, coating himself with my heat. He groans and presses blunt teeth into my back. The idea that Raum is touching me is revolting, but it has been so long since I've been touched and I shudder. I should fight him, but the heat from his body strokes me, just like everything else.

"Raum." I can't find the breath to say anything other than his name. Words like "no" and "stop" aren't possible. The last time a demon had me like this he nearly killed me. The last time, I had not been willing. I press my hips back into Raum before he can enter me and he growls. The snarl is followed by a hard nip that I know is going to leave a nasty bruise.

He moves his tongue over the imprint and presses his forehead into my back. "Let me thank you," he says thickly. "Let me be kind to you." He presses his hips forward and grabs one of my breasts, massaging it sweetly, and takes a nipple between his fingers, rolling it around.

I shouldn't. This monster keeps me at his side with nothing but cold threats. But it has been so long and I don't think I can sleep now, or be in my right mind if I pull away. He is not like the rest. Though his teeth are no longer in me, I feel like I'm on fire. If I don't have Raum inside of me, I'll explode.

I lean my hips forward and he hisses with approval. Once again, he slides between my thighs to coat himself and then presses himself against me and pushes. I don't know what I expected of Raum, but he is much bigger than I imagined. I tense as he stretches me, and he lets out a throaty moan. He grabs my hips and pulls me back until my ass is pressed against his pelvis. I'm torn between pain and pleasure as he moves in and out. I feel like he is going to break me, and he has hardly done anything at all.

He licks the sweat that has gathered on my back. He fills every inch of me and still tries to push deeper even when there is nowhere else for him to go. When his thrusts become more urgent, my body convulses and I let out a cry of sheer ecstasy. I tighten around him as wave after wave of pleasure runs through me and, still, he doesn't stop. He draws out my orgasm with quick, hard thrusts that make my legs and arms shake. I fall forward on my chest. Raum growls. It is not like the sound I heard him make moments before. It is much more sinister.

This position gives him better access and he finally pushes past the wall he couldn't before. It doesn't take him long to find his release. I don't even realize it until it's too late. I reach back to grab his hips. He slams them forward with a moan that makes me cry out with brazen pleasure.

Once he finishes, he thrusts a few more times, each movement drawing a little sound from my lips. I drop my hips to the ground and he follows me down, laying us on our sides.

I breathe heavily. I can only focus on the fact that he is still inside of me and that I'm full of his cum. Can I get pregnant from this? He doesn't try to burn me the way Leyak did when he was finished with me. At my discomfort, he thrusts forward and kisses my shoulder.

"Thank you," he says softly.

I touch my neck where he initially bit me and look at the blood on my fingertips. His venom must be inside of me. Otherwise, I wouldn't have been so willing. Rational thoughts suggest I push him off me, but I don't say anything. I enjoy the way he feels between my legs.

"You said… you wouldn't," I say between breaths.

"And I didn't. Your blood is still clean. Ah, Leah, don't pull away from me," he says, running a hand down my legs. "Let me stay inside of you tonight."

I don't know how he hasn't softened yet. He had been moving gently, but now his thrusts are more known, slow and deep. "Tonight," I agree.

I wake up in pain. It feels like I've been ripped apart from the inside out. I look down to see bite marks cover my chest and thighs. By the soreness across my back, I imagine they're there too. But, as I look closely, I notice they're human bites. Not one bit of my skin has been pierced save for the patch on my neck.

Raum is stretched out in front of me, watching me with a look so dark it chills me. His countenance changes to smug satisfaction and I instantly feel guilty for what we've done. Red nail marks rake across his hips where I must have been holding onto him. That isn't the only red on him, though, and my hand finds my stomach. There is dried blood on him and between my thighs.

"What did you do?" I dab my hand over the invisible wound.

Raum stands with a grin, his black eyes flashing mischievously. "Clearly, I gave you the best night of your life."

"There is blood on us!"

He shrugs and slips his pants on. He goes about picking up my clothes and then crouches in front of me, holding them out. "You are very small and it was hard not to get carried away. You'll be fine."

My face heats. I snatch the clothes from him and try to put them on as quickly as I can. My hands are shaking so bad that I do more fumbling than anything. "Fine? You don't know that! This isn't normal!" My eyes fill with tears. I lean my weight into one of the trees to steady myself. It feels like I've been beaten.

"You are bruised, nothing more. I haven't done any lasting damage. I'd like to fuck you again, after all," he says.

"Absolutely not!" I snap.

Raum closes the space between us in the time that I blink. I turn and dumbly press my back against the tree. He doesn't touch me, but his heat caresses me delicately. "Even in pain, you still want me. I can smell you, Leah, and it's delicious. Say the word and I'll bend you over." He grabs my face and licks the side of it.

I jerk my face free. "I don't," I say through gritted teeth. I *am* aching for him, but I refuse to give into the desires he is forcing on me. I shove his chest. He grins wickedly before snapping the air in front of my face.

Cold dread settles over my shoulders as he turns away. What have I done?

V

Much to my humiliation, Raum teases me on our journey. One would think I'd get used to the pain, but I don't. Not for the next few days, at least. Every movement is agonizingly stiff. I'm constantly reminded of what we did together, without him taunting me about it.

"I love the look of pain on your face," he comments. I scowl and he flashes a sharp smile. "Because I know, whether you like it or not, you're thinking about me."

"I'm always thinking about you," I snap. "I can't get away from you!"

It seems like the wrong thing to say because he suddenly grows quiet and his eyes seem blacker than ever. They become hungry and angular. The way he looks at me is as if he knows something I don't. He has been docile compared to when we first met, but he speaks with the same threatening tone he used before.

"You never will, Leah."

Fear is the word I would use to describe the emotion that fills Raum's face, though it is not a look I ever imagined to see on a demon. I sidestep past him as he stops short and his head whips up, twisting his neck at a grotesque angle.

He hisses, a long hostile sound that thickens my blood. "Hush," he says, halting the retort I was about to throw at him. He inhales and flicks his tongue across his lower lip in unison. The look that falls into his eyes is enough to frighten me to his side.

Raum grabs my hand and pulls me in the direction his eyes have been fixated on. I don't know what he smells but he is frightened, so I don't protest and do my best to keep up. What does a demon have to fear? Every few paces he pauses, listening for whatever it is I can't hear.

Then he stops.

I follow the path of his eyes. At first, I miss it, but after looking closer I see dark wood walls peering at us between the trees. A cabin, a few hundred feet away. I touch his arm with my free hand and press him forward, but he doesn't budge.

"Wait here," he says and lets me go.

I resist the urge to look over my shoulder for the prickling feeling at the back of my neck. I don't want to lose sight of him. The smooth handle of my tracker knife finds its way into my hand as I wait. I feel a little bit better, but not much.

Raum circles the cabin with hunched shoulders and his head stuck out low like a wolf. When he is satisfied with the grounds, he steps onto the front porch and pushes the door open. Even where I'm standing, I can hear the creak of the home that has been shut up for too long. It takes him less time to search the interior and he steps out to wave me down. It's only then that I finally look over my shoulder to the empty forest.

A mixture of dread and relief fall over me as I step inside the cabin. The air is stale, musty with age. By the thick layer of dust covering everything, this place has been abandoned since before the Possession.

I make a beeline for the kitchen as soon as I catch a glimpse of the sink. I turn on the faucet. The spigot spurts and sputters with thick ooze and then the water runs, brown and ruddy. A little laugh escapes and I beam at Raum.

His brow furrows and then he turns away, looking for something. "A well."

"Yes!" I run my hands in the sink and wash the dirt from them. "It's not safe to drink, but it's something."

"I'll look for it. I'll clean it out and boil it." He nods to the pantry. "See if there are any canned goods for you." I'm already going through everything before he has finished.

I find an assortment of beans and vegetables. Glorious tin cans that have become more valuable than silver. There is enough food to last me a month. I won't be able to take all of it with me, but I can carry enough that I won't have to worry about going hungry—providing Raum continues to feed me.

I scan the darkened rooms, dusted and broken down by neglect. There are two guest bedrooms and a master, all covered with white sheets. I pull my bandanna from my pocket and tie it around my face before stripping the sheets from the master bedroom. Once I gather everything outside, I shake them, squinting my eyes so no dust bunnies can invade them.

I leave the sheets on the porch and set about opening the back windows and cleaning the area I intend to sleep in. Raum doesn't know it yet, but we are going to stay for a few nights. If he can clean the well, I can wash the sheets, towels, my clothes, and myself. My body tingles with anticipation. Clean water and soap to wash with! Bless whoever left this behind. I stop myself as soon as the thought enters my mind. God help whoever left this behind.

I step out into the hallway. This must have been a shelter. There are no signs of a struggle, no reason for the home to be empty other than whoever lived here before never made it. I pause at one of the many photos hanging on the wall. I drag my thumb through the dust to reveal the smiling faces of a husband and wife with three children. The oldest child can be no more than thirteen.

"It's clean." Raum's voice startles me. I jerk my hand away from the photo. There's a curious look on his face, but he does me the courtesy by not saying anything.

"Thank you," I say absentmindedly. I turn away, hardly noticing he follows me to the bathroom.

Cleaning the tub takes the most work, but by the time I am finished it is more white than black. I wash the sheets next. I'd like nothing more than to bathe myself, but the bedding needs to dry. Besides, bathing has become more of a privilege than a necessity, as cringe worthy as that sounds.

Raum has perched himself on the windowsill beside me, his dark eyes enveloping me as I dunk the sheets in for a final rinse. The corner of his mouth quirks up in amusement that doesn't quite reach his eyes.

I snap at him, my soapy fingers sliding together, as I try to gather my thoughts. Raum's curious look hardens. "Will you hang a line? You're taller than me," I say quickly.

Raum looks at me, unblinking, before rising. He leaves without a word, the smell of sulfur trailing after him.

He hasn't said anything since I started cleaning. I know I can't make him stay, but I deserve this little pleasure after what he has done to me. I pull the plug and sheets out of the water and carry my soaked bundle down the hallway, nearly running into him.

"It's to the right," he says, pushing past me.

I shouldn't do it, but I can't help it. I smile. I look back at him as he disappears into the bathroom.

I've kept my time in homes limited. They're too obvious. But my worst fear is a demon finding me, and Raum already has me. I can allow myself to enjoy the simple things like washing clothes and bathing now that I'm facing the worst of my fears. It's incredible what you take advantage of when you feel entitled to tomorrow.

The sound of the water splashing against the tub thrills me. I set a robe aside I found and washed earlier. It's damp, but it will have to do until I can wash my clothes. I've already showered to clean off most of the grime and blood so I can soak.

The cold water tightens my skin and catches my breath. It's *so* good as I slide beneath the surface. It's so clean! I'm shaking by the time I set myself under the water, but I welcome the chills that spread along my skin.

"It would feel better warm."

I jerk my knees to my chest. I don't know how I forgot about him. He's massive, his presence is like a giant storm cloud. Raum appears from a dark corner I hadn't noticed. He slinks to the ground, cupping the curve of the tub with his large hands. I'll never get used to his antics.

I peer over the edge as the water warms. "Are you going to cook me?"

"I prefer my food raw," he says darkly.

"Lucky me."

Raum settles back on his heels, his eyes intent.

"Get out," I snap.

"Or what?"

The heat that creeps up my neck might as well be his hand strangling me. Against my better judgement, I give him my back and slip deeper into the water. He's already seen everything, but that doesn't mean he gets to see it twice.

Washing in a river is nothing compared to soaking in a hot tub. The grime I couldn't get off in the shower falls away to reveal my suntanned skin as I line it with soap. I dump a dollop of conditioner into the knotted mess of my hair and lean back. How simple yet wonderful. I close my eyes.

I imagine I'm back in the little one-story house James and I lived. There the tub was smaller with acrylic resin; it wasn't a nice claw-foot like this one. If I stretched out, my feet would hang over the edge. James would rub my feet when he sat with me. I can almost feel his touch again, though I remember it to be softer.

The touch is nothing like I remember it. The basin is large enough that, even though my legs are outstretched, they are entirely covered by water. The touch slips beneath the water and traces the arch of my foot and around my ankle to the curve of my calf. An ominous feeling looms over me.

I struggle to retain the image of James' face, but the dark feeling becomes more urgent when the pale complexion is replaced with teak skin and Raum's face. The warmth of his hand chills me as it moves up to the plump flesh of my thigh.

It's hard to breathe. I squint my eyes tighter, willing James' image to come back and for Raum to stop touching me. I could tell him to stop, but my tongue has forgotten how to form words. His hand slides farther still. His warmth caresses the side of my face while his fingers brush the sensitive spot between my thighs. A little sound escapes my lips as I let out the breath I've been holding.

Raum pulls away and the image of him as James shatters.

My eyes fly open. There's a sinister sneer on Raum's face that leaves me feeling shamed. "Get out," I hiss.

"You shouldn't deny yourself what you really want," he says smoothly.

"I don't want you."

"Why not? Because I'm a demon?" He chuckles and brings his fingers to his lips to lick the tips.

"Exactly."

"You should have thought about that before you gave me your blood," he sneers.

"You tricked me!"

Raum shrugs, his lips turning up as he silently laughs at me. "The truth is, Leah, I wouldn't have raped you had you said no. But now that I've had you, you belong to me whether you like it or not. And I do know that you like it, or you would not be blushing."

"Get out," I say through gritted teeth. I'm not blushing from embarrassment. My face is heated from the anger boiling inside me. I splash water at him with a loud smack across the top. "Get out!"

Raum's lips press together as I continue to amuse him, but he leaves me.

It's impossible to enjoy the warmth of the water any longer. My heart hammers so hard behind my chest that it hurts. The air has grown thin. I lean over the side of the tub as a merciless wave hits me and I sob. I don't know why I cry. Exhaustion, how much my body still aches from Raum, or the fact he has me at all. I scream out my frustration, sending an echo into the room. The only response I get is Raum's dark chuckle ringing back from down the hall.

The hem of my robe gathers around my calves as I step out onto the cool tiled floor. I'm still crying by the time I get down on my knees to wash my soiled clothes. I can't let him get to me. I can't let this monster manipulate me, not while I'm still free and capable of refusing him. I press my forehead against the tub and suck it up.

A dark presence hits me as I enter the hallway. I look down between the faded walls, expecting to see Raum waiting for me. There is no one. I curse him silently for playing tricks on me. He has done a good job of scaring me stiff, but I force myself to walk outside to check on the dampness of the sheets. I think I see him in one of the doorways, but if he was there, he is gone by the time I look.

Raum has cleaned away a small patch of earth beside the sheets where a low fire burns. I don't mind that the linens will smell like smoke because the heat of the flames will help them dry faster. I run my hands down their length. Still damp, but by the end of the day they will be dry.

Much of the evening is filled with silence. Raum tests my limits with mild touches and dark looks that turn my blood cold. At one point, I whisper the Lord's prayer when I feel his eyes on me and he laughs.

"That does not work on us."

"I thought demons were supposed to be repelled by God." It was worth a shot, at least.

"God would have to exist first, wouldn't He?"

I fold my arms over my waist. "What are you implying?"

"Only what you've known from the beginning. Evil is winning."

That's not how things are supposed to go. Goodness, God should win. What *if* God is gone? For someone who never believed in God before the Possession, I think of Him often and pray for the best and that this nightmare will one day end.

I check for bugs and other critters that might inhabit the mattress before tucking the sheets in after I eat. The bed can't be any worse than the deep forests and dark holes I've slept in. As I finish, the uneasy prickle at the back of my neck straightens every hair on my body. I turn slowly and my heart drops to the pit of my stomach.

Raum leans casually against the doorframe flipping through a leather-bound book. *My journal*.

"Where did you get that?" I lick my lips to wet my mouth that has suddenly gone dry.

"I took it the same day I took you," he says without looking up. "You've got quite the voice."

"That's private—"

"Is it? I don't think there are any secrets between us, Leah." He snaps the book closed and looks up at me. The movements are so quick I jump. "I find it curious that you've had time to write about me."

I swallow. It's true. I had been sneaking entries whenever I thought he was asleep. I knew I couldn't steal a knife without him noticing but adding a few lines of ink here and there seemed harmless. It was the only place I thought I could escape without consequence. As silly as it sounds, I wanted to document as much of my life as I could before he ended it.

"You've been going into your bag without permission," he says coolly.

"You should be flattered," I say, but my voice betrays me by quaking. I had written about our time together, how he terrifies me and that when I have the chance I am going to kill him unless he ends me first. I can tell by the look in his eye that he has read that part.

Raum is grim as he approaches me, his steps slow and steady like the predator he is.

"It's the only thing I have left," I whisper under the weight of his power. "I have left my knives alone. I have eaten and drank when you permit me to. Don't take this from me." I know he is going to, though. He is probably going to punish me for it and break my bones like he promised. His blank expression frightens me because I know he can choose to be kind or wicked without a moment's notice. One a lie, one painful–both cruel.

"I enjoy when you are afraid of me, but it does not suit you to grovel," he hisses. He jerks his chin to the bed. "Lie down."

"What are you going to do?" I step back slowly, the back of my knees hitting the edge.

"Lie down," he repeats.

As I crawl over the pale sheets, I get a vivid image of how my blood will look in contrast. Sprawled out and dismembered with my hair fanned out like a broken halo. My hands shake as I ease down. The bed gives under his weight as he follows me.

Raum settles his chest against my back and wraps a strong arm around me. He presses his face against my neck and the bottom of my cheek. I brace myself for the blow of his fangs as his tongue traces the line of my jaw.

A purr of satisfaction rumbles through his chest and vibrates against my back. He pushes one of his legs between mine and lifts his face so my head is tucked neatly beneath his chin. A wave of tension rolls off his body into mine and then he stills.

Quiet tears trickle down my face as hysterical relief washes over me. God, or whoever is listening, thank you! I find no comfort in my enemy's arms, but the fact that he uses them to hold me instead of breaking me brings me a sort of peace.

I take a few deep breaths to steady the flow of water down my face. Exhaustion, both mental and physical, overtakes me and I shut my eyes only to be greeted by the sweet stinging one gets when they're too tired. I place my hand over Raum's and allow myself to sleep. If I hold onto him, he can't hurt me

VI

I'm still firmly wrapped in Raum's embrace when I wake. At first, I forget about what and who he is. I allow myself to enjoy the foreign comfort of being in someone's arms. The swell of his bicep rests against the side of my ribcage, his chest rising and falling into my back. And then he stirs, tightening his grip around my waist in a way that aggravates the internal bruise. My stomach clenches.

How long will this go on? I've heard of Babel, but part of me believes it's a myth. Will he keep me alive long enough to see it? Why *am* I alive? Why hasn't he marked me? He refuses to answer my questions, no matter how many times I ask. Whatever the reason, nothing good can come of it. Raum treats me too poorly to have my best interests at heart. For a demon, he is kind, but that does not change what he is and all he can do to me, and will, if I continue to fight him.

A low growl emits from the back of Raum's throat. He presses his nose into my neck and nuzzles me affectionately and then his lips follow. I have no intention of giving into him like I did in the woods. It was a disgusting mistake that all the soap and water could not wash away. The sharp edge of his nails move against my waist again, trailing farther down.

I roll over. Raum's dark eyes crinkle at the corners as he smirks. There's a spot of dried blood at the corner of his mouth. I open my mouth to say something then stop. What is that? I reach around the back of his neck to a dark object sticking out beneath his hair. I touch the soft line and curl my fingers back as I realize it's not braided into his hair but growing out from under it.

It's a feather. I stretch my fingers across it, then to the other side of his neck and yes—there are others. I tick my index and middle finger over them, counting blindly. Eight feathers, maybe more, extend from the base of his hairline and fan out over his neck. His hair covers them so it's no wonder I haven't noticed them until now.

The whole time Raum watches me. I can see him staring intently from the corner of my eye. I stop touching them when I realize this might be an intimate gesture. Is it? I have no idea, but something about it feels like it could be. Can demons feel anything?

"They grow from beneath your skin," I say.

"Do you like them?" he asks. He turns his mouth into my arm and presses sharp teeth against my wrist.

If this is Raum's way of trying to connect with me, I don't like it. This feels like another game I don't know the rules to. I've never been a gambler strictly because my poker face is horrendous. But it's not entirely a lie when I answer him.

Yes," I say softly.

He runs his hand on my stomach to the underside of my shirt, flattening his palm over my belly. "They are much longer on my real body. They run down my spine."

I swallow. Raum's touch firms as my stomach tightens. I hate the crooked line his mouth makes when he laughs at me. It only happens when he is laughing at me, vocally or not. It's when I'm staring at his mouth that he whips his head towards me. It's so quick that I gasp, inhaling the warm breath he lets out as he hisses.

Before I can pull away, his hand latches to mine that has found its way back between his feathers. He clenches his fingers around mine, turning my hand into a fist. The ugly line of his mouth twists higher. I jerk my hand, but it doesn't budge. I push against him, slamming my other palm to his chest.

"Stop," I pant. The word sounds mangled as it comes out. It was nearly impossible to say, but I've managed it.

A sinister shadow passes through Raum's eyes. He removes his hands from my body and sits up, rolling me on my back by the force of his power so he is leering over me. The soft curve of his lips hover over mine. They move down across my neck and chest, down to my belly button. He doesn't touch me, but he might as well. As warm as fire, heat runs over the length of my body. His eyes snap up to me.

"Go. Before I change my mind," he hisses.

I slip out from under him slowly, afraid that touching him will cause him to strike me. Once my feet touch the floor, though, I'm gone. I don't let out the breath I've inhaled until I'm at the front door. With it comes a series of tremors that make every part of me shake. I'm going to be sick.

Gray wisps of smoke trail into the air from the fire that died during the night. I brush my shaking hands over my thighs as I stalk to it. Tending to the ashes will give me something to do. I can't describe the feeling rushing through my blood. I knew what Raum was going to do and it had nothing to do with marking me. My stomach rolls. If I hadn't found my voice, I might have let him.

He comes out of the house shortly after I've collected most of my thoughts and started a new fire. He mentions something about scouting the perimeter. I watch him go with my bag slung across his shoulders. The shadows of the forest reach out their long arms, welcoming him as he disappears into the tree line.

He let me keep the knife from the hunt. It's my best knife and I could survive without my others, though I'd prefer to have my karambit as an attack weapon. I slowly stand. This might be the only opportunity I have to escape him. I throw a couple more branches onto the fire before darting back into the house.

I dig through the closets and beneath the beds until I find a suitable bag that will carry food. I pause as my fingers brush cool metal at the back of a closet's top shelf. I stretch higher, but I'm too short to grasp the barrel. I curse under my breath.

Raum's presence washes over me. I reach for it again as I feel him draw closer, moving somewhere within the house, coming for me. I jump up, brushing my fingers once more across the gun, shifting it a little bit closer to me.

"Come on." I grit my teeth.

I know Raum is behind me before he even takes the gun. As his long arm reaches over me, tears of defeat burn my eyes. I watch the rifle lift over my head, then the box of shells evidently tucked in the corner.

"I thought we might be able to use it," I say as I turn around.

Raum's countenance remains void. He isn't stupid, so I'm not surprised that his eyes are full of anger when I finally meet them.

"*We*?" he asks.

I nod. "For protection."

Raum's eyes narrow. "I'm all the protection you need."

I nod again, not really knowing what to say. He caught me fair and square. Would I have shot him? I've never shot a gun before. If anything, it would have pissed him off, much more than my attempt to get it already has. I fold my hands behind my back reflexively. I don't want him to break them.

"Stay here," he commands. "When I get back, I expect you to be doing something more useful with your time."

I slam my fist into the wall as he leaves. I wasted precious time trying to reach a weapon he can probably survive. A mangled yell leaves my throat when I strike the wall again.

All the anger and pent-up emotions that threaten to break a seal of tears build up inside me. There is only one way to exert the energy in such tight confines. I find a room with more suitable space before dropping to the floor. I haven't worked out since Culsu stumbled on me. I push up then back down, forcing all my anger into the floorboards beneath me.

The last thing I wrote in my journal was that I'm going to kill Raum. I'll find a way to do it. It'll have to be soon. I fear I've fallen out of any favor he might have had for me.

"What are you doing?"

The sound of his voice makes me flinch. I look up from my plank position, meeting his inquiring expression complete with an arched brow. I lower slowly, completing the set of push-ups I started, and stand. Bits of dirt stick to my palms that I wipe across my thighs. It's a nervous habit I acquired over the years to hide when my hands are shaking.

"Something useful," I say bitterly.

Raum cocks his head. The corner of his mouth twitches. He follows me to the next room where the top of the doorjamb is broken. I noticed it earlier and want to see if it has a decent grip. I hop up, doing my best to ignore the demon's eyes drinking in my every move. The wood creaks, but it will hold my weight. I pull myself up, lower slowly, and back again.

My fingers dig into the wood, turning my nailbeds and knuckles stark white with effort. Part of my sweat laden shirt has ridden up across my stomach; the rest sticks to my back. I try to focus on these things instead of Raum. It becomes harder to concentrate when he steps under me as I pull myself up. The wall blocks him from view until I lower myself down, his dark eyes following up and down. Up and down. I hold at the top of a pull-up as I count backwards to end my set.

His warm tongue flicks across the exposed skin of my stomach. My fingers slip, and I kick my foot out. Raum is much faster than I am. I'd have fallen on my ass if he didn't catch me. He shoves me against the wall, pinning me in an awkward position where my feet can't touch the ground.

"I can think of better ways for you to stay in shape," he says suggestively.

"Put me down," I hiss.

Raum's eyes narrow. All playfulness is devoid from his expression as his grip hardens. My back slides against the wall as he pulls me down, bending one knee and then the other. I grip his shoulders as he turns us until I'm lying flat on my back and he is caged around me. I don't know how Raum does it, but somehow he manages to instill a new wave of fear into me.

"Is this better?" he asks.

The sound of my blood pounding in my ears is deafening. "No," I say. The punishment I thought I escaped for touching the gun is close.

He hisses. "I have been so kind to you. Don't you want to thank me?"

Arrogant bastard. He licks the sweat from my collarbone. The long red tongue feels like sandpaper as it laps the salt from my skin. His lashes lift as I clench my jaw. As much as I hate him, I'm too afraid to answer him. Already, I can feel my body warming to his rough touch shamelessly.

"You will not deny me a third time."

No. I don't think I can.

We eat in silence. I watch the light fade from the sky as Raum watches me. The brighter the stars become, the sooner it will be for us to go to bed. I take a chance to glance at him now. His attention has finally turned to the flames. They dance back and forth, whipping their red and orange tendrils like a dancer's skirt.

"We should get an early start tomorrow," he says.

I agree. I look at the cabin that has started to fade into the night. I wish we could stay. I want to feel human, normal for a little bit longer. But I can't deny the urge to start moving again. Though I'm not particularly fond of our trip, it will be nice to get back on track.

The sky is clear save for the millions of stars sprinkled between the dark branches of the canopy above us. It's times like this that I find it easy to forget what the world has become. Even in total destruction, beauty refuses to be erased.

It was on a night like this, about a month after Sin swept through, that James and I were lying on the back patio of our house when the same image was shaken.

A scream. To this day, I have never heard a scream like the one I did that night. So piercing and abruptly cut off. It was powerful enough to freeze the blood in my veins, despite it being nearly one hundred degrees out.

I followed James four blocks before we saw what caused the sound. I told him we should go back, but he wouldn't have any of that. Instead, we continued forward, ignoring the white-stricken faces that blew past us.

A man was hunched over a woman. It looked like he was murmuring something in her ear; I couldn't quite hear the words, but he made a sound against her. It wasn't until I scuffed a piece of gravel and saw the bloodstained face when it whipped towards us that I realized he had been feeding from her. I've seen people eat bodies before, but this was different. When he looked at me, his eyes were jet black. Empty. Deadly.

His lips curled and revealed pointed teeth and two long, extended canines.

That monster wasn't so different from the one in front me.

"I'm going to wash," I say abruptly, shoving the memory aside. I stand before Raum can say anything. I might as well enjoy the luxury while I have it.

It's a scary thing to bathe in the dark. I never thought it would spook me so much. Raum is the only dangerous thing out here, but part of me is afraid of something else. Something unknown. I scrub as quickly as I can, sloshing water over the edge. It's a strange feeling when I'm actually comforted by Raum's dark presence as he enters the house.

The power of him hits me like a wall when I go to the bedroom. I let my eyes adjust to the moon's light as they settle over his form that is already stretched across the mattress. I can feel his eyes roving over me as I crawl in on the other side. I slipped on the most unflattering nightgown I could find. It's thick cotton with a vintage floral pattern and a high collar. It's not practical, but neither is it appealing.

I face Raum as I lay down. The sound of our breath intertwines, reminding me of the gentle waves from the lake back home. It's a distinct sound the water makes whenever a boat cuts through it. This whole time I have been trying to think of places he might have put the gun. I've thought about cutting him with my knife while he slept. I hate him for taunting me.

None of those thoughts stop me from touching his feathers. They are like fine velvet beneath my fingers. So unique and strangely beautiful even though I can't see them. I remember their color to be the same as his hair, black with a blue sheen.

Raum slides the bottom of my dress up to grip my thigh. I don't protest as he pulls my leg across his hip. I tilt my head back as he leans forward and presses his lips to my throat. A growl of appreciation vibrates through the cords of my neck whenever I grip his feathers. My hold is to threaten him, but it only encourages him. We fall asleep like that, with his lips and teeth resting against me and my body straining from his touch.

Something strokes me from my sleep, easing me out of dark dreams in long, luscious sweeps. It takes me a moment to realize the gentle lapping comes from between my thighs. He must sense that I'm awake because Raum's grip on the outside of my hips hardens. His tongue delves inside of me and I gasp.

Now I'm awake.

He growls with satisfaction and the vibrations tingle against my skin, giving a strange but delicious sensation as he moves his tongue in and out of me. My legs tighten on their own and I grip the sheets. I should kick him away, but I find myself reaching down to his dark mane and lacing my fingers between the locks.

"Yes."

His tongue withdraws from me and he runs it from top to bottom, agonizingly slow. "What do you want, Leah?" He nips the inside of my thigh and I look down at him. Even in the dark I can see his glistening stare looking back at me. He swipes his tongue across me again. I groan.

I want him to stop is the right thing to say. But with his tongue constantly moving over me, I can't think clearly. All I can think of is his name and how badly I want him. His tongue, his fingers, *him*; any part of him that will fill me and take away this desirable pain that's building. Everything else is entirely forgotten. I feel his teeth against me and I brace myself for the pain he is about to inflict.

"You," I gasp as he parts his teeth for his tongue to flick up my slit. "Raum."

With his name fleeting across my tongue comes sweet ecstasy. I come instantly; my legs tighten around his head and my back arches. A strangled cry leaves my throat as he laps away everything I give him.

Raum pries my legs away and pushes one back, extending it over the front of his shoulder. He wastes no time in filling me. I'm still sore from before, but the pleasure he gives me is stronger and I push through it as he pushes forward. I pull him to me, moaning as he moves in and out; intentionally slow like he is trying to please only me.

Unlike our first time together, I'm not in pain by the time he finishes. I find that surprising since he was anything but gentle. I remember seeing bits of my skin in his teeth, but that must have been my imagination because my skin is smooth and unbroken. I run my hands everywhere just to be sure. The only marks are a few bruises here and there, but they are nothing compared to before. Even my shoulders feel smoother. I shudder to think what I imagined could have been real.

"Do you intend to make this a regular occurrence?" I turn to him, startled to find his inky eyes staring directly at me.

"So long as you keep forgetting the word 'no'," he says.

I blush shamefully and look away from him. I'd know if Raum had bitten me. I would swoon over him unabashed. Guilt and fear would not be the two prominent feelings I have towards him. I can't help but wonder if he has, though, but only because I have given into him so easily.

I am weak.

Raum's laugh pulls me from my thoughts. "You look as if you are tearing yourself up." He rolls us over, pinning me beneath him. "Unless the circumstances become dire, I have decided to keep you alive, Leah. I know you enjoy being with me as much as I do you. You have no one that will judge you, no one to turn to with these feelings eating you. Allow yourself to revel in me and I will be kind to you."

I bite the inside of my lip and shake my head. "You're a monster, Raum. You're wicked."

"Which makes it so much sweeter." As he says it, he runs his nose along my face. His words come out as a hiss, the S's trailing longer than the rest. "We both know you want to. Why fight it?"

I close my eyes as he wanders across my face with his. "Because I might lose my humanity."

"I can fix that for you." He inhales beside my neck. The pressure of his teeth make my eyes fly open.

"No," I say.

Raum chuckles and nips me, but he doesn't break the skin. He doesn't inject me with his venom. "Humanity is not doing you any favors, but I will allow you to keep it. For now," he adds.

VII

I hate to leave the cabin, but I feel safer once we start moving. It's only been two nights tucked away, but I've gotten used to walking endlessly and it pleases my restless legs to adventure on. It's hard to believe we have been together nearly two weeks. A crack of thunder rings out over our heads and my eagerness to get a move on vanishes. We look up at the sky. There are no dark clouds.

A cool breeze moves through the heavy foliage. I can smell the rain on the wind.

"We will keep moving," Raum says.

"In the rain?"

"We have already wasted too much time."

He wasn't complaining last night.

"If we keep moving, we can reach the edge of Nevada in a few days," he says.

My brow rises. I hadn't thought about it, but Raum is right. With the pace he has set for us, it's no wonder we hadn't ended up there sooner. But why Nevada? There's nothing there but desert, unless he means for us to pass through California. It doesn't make sense. The shortest distance to the coast would have been through Idaho and Washington.

"Raum, I can't go through the desert." I slow my pace, taking in the trees around us. We are still in the mountains, but I realize the slopes are thinning, the trees growing sparse. Raum must be taking us the long way, otherwise we would have already hit plains.

"You can and you will."

"We don't know if there will be any water." He keeps walking away and I grab his arm. "Do you even know where you're going? We need to cut across to Oregon. We can still get to the coast from there."

He pulls his arm from mine and lengthens his stride. I have to jog to keep up with him.

"Raum! Why are we taking the long way?" I step in front of him and throw my hands up to brace against his chest. He shoves me to the side so hard I nearly lose my footing. Blood pounds against my eardrums. Raum is afraid of something. The idea constricts around my heart and I run after him again, suddenly scared to be left too far behind. He has the same look in his eye as when we came across the cabin.

Soft pitter-patters fall from the leaves and splash over my face. The drizzle turns into a downpour as the sky opens in a sweep of dark clouds. The storm is torrential, whitening the air around us so we can't see more than a few feet ahead. Raum is slow and careful for me, though his sense of urgency remains. He constantly looks back to make sure I'm following.

I slip on a stone and he moves with lightning speed to catch me before my face can smack into the rock. I grip his bicep and pull myself up. This is maddening. We should at least build a temporary cover until the storm passes. This rain could last for an hour or days.

When I left Michigan, I had to take shelter for five days before a storm passed.

"We can't see where we're going. We'll get turned around!" I yell. I know he uses his nose for direction. I've seen him sniff the air all too often. Not even he can lead us if his acute senses are hindered.

Raum ignores me by lengthening his stride again. This time I keep my pace. If he wants to go then he can, but I'm not going to exert myself during a monsoon. Maybe I'll get lucky and he will lose track of me. The idea sparks a light inside of me and I stop walking. If Raum is lost, he could easily lose me too.

A feeling of unease sweeps over me as soon as his shadow vanishes into the mist. I curse. Raum is afraid, so I should be too. I pick my way over the slippery ground in the direction I last saw him. I call out his name, but my voice is lost beneath a clap of thunder.

Another wave of unease touches me, this time stronger. I let out a sigh of relief as I see the familiar silhouette standing a few yards away. A second and then a third come to stand beside him and I stop. It's not Raum. None of them are. I can't make out their faces or any particular details, but I know they're demons. The feeling of darkness is more powerful than when I'm with Raum. The rain is cold, but I'm sweating. I can feel the heat from them pooling around me. Their power is like the storm itself, dangerous and lashing.

Someone touches me from behind. I'd scream if their hand didn't clamp over my mouth first. Their other wraps firmly around my bicep.

"Shh," they whisper.

I crane my head back to look at Raum. He watches the visitors with parted lips. "I need to bite you," he says.

"What? No!" My refusal is muffled behind his hand.

His fingers constrict around my arm. I bend into him, gasping soundlessly as he threatens to break it. "One of them could be sick and decide you are a better host." He moves his hand slowly as I try to catch my breath.

"Make something up! I'll do whatever you say, but don't bite me." I look back to the trio. They've vanished. I look about us wildly, trying to find them, while at the same time I fight to free myself from the demon who already has me.

"I will bite you without giving you my venom, just like before, but this time it will hurt. I am going to burn you so the mark looks real. Trust me," he says sternly. He is looking off to the right now. I wonder if he can see them. Are they watching us?

"I don't trust you." Raum tries to silence me by giving my arm a good squeeze, but I push through the pain. "You've never given me a reason to. You are a liar, deceitful— Ah!" I cry out as the bone in my arm splinters. It's a hairline fracture, but it's enough to shut me up. "An abuser," I whimper.

Raum pulls my arm back and covers my mouth with his other hand. He twists my body so I'm helpless against him and my neck is entirely exposed for the blow of his fangs. I scream into his palm as his teeth sink into my skin with a sickening pop. It's excruciating. It starts as a pinch. In the next instant it feels like a thousand knives cutting through my veins. I cry as his fangs sink deeper than I thought possible. I feel them scrape against something as he works his jaw, wringing my neck. My stomach wretches and I lurch against his hand. He withdraws from me before I can vomit. I expel what little food was in my stomach.

"You will do exactly as I say whether it is a command or a suggestion. Do you understand?"

"Fuck you," I wheeze. I wipe the back of my hand across my mouth and shudder as the pain needles into my neck.

"Believe it or not, I am doing you a favor," he snaps and pulls me with him. I whimper as he jostles my arm.

We walk a few yards before the three appear again. They're to our right, where Raum had been looking. I want to flee as Raum walks towards them, dragging me along. They greet each other in their dark language and each nod their heads to one another. Two are dark skinned and the other bears a soft tan. The one in the middle jerks his chin towards me. His long-braided hair is the only feature I can make out through the haze.

"Ozien," Raum says.

Their leader nods and turns away, leaving the rest of us to follow him.

I touch Raum's hand as we follow and hope they can't hear me over the rain. "What is that word?"

"Mine," he says.

We stick with our new companions for a few more hours. I don't know whether to be grateful or worried that no one speaks. The storm continues to hound us. I shake with the cold seeping into my bones, despite the heat rolling from the demons. I shake with the fear that comes from being caught between four demons.

Eventually we stop and the fair-skinned demon and his companion set to making a camp. They clear a patch in the ground, removing all leaves, straw, and debris. They come together and lay their palms together then step back and clap their hands over their heads. The sound strikes lightning across the sky.

They pull their hands down and step back until we are all covered by their power. It has stopped raining. I break away from Raum and look at the space around us, to the sky and the rest of the forest. They've created a dome. Rain splashes and rolls off the top. The invisible cover shelters us, but it does not muffle the sound.

Their leader, the one with the braids, leaves the dome and comes back with an assortment of logs and debris. He pulls the water out of his load and starts a fire with the snap of his long fingers.

I've never seen anything like this before. I've always known demons have powers, but I've never known the extent. Do they all have the same ones? I doubt it, I think as I look at Raum. He said he could do anything, but he hasn't exercised much of said power. Maybe he was lying.

The two who created the dome strip off their shirts and lay beside the fire. They stretch their long limbs, flexing their fingers and toes like animals. The first with darker skin is lanky with well-defined muscles. His hair is cropped on the sides with a jagged pattern that digs into his scalp. There is a scar running from his brow bone and across his nose and opposite cheek.

I get the vague distinction that I know the second one, but I can't place my finger on where I might have seen him before. Something about him makes my hair stand on end. Before I went into hiding, I kept a safe distance from the demons as best I could, studying from afar or listening intently to someone else's encounters. My run-ins have been few and far between. Raum and his companions are the first I've come face to face with since I disappeared.

"Thank you, brothers," Raum says.

The one with the braids nods. He is more solid than his companions and of skin as black as soil. He has wide-set brows and a generous smile. He flashes two striking white rows of teeth at Raum. "Of course. It has been a while since we have seen another. What do you call yourself?"

"It has been some time for me as well. I am Raum."

He gives a closed smile and looks him over. Like the other demon, he has a scar on his face and a few more that creep down under his shirt. "I'm Eblis," he says, then turns his attention to the other two. "Mara and Leyak have been traveling with me for the last six months."

My blood goes cold as I watch Leyak tip his head to his name. What is he doing here? How? A million questions ring an alarm inside my head. Now that I'm looking at him, I can see traces of James' features, though most of them have been marred. My heart doesn't know whether to pound or sink as I take him in. I'm terrified of Leyak, but seeing him like this, with his true face, I realize that James is gone. Devastation is the only way to describe the feeling that washes over me.

Where James had a full face, his cheeks are now gaunter, the bones high and sharp. His beauty, though I hate to admit it, has been enhanced by the supernatural creature wearing his skin. One thing more peculiar than his enhanced features are his lack of muscles. The body seems to have taken on James' natural frame, sturdy but thin. It doesn't bulge with the power of darkness that I remember appearing under my hands.

"See something you like?" Leyak asks.

I blush, not realizing I've been staring. I look up at Raum and see that he is watching me with a keen eye. I can't read his expression, but I'm sure he isn't pleased that I've been looking at someone else. He must understand that this is the same Leyak I told him about.

Regardless, Leyak doesn't seem to recognize me. I don't expect him to. To him, I'm another face not worth remembering. This gives me little comfort, though, because if he does end up remembering, Raum is going to have a whole lot of trouble on his hands. If Leyak is the same as he was when I knew him, he is a terribly wicked creature. I have no doubt he will feel entitled to me once he is smart enough to put the pieces together. Just because he let me go before doesn't mean he will do so again.

I risk another careful glance at Leyak. Raum's words whisper through my head. One of them could be sick, he had said. Leyak reminds me of Culsu. I wonder if he would be as easy to kill as the younger demon had been.

"What are you doing with her?" Eblis asks. The question startles me, and I turn back to the first demon. As soon as our eyes meet, I break away. Eblis' eyes hold a dark power. They hold death. I get the sense he is much older than the others.

"I found her in Montana," Raum says, easing his eyes off me. "Would you believe it if I told you she's been hiding for three years?" He gives my neck an affectionate stroke. I admit I don't know much about being bonded to a demon, but I heard from a neighbor that those tied become completely infatuated. I feign admiration as I look up at him, which makes him respond darkly by caressing my throat.

We sit on the other side of the fire, closer to Eblis and away from Leyak.

Eblis' eyes widen and Mara chuckles. "Three years? So, she has no idea?"

I have no idea what? I look at Mara, whose face is split wide with a menacing grin.

Eblis regards me and smirks. "How interesting, and fortunate for you, my friend." Yes, how fortunate I am to have fallen into the hands of such a conniving monster. What does he mean?

Raum gives my arm a gentle pull and lays me across his lap. His fingers play with the tender wound on my neck. My blood boils and it takes every bit of self-control I have not to retaliate. The other demons take note of the mark, their leader switching the subject off me when he realizes I am unavailable.

"Where are you heading?" Eblis asks.

"Babel," Raum confesses, almost sheepishly.

The three look at each other and Eblis frowns. "That is a long way."

"Yes, but if there is a way to strengthen our power, it is worth it."

"You should continue southwest. Portland and most of the Washington area are no longer safe," Eblis says. My ears perk up at this, but I try my best to feign disinterest. Nothing is unsafe for a demon unless there is some new power coming into play. For once, I regret shutting myself off from the world for so long.

"I suspected as much," Raum hisses. "I will continue through this land, cutting through the desert until we reach the California coast. I have not determined if it should be the north or south coast, though, I must confess."

Mara digs long black nails into the earth and bares his teeth. "It is anyone's guess."

They continue to talk nonsense, discussing where each is going or coming from and politics. I care nothing about the political side of things and tune out, losing myself in the fire. Cities continue to fall. It's the same thing I heard before I went into hiding. The demons are still winning the war and I can't bring myself to listen to it again. Their stories are full of blood and pain and I can't even weep in front of them to mourn the loss of my kind.

I smile at Raum as he pets me and, though he tells me I am a good girl, I remember there is fire inside me. I remember to hate him.

VIII

Raum denies me food, despite how loud my stomach growls. I can only figure it's because we are in company and, though it won't satisfy the demons, they might want some. I'm used to not eating, but these last few days of being spoiled are making it difficult. Has it really been so long? Being with Raum has kept me distracted.

Both Mara and Leyak steal glances at me when they think Raum isn't looking. Leyak's are briefer, but then it happens. A light of recognition passes across his colorless eyes and the corner of his mouth twitches. I hold his eyes in fear that looking away will give him power over me. He won't win, not this time.

His chin lifts a touch as he looks above me. It's hard to tell where his eyes are directed, but I have a feeling he is looking at Raum, sizing him up. This could turn nasty. Raum favors me despite his abuse. He will tear Leyak apart if he tries to take me.

"Where did you say you found her? Montana?" Leyak asks, cocking his head to one side and then the other like a bird. His lips are parted enough that I can see his teeth have sharpened. Shit.

"It is so," Raum says evenly.

"I used to have one like her." Mara, who has spread himself across Leyak's outstretched legs, glances back at my former tormentor, his scarred brows furrowing. Everyone seems to be watching Leyak except for Raum, whose eyes I can feel on the back of my head as he plays with my hair. Chills run down my spine when Leyak's gaze slips down to me.

"You are suggesting that this is the same girl," Raum says quietly. "Surely one baring your mark could not have run from you."

When Leyak smiles, it does not reach his eyes. And when he laughs, it is with all the venom he wishes flowed in me. "You are right," he says. "I am sure what is mine is long dead."

He is threatening me, possibly both of us.

"Surely," Raum muses.

Eblis chuckles as he swipes his tongue over his full lips. "Even demons can become confused when in the wilderness too long," he says.

I glance at him then back to Leyak. Eblis is in charge, unless Leyak is feigning rank, though I don't know why he would. In the time I knew him, he was equivalent to a king. Are they all rogues?

As strange as it might seem, demons are cordial when it comes to each other. They don't like to offend, and even the lowest-ranking demons treat each other with high respect. Raum exudes power even if he doesn't blatantly show it. If things are as they were three years ago, attacking a guest—us—would be with great consequence.

If they are rogues, there is no cause for courtesy.

I feel like I'm going to be sick.

"When did you last feed from her?" Mara asks, breaking into my thoughts.

The constraint that has been around my heart since we joined their party tightens.

"This morning," Raum says thinly.

Mara shifts uncomfortably and looks at Eblis before turning back to Raum. "It has been months since—"

"Mara," Eblis snaps.

The demon pouts and dips his head. The movement makes him look younger than the skin he wears.

Months is a long time for a demon to go without feeding. It's not impossible, or even dire for them to do so, but it is rare. They must be hunting humans who have fled the cities. It doesn't explain why Leyak is here, though. I find it highly unlikely he would give up his throne. Something doesn't add up.

"Forgive him," Eblis says coolly. "It has not been so long that we should put our troubles on your shoulders."

I let out a short sigh. Eblis is in charge if he can command them. I just hope his power is strong enough to hold Leyak at bay.

Raum doesn't strike me as someone who likes to share. I'm thankful for the tight smile he flashes Mara before he says, "I need her if I am to make it to Babel." It's straight to the point. I am Raum's and none of them are going to get their fangs in me.

Mara huffs and leans against Leyak, who still looks ready to pounce on me.

"A drink wouldn't hurt her," Leyak says. "One swallow for each of us, to get by a little longer."

Eblis' eyes narrow, but he doesn't say anything to scold him.

I look up at Raum. *Don't let them touch me*, I try to convey. I can withstand Raum's rule over me. Maybe I could suffer Eblis' and Mara's bite, but I know Leyak's touch will cripple me. Once he has me, he will not let go.

Raum strikes faster than I thought a demon could move. I wouldn't have known he moved at all if it weren't for the burning pain in the side of my neck. All three demons sit up straight, leaning towards us as he pierces my already sensitive flesh. Lashing pain explodes from my neck and I make a restrained sound, encouraging the demons to draw closer still. It is over as soon as it starts, and the retraction of his fangs is as raw when he rips them from me. I fall against Raum and clamp my hand over the side of my neck.

Leyak's upper lip quirks. "I do not think she will be able to feed anyone now."

I lurch to my feet and steady myself against Raum's shoulder when I stumble. The urge to spit my fury at him comes to surface. The challenge is juvenile. How dare he flaunt me in front of Leyak when he knows what he did to me. I turn away before any of them can see that I'm crying, and I tell Raum I have to use the bathroom.

A look of annoyance flashes across his face, but he lets me go. I step outside of the dome where I'm instantly drenched by the raging storm, darting to heavier foliage to contemplate my escape. I can't see a clear path through the rain. I'll likely break my neck trying to run from them, but it would be better than being ripped apart by claw and fang.

If I stay here, I'll be killed in whatever brawl takes place between Leyak and Raum. Raum has plans to dispose of me anyway. The storm will obscure his senses long enough for me to run. This is the only chance I have.

"Don't even think about it," a throaty voice warns.

I spin on my heel.

Raum was right to follow me.

"We need to leave," I tell him. My voice is heavy with the tears I've swallowed.

"We are staying."

"Leyak is like a child. I'm something that he wants only because you have me. He won't be satisfied until he has me, and he won't keep me alive as long as you have." I glance nervously at the dome and hope they can't hear us over the rain. "Leyak knows who I am, and I will not let that *monster*," I point towards him, "touch me again."

"You think I haven't noticed the way he has been looking at you? I assure you that if any of them touch you, they will not live through the night."

Raum closes the space between us, our chests brushing together. He turns his head down, casting raindrops from his face onto mine. The words offer me no reassurance. I shake my head, chewing on my lip.

"I don't trust you, Raum, but you better fucking protect me from them," I say.

He nips the top of my cheek with a purr. "When you die, it will be by none other than me."

I turn my eyes up to his. A wisp of hair has broken away from its tie that Raum curls around his finger. He pushes it away from my face as he cups my chin and pulls me closer. Our lips brush together and then he kisses me. It's undeniably sweet, so sinful that my lips tingle. Something about it makes me cling to him. I have the feeling that this will be the last time he ever kisses me.

We all sleep together. They tangle their limbs with each other. I'm now certain that demons are from snakes. The way they wind and writhe about each other is as intriguing as it is repulsive. What is worse is that Leyak sets himself at my back while Raum holds me close to his chest. My demon hisses a warning at Leyak as he nestles his face against my shoulder blades. Another slings their arm over Leyak, their fingertips hanging above me.

My heart pounds so loud I'm sure everyone can hear it. I have a hard time sleeping in the company of one monster, and now I'm caught between two, with two more lurking at the edge of our entanglement.

I don't know whether to feel safe with Raum holding me or frightened. Either way, my future is grim. Hands roam over my curves. I press my face as close to Raum as I can. I pray that is all they will do. I force down the bile that rises in my throat when the familiar burn of Leyak's touch scalds me.

I don't sleep. Every bit of my body begs me to succumb to the darkness, but I must not. Something terrible is going to happen to me as soon as my guard is down. I hear movement somewhere in our nest. Skin to skin. It must be Mara and Eblis. I dare not draw an image of what they could be doing.

It isn't long before Raum falls asleep. His hold around me slackens and he turns his face away to breathe in the night air. Then Leyak makes his move.

He presses his face against my ear and flicks out his tongue when he speaks.

"I've missed you," he purrs.

He pulls at my hip to turn me over. I reluctantly let go of Raum and face him. Leyak *is* sick. I guessed it before, but now that he is up close and hovering, I know it to be true. His black eyes do not gleam like Raum's. They do burn, though. There are little red fires in the black abyss, hungry with flames.

I brace him as he slides over the top of me, leaning into my palms. The last time we were like this, he was full of muscle. Even James had been more solid. Now Leyak feels bony. I can still see the definition of muscles, the sharp lines of the supernatural, but his *strength* is not the same as before.

"Where have you been hiding, Leah?"

"Away from you," I whisper. I don't want to wake Raum, not yet.

A husky growl comes from Leyak's throat as he chuckles. "And here we are." He lowers to one elbow so he is half on top of me but still partly off to my side. "It's a shame you wear this now," he says, nuzzling the bite mark on my neck.

"It's better than having one of yours." I turn my face away, trying to break his touch.

"Yes, I should have bitten you when I had the chance. No matter, we can still finish what we started." His tongue touches Raum's mark and I tense. "We miss you," he says, using James' voice.

"Go to Hell," I hiss. I curse the tears that spring to my eyes.

Leyak pushes against me harder. "I'm taking you with me," he purrs. His tongue snakes across Raum's bite, probing the divots, savoring me. He lets out a huff when I shiver.

When Leyak slides his hand underneath my shirt, I'm thrust back to the past. I'm paralyzed, caught up in the nightmare I tried so desperately to hide from. He stretches out his elbow so he is completely over me and slides his body suggestively against mine.

His warm lips trail across my eyes, his sharp teeth grazing my lids, when suddenly he stops breathing. I look up hesitantly to see he is looking past my head at something in the shadows. One of his hands is on my breast and the other is sinking into the ground next to my head.

"What is it?"

Leyak's nails scrape against my skin as he re-moves his hand from under my shirt. "Shh," he hisses, sounding more reptile than human.

I glance at Raum then back at Leyak. The corner of his mouth quirks and his eyes narrow. Leyak slides across me, half crawling, half slinking over the ground into the shadows. He's stalking something. I know be-cause I've seen him move after me in the same way, with slow, precise measures.

I try to keep my eyes focused on him, but he blends in with the shadows outside the glow of the fire. I can't hear him either. Like every other demon, he is soundless. I hold my breath, straining to hear whatever it is that caught his attention.

I inch forward, hating how loud it sounds when-ever I move. I tense but Raum doesn't budge. I think his breath has changed, but I can't be sure. I don't have time to check if he is awake. Where the hell is Leyak? I'd be stupid to go after him. It's a trap if I've ever seen one. It is unlikely someone else is hiding this far out in the mountains, and even more unlikely they would come so close to a demon camp. Still, Leyak has gone after something. I'd recognize that look in his eye anywhere.

I crawl on hands and knees. I wish I was like a demon in the sense that I could be soundless. I nearly scoff at the idea as soon as it enters my head. There is nothing worthy of a demon, no matter how convenient it might be. Still.

I stop at the edge of the dome. The storm is louder now that I'm at the end of the barrier. I glance back to the nest before slipping through the invisible wall, into the rain.

There are no tell-tale signs of where Leyak has gone, but I work my way in the direction I think he might be. Even with the rain masking any sounds I might make, I'm careful, making a point to walk heel to toe. A streak of lightning illuminates the forest, making me drop to the ground before Leyak can see me.

This is stupid. I shouldn't have come out here. I could run while they're all distracted. I shift my weight to steady my crouch and shut my eyes and listen. Too many thoughts hound my mind and only one matters. I have to find whatever Leyak went for. It is important. He wouldn't leave me if it wasn't.

I feel blindly through the underbrush. Thorns and branches grip my clothing, making my effort more difficult. I'd do better standing, but the fear of Leyak finding me keeps me on my knees.

Another flash of lightning illuminates two dark eyes set inside an oval face a few feet in front of me. I fall back before my mind can register that the eyes are clear, not black. Even when the light passes, I can see her silhouette hiding in the shadows.

What is she doing out here? How? What is she doing so close to our camp? Where is Leyak?

She leans away from me and I grab her with one hand and put a finger to my lip with the other. "Quiet," I mouth, though I doubt she can read my lips in the dark.

She's so thin that my hand encircles her arm completely. My gut clenches. I knew it was possible, but I never really considered someone else fleeing into the wilderness like I had.

"Your eyes," she says, her voice as frail as she appears.

I press my finger harder to my mouth and shake my head.

"You're human," she says, her voice rising.

The presence of evil sweeps over me and, before I can jerk the girl toward me, she is ripped from my grasp. A piercing scream leaves her throat. I lunge after her as Leyak drags her through the foliage by the end of her hair.

"Leyak! Don't do this." I chase after him. "Please, don't."

The girl clutches her scalp and lets out another piercing scream. If the other demons weren't awake before, they are now.

Leyak chuckles, the sound sinfully dark.

The amber glow from the fire lights the path to the nest. Once we are back, it's over. He'll torture then kill her. The others will help because, unlike Raum, Leyak likes to share.

"Leyak!" I've never been brave enough to attack Leyak, not after the countless times he brutalized me. That spark of fear, the consequences of what I'm about to do, makes me falter, but I'm already lunging at him. I throw my entire weight into his back, pushing him beneath me and relieving his grasp from the girl's hair. The three of us tumble within the shelter of the dome.

The demon twists, reaching for the girl while trying to bite at me. His teeth scrape the top of my cheek. It stings more than anything, but the stench of his hot breath makes me recoil.

Hard hands grasp me by the waist and lift me away. By the snarl on Leyak's face and the possessive hold, I know it's Raum who has me.

"What have you caught?" Mara circles behind the girl, who is struggling to free her wrist from Leyak. Mara's movements are unusual. He switches between his feet to hands *and* feet. His arms are nearly as long as his legs.

Raum presses his lips against my ear. I can't feel them move, but a threatening hiss still manages to escape his lips when he tells me not to move. Every muscle in my body strains against him.

"Where was she?" Eblis asks.

"Hiding beneath a shallow hill," Leyak says.

Eblis presses his nose to the curve of her neck and inhales. A shudder runs through his body as he trails farther down, sniffing and rubbing his face over her. "Strip her," Eblis commands, stepping back. His eyes rove over the young woman, searching.

My gut clenches. He wants to know if she's marked. Even if she is, they'll take her. This isn't about respecting the demon she might belong to. It's about humiliating and degrading her.

"Please," the girl whimpers. She drops to the ground and wraps her arms around her knees.

"Keep begging," Mara says, latching onto her wrist.

"We'll be gentle," Leyak taunts, hauling her to her feet.

When Mara slashes into her sodden attire, he is anything but gentle. He purposefully cuts deeper than her clothes, marking her skin with fresh red lines. She flinches from every touch, pressing herself closer to Leyak.

Where did she come from? She must have seen our fire and drew closer to investigate.

I reach for the dagger still hooked to my belt. Consequences be damned. I can't do nothing.

Raum's warm hands move up to encircle my shoulders. "Don't," he croons. "They deserve this."

Leyak sinks his teeth into the girl's neck and pulls his head back and forth. Blood spurts from between his lips onto Eblis' chest. The red makes his dark skin glisten, accentuating the power behind his muscles.

"She doesn't," I choke.

"It is our way," Raum whispers, his voice caressing me. There's something in his voice that makes me look at him. Raum's eyes look glazed. His mouth is parted enough to reveal his fangs resting on his lower lip.

"You like this," I accuse. I twist under his hands, but he doesn't budge. "Do you *know* what is going to happen before they kill her?"

The girl is in nothing but her skin. Leyak throws her face first onto the ground. Dirt cakes to the fresh blood oozing out of a cut on her cheek. She flinches when Mara shoves his nose into the wound.

"Do something," I hiss. Pinpricks heat the back of my eyes as tears form.

"This is their kill. They have not touched you, and so I may not do the same. I cannot help her." Raum looks down at me coolly. "Nor do I want to."

Mara swoops at her again and presses his crude lips against hers. The girl's face twists when he forces his long red tongue into her mouth. Beside him, Eblis whispers something against her ear. I can't tell if she is crying because of what he is saying, or from Mara. Maybe both.

Leyak strikes as soon as Mara pulls away. He gathers the girl's muddied brown hair and wrenches her head back so hard her vertebrae pop. A gargled sound leaves her throat. She leans into him, twisting onto her side, but she has no idea she is lining herself up for a fatal blow.

I hold my breath when she looks at me. The little bit of hope she has left leaves when her gaze drops to my neck. No, I want to tell her. I'm not like them. And yet I do nothing when she shuts her eyes to resign herself to the demons.

Leyak runs his nose along the side of her face, smearing her blood into her skin. "I'm going to call you Leah," he says, his voice husky. His lips trail down to her collarbone until he comes to rest against her chest. He kisses her. "My name is Leyak," the demon whispers. "Say it."

It's as if his words blot out any other sound. The thunder from the storm is nonexistent. The wet sucking sounds from the other demons, gone. I can only hear Leyak's voice and how loud my pulse beats in my ears.

The girl tries to cover herself while still leaning into his hand. Leyak's mouth twists into a sneer and he gives her head a hard shake with the snap of his wrist.

"Leyak," she croaks.

"Good girl, *Leah*," he says. Leyak's hollow gaze slides to me, freezing the warm blood in my veins. His hand slides up the inside of her thigh. "Now I want you to scream it for me."

In the moment his talons slice into her skin, it is me screaming. Her mouth widens into pure agony as Leyak invades her sensitive flesh with his hooked claws.

I can't breathe. There is so much blood. It's all over me, my chest, thighs, in my hair. It's happening again, just as I remember it.

Leyak holds my eyes as he pulls his hand away from the girl and rather obscenely slings her blood through the air at me and Raum. It scalds the side of my face and reeks of burnt flesh.

All the noise that was blocked out comes rushing back when my knees hit the ground. Someone is screaming. I clamp my hands over my ears. God, no. This isn't happening again. I can feel Leyak's claws, his teeth, and his horrible skin on mine.

"Leah."

It's not me. It's not me. I can save her. God, help me, I can try to save her, but I can't see past the horror in my head.

"Leah."

Eblis, who has been collected from the beginning, succumbs to the bloodlust rising in the air. He falls on the girl's neck like a vampire, clamping his mouth around her throat, cutting off her scream so it is nothing more than a strangled gasp. It's then I realize that I am still screaming.

Mara shoves his shoulder against Leyak, pushing the lighter demon off balance so he can tear into her belly. They snarl and snap at each other like wolves over the spilled entrails.

Mara shoves his face into her white belly—

"Leah!"

I finally turn my eyes toward the sound of my name. Raum's hands cup the underside of my face.

"Do not look away from me," he commands.

I don't know what he does, but suddenly I can feel Raum. Not just that he is touching me, but *him*. It's like a dark wave that envelops me. I let it drag me under, leaning into the calloused fingers that hook under my jaw. He feels so good.

Movement draws my attention to the right at the same time Raum's kind eyes harden. Leyak might be sick, but he is fast.

He slams into my ribs and pulls me from Raum's hands. Sharp teeth tear into my arm. My bad arm, I realize, though it is not the bone that hurts. Before I can register the difference in pain, another shock of fangs tears into my shoulder and sends me to the ground. The bite doesn't pierce the leather of my jacket, but it doesn't make the blow feel any less like a gunshot.

"I am going to drain every drop of blood from your worthless body," Leyak spits, covering the side of my face with red spittle.

My head is foggy, my movements too slow. Leyak shifts on top of me and I swing with my free arm to deflect him. He's going to eat me, just like—

Another weight is added to our pile, forcing the breath from my lungs. Someone knees me in the back when I try to get up. Leyak rolls off me, only so whoever he faces can pin me down. I push whatever demon is on me up so I can slide out from under them when I realize they're fighting on top of me. The tearing of clothes and flesh sound identical.

A violent snarl cracks through the air, making every hair on my body stand up as I crawl away from the entanglement.

Eblis is on top of Raum, shredding the shirt off his back while Raum sinks his teeth and claws into Leyak. Raum doesn't seem to notice Eblis is attacking him. His talons are embedded into Leyak's shoulders, pinning him to the ground. Blood spurts through the air when Raum strikes Leyak's throat.

An iron grip latches my ankle and jerks me back. I kick, but Mara is faster. His face is covered in blood. He reeks of death and fear. I can smell my own fear in the air. He shoves my face into the dirt as he climbs on top of me, pinning me beneath his weight. I twist in an attempt to free one of my hands. I need my knife.

Mara bites me, the pressure of his teeth makes me arch into him. He tears into my jacket, moving erratically as he tries to find flesh to bite into. I throw my head back as he gets closer to my neck. The back of my skull smacks into his nose and he jerks back with a hiss.

"Raum!" I twist again, throwing my weight around. The world spins and I lose focus on Mara.

Eblis falls on his back as Raum turns his attention to me. What is left of Leyak claws at his neck and chest. His flesh is torn open and gaping, exposing fatty tissue and bone. His hands slip through the blood flowing across his skin as he tries to push the broken pieces together. He has been marred beyond recognition from Leyak or James.

Eblis looks at Raum, then to me and Mara. He doesn't know what to do. I imagine if Eblis was mortal, the whites of his eyes would be large with fear. Mara rips the jacket from my back, twisting my arms, and I cry out.

"Mara! Don't!" Eblis yells. The invisible white parts of his eyes nearly shine.

Mara finds skin and bites. The pain that runs through me makes me scream again. He jerks his head back and forth like he is trying to tear a piece off. His teeth scrape against bone. Liquid heat courses through me as blood spreads across my back. I can't stop screaming.

It feels like a train hits us, and when it does, it takes all the air from my lungs. Mara and I fly apart. Roars follow me as I heave myself up in preparation for another blow when Raum and Mara roll my way.

Everything hurts. I jerk my arms free of the jacket restraining me with a grunt of agony. The back of my shoulder is scorching. I think Mara has taken a chunk from my back. Oh God, he's torn me open.

Mara backs away from Raum on hands and feet. His scarred face twists into what can only be a glimpse of his true face. It's nasty and wrinkled. His nose lengthens and his chin juts out. When he snarls, his fangs are at least two inches long, too large to fit inside his mouth.

Raum falls on top of Mara with a vengeance that shakes the ground. They are a tangle of limbs and flesh. It doesn't take long for Raum to overpower the smaller demon when he lands Mara on his back.

Eblis grabs Leyak from under the arm and hauls him to his feet. Leyak's head tips forward, but he stumbles with his companion into the rain. I get only the briefest satisfaction seeing Leyak that way. There is no way he will survive the wound. Demon or not, he will be dead by morning.

I sway on my knees as I try to stand, and I fall forward. I might be dead too if I lose any more blood. My back is hot and wet with it. I crawl towards the demons.

Raum's mouth is fastened firmly over Mara's throat. I reach for them and push myself up, using Mara's legs as an anchor. Raum twists his body around and looks at me, his dark eyes searing into mine. A sharp ringing burrows its way into my ears. I nod. Without saying anything, I know what he wants me to do.

I undo Mara's pants and give them a hard yank. He bucks his hips and kicks me; his heel connects with the curve of my jaw. It jars my skull and I fall back, pulling the denim with me. I sag forward and jerk them again, exposing Mara down to his knees.

Raum folds Mara's arms across his chest as the creature screams. He tries to kick again, but his legs are bound by the ankles. I give a final pull to free his feet as Raum turns his body. He releases his bite only to reapply it over the top of Mara's head. Mara's eyes widen as he realizes what is about to happen. He strug-

gles wildly, kicking and thrashing. He jerks his head to
the side to try and free it from the sharp teeth that pro-
trude from Raum's gums.

Raum's jaw unhinges and his teeth lengthen. The
bones of his face shift, and his mouth stretches into a
grizzly gaping hole as he pulls the demon inside of
him. Mara's screams are muffled as Raum's mouth en-
gulfs his head. It's not until Raum's teeth are centered
over Mara's chest that he bites down. Mara's shriek is
cut off. His flailing body goes limp, save for one hand
that twitches as Raum consumes him.

I let go of Mara and scramble back to a tree. I draw
my knees into my chest and sob. The sound of Mara's
body sliding across the ground unnerves me, but it is
the crack of bone that sets me on edge. I throw my face
into my knees. Make it stop! Make it stop! My sobs
turn into screams. I clamp my hands over my ears. I
can't block out the sound of death.

I flinch when something touches me. Please stop.
Go away!

I look up, still sobbing, into Raum's black eyes.
Blood covers the bottom of his face. I break away, half
expecting to see part of Mara lying on the ground, but
there is nothing, only an empty patch of dirt that has
been torn apart by a struggle.

I turn my hands out to Raum. "Get it off me. Get it
off me!" I cry. Mara's life stains them like inky black
webs. I know I'm the only one who can see them with
the way Raum looks at me. His brows are heavily
drawn and there is a worried line in his now perfect
mouth.

Raum closes my shaking palms. Something like a
groan leaves his throat as he drops to the ground beside

me. He sways into my lap. I can't stop shaking. He pulls one of my hands to his mouth and presses his lips over the knuckles. A new wave of hysteria takes me and I let out a mangled sob again.

"Oh God!" I cry.

"I told you what would happen," Raum says.

I didn't imagine it would end like this. We could have run instead. That's not what happened. This is worse than when he ate the deer. I saw a demon so human that raw fear burst into his eyes as he fought for his life. Raum could have ended it with a swift snap of his jaws, but he didn't. And I helped.

"You're a monster," I choke.

He rolls on his stomach and crosses his arms over mine so I will lie down. He looks up at me, searching for who knows what. The cruel look in his eyes has softened to something that could be mistaken for pity. I can't stop shaking. The images are a constant replay in my mind's eye.

"I am," he says.

He weighs heavily on me. His limbs have not stretched like before, but he feels more solid, more powerful than before. I can feel it ebbing through him like a river. It pounds with a strong current in time with the beat of my heart.

He slides one of his hands beneath the hem of my shirt to the flat of my stomach. "Mara's life will sustain me for months. Consuming him has bought you more time."

I don't want time. I don't want this life anymore. I'm tired of surviving. "I don't care." I sniff. "I don't care."

"Oh, Leah," he croons. "You can't get away from me that easily."

I cry until I fall asleep. My dreams are full of horrors that I've never witnessed and they all happen at my hand. I take the life of humans and demons alike. Blood flows like a river and fire rains down from the sky. Everything is red.

IX

I wake up to see the world has turned upside down. It takes me a moment to realize that Raum is carrying me. I wrap my arms around his neck and breathe him in. Sulfur and dirt, he smells like the earth on a rainy day. The length of his stride slows and I look around. The land stretches into gold and pastel green fields with the occasional rocky surface peeking out.

"How long have you been walking?"

"A while."

I don't know what that actually means, but I suspect it has been at least a day. Raum is speaking, but I'm not listening to anything other than the rumble in his chest. The red stain on his collar cruelly stares back at me. It seems like so long ago. I don't want to believe what happened actually happened. Why had I jumped to help Raum?

"Are you hungry?"

"No," I honestly answer. Stress will do that, or depression. Or was it trauma? Something will do that. I can't remember what.

In fact, I can't remember what led to the demons attacking us. The more I try to remember, the more my head hurts. It starts with a dull throb but soon turns into a swift pounding.

Raum sets me down once we happen upon a small lake. I rinse my hands off and throw water in my face. I know the water hits my skin, but I can't feel it.

"Why did they attack us?" I ask softly.

Raum's mouth presses into a thin line. He looks sharply at me and then shrugs. "You were right about Leyak," Raum says.

What is he keeping from me?

I let it go when the pain intensifies.

I eye Raum through the glassy surface as he steps beside me and strips off his clothes. He wades into the water and rinses his body. The water turns a light pink around him as he scours the dried blood from his skin. Despite my better judgement, I do the same in hopes the water will wash me clean.

Don't people believe water will wash them clean? The blood of Christ. I laugh as I fall into the stains Raum has left behind. There is no salvation, only darkness. Only Raum.

He snakes his arms around me as I come to the surface. Hot lips graze my neck and shoulder. Revulsion ripples through me. I pry his hands away and slap him. How can he touch me when we just killed someone?

The corner of Raum's jaw ticks. He grabs me by the hair, and I grab his when he pushes me against the bank. In the water and mud, I fall open to him. I don't even protest when he bites me.

It's disgusting how aroused he is. What's worse is that I willingly fall into it. I hate Raum, but it's like I'm addicted to him. When he isn't paying me attention, my fear and loathing for him come in waves. But when he touches me, I'm enamored and lose myself in the moment. Raum is the only thing I can feel.

We dry quickly and dress before heading south. I no longer fight him on cutting through the desert. I've accepted that Raum will keep me alive, no matter what. He supplies me enough food and water to keep me moving throughout the day. I still thirst and hunger, but it's enough to sustain me.

We make a camp late into the night. I turn away when he strokes the back of my head. He unties my hair and smooths it down over my back and shoulders. His nails scrape against my scalp all the way to the ends.

"You should keep it down," he says.

"It's not practical."

He hums quietly. "Perhaps, but it suits you."

I run my tongue over my teeth. I can't let him needle his way beneath my skin further than he already has. "Just leave me alone."

"Is that what you want?" he hisses.

"Yes."

I close my eyes. His caress becomes softer. His fingers curl into my hair as I lean my head back. It feels so good when he touches me. He hums the song I remember from the day we met. It's the lullaby I need to fall over the edge into sleep.

When I wake, Raum is gone.

My heart skips a beat and I find my feet but stay low to the ground. It's dark out, the canopy so thick I can't even see if the stars are out. The fire has not been fed in some time; the flames are cooling. I toss a couple of logs on it. Has he really left me? I look around, but there is no sign of my bag. I scour the area, turning over logs and brush, but he hasn't left me anything. That must mean he is coming back.

Right?

I call out his name. My voice fades into the shadows. Not so much as a birdsong or insect's chirp comes back to me. Though it has been a long time since I've heard either, the silence frightens me.

This is fine. Raum will be back. But what if he doesn't return? I have no food, water, or weapons except for the knife on my belt he never took back. I have no idea where we are. I take a deep breath and hold it. I can't panic now. God, I can't panic. Not after everything I've been through. Raum abandoning me isn't the worst thing that can happen.

I rest my head in my hands. This isn't the end of the world. That's already happened.

I lie back down. If he is not back by morning, I'll leave. It's my only option. If I stay and wait for him, I could starve. If I've learned anything, it's to constantly move. I only stayed in the cave for as long as I did because it was convenient. If Raum doesn't come back, I'll have to start over.

A branch snaps deep in the forest. I sit up again and peer in the direction I think it's come from. I curse Raum for taking the water. I have nothing to put the fire out. The ground is too hard and dry to throw dust over it. What if Leyak or Eblis are looking for us? I wouldn't put it past them, Leyak least of all, to hunt us down for what Raum did, if by some slim chance he managed to survive.

A quick brushing sound comes from the shadows. My eyes widen and I jump to my feet. Not brushing, running. Someone is running towards me! I bolt in the opposite direction and veer sharply to the right to try and throw my pursuer off.

They tackle me, sending me face first into the grass. A bag slips over my head and a strap tightens around my neck. I scream and they kick me in the stomach, sending a whoosh of air out of my lungs.

"I've got her," they hiss.

I hear another, maybe two, coming near. My attacker hauls me to my feet. A blade slides across my throat. "If you scream, I'll cut your throat," they growl. It's a man.

I groan, still hunched over from the blow he gave to my stomach. Are they humans or demons? They smell of sulfur, but what reason does a demon have to put a bag over my head? I know for certain that none of them are Raum. Neither are they Eblis and Leyak.

"Is she hurt?" a male asks.

"I had to shut her up," the first says.

Someone relieves me of my knife.

"Hurry up," a female says as someone ties my hands behind my back. Without my knives, I feel naked in defense, but losing my hands leaves me entirely helpless. I test the binds as soon as they let me go. They're strong and secured with a good knot.

I lose track of time as we walk. Gold rays peek through the cotton hood when morning comes twice. My kidnappers grumble that we are moving too slow. I tell them it would be faster if they took the hood off my head. They ignore me. No one says a word to me, but they talk about me. They're trying to figure out if I'm marked or not.

"She has a bite on her neck," one of the males says.

"It's healing," the female points out.

I want to tell them no venom poisons my veins, but if they are demons they could bite me and make a bond themselves. Perhaps even save me for one of their other friends, if they have any. I find it funny they are as untrusting of me as I am of them.

"What are you?" I finally ask.

They grow quiet until the female speaks. "Human," she whispers.

"Devon," another hisses.

I stop abruptly. "Are you sure? Let me see you." I sound a little too hopeful. I haven't seen unclouded eyes in a long time. If they're not lying, I need to see them. "Please." They whisper amongst themselves and I pull at my restraints. "Please," I choke. I don't mean to beg. I've gotten better about it with Raum, but I *have* to see these people. Humans!

"It won't hurt anything," Devon says. She pushes whoever is standing beside me away and pulls the bag off my head.

My eyes slowly adjust to the stark light. Devon has a round face with a full mouth and button nose. Her dirty-blonde hair is pulled back in a fierce ponytail and her eyes are blue. I sway forward as I lose myself in the color and she grabs me by the shoulders. They are as blue as the deep lakes of Michigan.

"Oh my God," I cry and fall to my knees.

Someone pulls at my hands.

"What are you doing?" one of the men asks.

"She's not bonded. She wouldn't respond like this," they say. The binds fall free from my wrists.

Devon drops down in front of me. She has a kind face and an even kinder touch. As soon as my arms are free, I throw my arms around her. I can hear the smile in her voice as she hugs me back. "You're safe now." I have a vague awareness of the other two moving

around us, but I only notice the deep hue of her irises
and the harsh white around them.

Devon lets me cling to her, but I pry myself away
to look at her two companions. One man is about my
age with dusty brown hair and a disgusted look on his
boyish face. His cruel eyes are brown. Farther down,
his lips are twisted into a sneer with a scar at the corner.

The other is at least a decade older than me, perhaps in his mid or late thirties. His short black hair is
greasy with sweat. His caramel face is full of stubble
with the hint of a smile lingering behind it. He also has
brown eyes, though his are much more comforting than
the first. There is a quiet wisdom about him that immediately gives him my respect.

Devon helps me to my feet, and I look at each of
them in turn. I never realized how much I missed people. I left because I didn't want to rely on other people.
Groups are easier to find and pick off. I realize I should
have risked it all along. I push the thought away. It
doesn't matter. They're here now.

"We need to get going," one of the men says.

"Who are you?" I ask.

Devon cuts a look over my shoulder and smiles at
me. "I'm Devon and this is Sebastian and Liam." Liam
is the one with the scowl. He looks mean, but he doesn't
intimidate me. Sebastian nods curtly.

"Leah," I say. "How did you find me?" As I ask, I
take in our surroundings. I grip Devon's hand. What are
we doing in a city?

The place seems completely abandoned. Buildings
that should have been well-kept are crumbling. The
streets are covered with cars, dusted by the wind and
lack of use. Where are all the demons? Aside from our

little group, there are no signs of life, save for the over-growth of vines and weeds sprouting through the cracks.

"Let's go. Walk and talk," Liam snaps.

"A scout saw your fire in the woods." She points up to a ridge as we walk. I glance that way briefly, but the mountains are not my concern. Rooftops, broken windows—there are too many places a demon could be lying in wait for us. Where is Raum? Did he really leave me?

Devon stops talking as I turn my attention from the buildings to them. All three are strapped with guns and on Sebastian's hip is my knife. "That's mine," I say, touching my naked belt.

"For now, I'm going to hold onto it," Sebastian says.

For now. They might be human, but that does not give them the right to steal from me. My temper sur-faces and I have to force myself to smooth it over. These people rescued me. I won't be doing myself any favors by trying to relieve him of my blade.

"What are we doing here?" I ask.

Liam jogs ahead, his gun raised as he scopes out the path before us. Someone says something, but I'm too distracted watching the boy with a gun. I don't know these people but already I dislike Liam. There's something about his body language that screams dan-ger.

"We live here," Sebastian says.

"What?"

"Boise." Devon smiles.

Boise? Had Raum really taken us so far? He must have carried me farther than he let on. I can think on that later, though. What are we doing here? Larger cities are the most dangerous, or they were when I left. What I don't understand is why this one seems abandoned.

"No, I don't understand. What do you mean you live here?" I want to run. Dread smothers me, making the fresh air thicker than it really is. "Where is everyone?"

Liam whistles and we fall into place behind him. Devon stays close to my side while Sebastian brings up the rear. "Let's just get back," Sebastian says. He looks away from me, but not quick enough. His brows furrow and his mouth thins. My questions have bothered him.

We stick close to the buildings until we slip into one that looks like it's been burned. It's one of many that have been destroyed. Clothes, appliances, and bags of chips are scattered about. It reminds me of an old department store, a mall. Half of the building has caved in on itself. At the back is an opening in the floor with chains that disappear into a black abyss. I peer over the edge as they sling their guns over their shoulders.

"Can you climb?" Sebastian asks.

"Of course," I say as I take the chain next to him and shimmy down. My eyes adjust to the darkness; a dirty hallway opens beneath us with what looks to be old railway lights. Sebastian reaches up and helps me land on my feet. The air is stale down here. Already, I miss the flow of the wind.

I watch Liam and Devon come down next. There must be another way in and out of here. I don't like the idea of being confined and that the only entrance is by climbing a chain. I feel trapped as we walk down a murky corridor. It's lit by old utility lights spaced a couple of feet apart.

We pass through three steel doors, all makeshift, but they seem sturdy enough as they creak and moan when opened and closed. This must be an underground bunker, but it has been worked on over the years. This sanctuary wasn't preplanned; it was built after the Possession.

Voices trickle down to us and I crane my head forward. "Sabby!" a female's voice rings out. I step over the threshold cautiously and am met by three pairs of eyes. Sebastian nods to a brunette who I suspect had been the one who called out his nickname. "We were starting to get worried," she says, and then her eyes fall on me. Her smile falters.

The other two men in the room do not seem as worried as the woman claims to be. They eye me suspiciously. I take note of the room. A few couches, a coffee table strewn with ink-scribbled notebooks. No windows. There are three entryways, though, the one we have come through, one that leads down a dark hallway with even more doors, and another with a bright ending. Sebastian touches my arm to lead me to the latter.

Sebastian looks over his shoulder. "Liam, will you update them?"

"I'm the one who found her," Liam says crossly. He clenches his gun as he brings it across his chest, throwing a spiteful look at me as he does.

"Exactly," Sebastian says. "So, let them know what is going on. Devon and I are going to speak with her."

Devon wraps her arm around my shoulders and leads me away. Sebastian's heavy footfalls follow us down while Liam's fade into the background. It's so strange to hear someone else walking. Raum had always been so quiet.

We congregate in a small kitchen. Sebastian takes a seat and motions for me to do the same, but I ignore him. I'm too anxious to sit down. Devon walks to a fridge and pilfers through it, coming back with a bottle of water and an apple. I stare at the red fruit as she hands it to me. I cup it between my hands and roll it carefully, inspecting it, afraid it will fall apart any moment. The skin is smooth save for a bruise at the top.

"Where did you get this?" I ask, looking between them.

They frown. Sebastian bites the corner of his lip. "Can you tell us what happened to you?"

"I don't know what you mean." I bring the apple to my nose and sniff.

"For starters, you have a nasty bite on your neck but you're not marked," he says gruffly.

"Oh, that," I say absentmindedly. I don't know why they care about the bite. It doesn't matter. I'm holding an apple! I have not come across one fruit since the Possession. Food like mushrooms and greens were the only thing outside of the occasional meat. I take a bite and hum. I suck on my lip to catch the stray dribble of juice.

"Yes, that," Devon says. Her brows are arched as she looks at me.

"I was lucky, I guess." I am lucky to be alive but not lucky to have experienced the horrors Raum shared with me. "Where did you get this?" I ask again.

Sebastian sits forward, his shoulders tense. "How long have you been in the mountains?"

I go to take another bite and stop. I look at Sebastian with new eyes. He's a perceptive man. He is also very handsome with worn laugh lines. If he allowed himself to smile, it would be a pleasant look. Currently, those lips are twisted so thin I can hardly see them. What a peculiar question to ask.

"Three years."

"What?"

"Three years," I say a little louder.

"Oh my God," Devon breathes. She touches her hand to Sebastian's shoulder, her other to her lips. "She has no idea."

Sebastian's eyes move back and forth across mine. It feels like he is searching for something, trying to decipher a secret code in what I've said. What is so unusual about my survival? The longer he looks at me, the more he wears me down.

"What?" I'm afraid. They're looking at me as if I'm an alien. A desperate need to escape builds. I break away from Sebastian and scan the room. There are no windows here either. Tension rises through the air. It spreads like wildfire and suppresses the breath moving in and out of my chest. Suddenly, I wish Raum was here.

"Did you have anyone else with you?" Sebastian asks.

"No." It's not a total lie. Before Raum, I was alone. "What's going on?"

Sebastian exchanges a glance with Devon. She looks at me with such heartbroken eyes that you'd think she was in mourning. "Come with me," Sebastian says. He rises with fluidity, not waiting on my answer. I follow him quickly, with Devon in hot pursuit. I hear her sniffle behind me.

A steady hum fills the room ahead of us. Sebastian looks back to make sure I'm following, but there is no smile on his face. His expression is grave, his chocolate eyes darker than before. What's wrong?

He opens the door and holds out his hand to me as he steps down a ledge. I take it and step beside him and down two flights of stairs. My fingers grip his on reflex.

The room is shaped like a cavern. At the top is a circular opening that filters light into the bottom. It fans out over a field of wheat and green leaves that hums so loud I swear I can feel the vibrations in my chest. I recognize the sound. I step past Sebastian, my fingers sliding across his as the soft grass surrounds me.

At the edge of the field are boxes with covered tops. They stand on tall stilts made of pine. I can smell the sharp odor from here. There are hundreds, if not thousands, of hives and, surrounding them, going to and from the golden ray of light, are bees.

X

Somewhere I'm in Raum's arms. I must be. Every honeybee is a dream flitting across my vision. The music of their wings is a song I thought I'd never hear again. My lips move, but I don't know the words.

Someone touches me. I turn, half expecting to see Raum, but it's only Sebastian. I blink slowly, coming out of my daydream. I try to ask him how, but I can't find my voice. I press my fingers into my temples and close my eyes. When I open them again, this will have been a twisted fantasy. Raum must be playing some cruel trick on me.

I open my eyes. Sebastian's brown eyes continue to look at me and Devon's blue irises capture my attention.

"They came back," Devon says with a shrug, holding up her hands.

"When?" I can't wrap my mind around it. This is not possible.

"Almost two years ago," she says softly, her voice a choked whisper.

"Two—" I can't. I turn away. This isn't happening.

"It's closer to a year and a half, but..." Devon starts, but her voice fades as I walk farther into the field. I'm vaguely aware of the gardens they have surrounding the hives, but I pay them no mind. It's the bees that hold me captive.

Fear drove me to do the most extreme thing: cut myself off completely. If I was alone, nothing could happen to me. For three years I have remained hidden, but for what? I sit between two hives and listen to the whirring of the bees move in and out of the boxes above my head. They're everywhere.

Sebastian sits next to me. I'm grateful he doesn't say anything. He doesn't even look at me, just sits quietly while I try to understand what the coming of bees means. The back of my eyes burn. I bite my tongue to do my best in steering the tears away. I take a deep breath as awareness creeps back in.

"Where's Devon?"

"I thought it best to give you a moment. Devon is not the best at handling emotional situations," he says.

I nod.

"I'm sure you have questions," Sebastian says softly.

"I don't know where to begin." I lean my head back against one of the posts. The hum of the bees vibrates through my head. I run my hand up to the bottom of the box to feel it through my palm.

"How about you listen then?" he offers.

"Ok," I say, opening my eyes. Stray tears run down the curves of my cheeks.

"It happened the same way they disappeared. We don't know how or why. We just know that it happened. Our group calls it the Salvation," he says with a tight smile. I smirk too. How fitting a name compared to the plagues that have swept over us. "When we got here, the demon population was large, but they were weak. It was like the bees returning made them sick."

One of them might be sick, Raum had said. I remember how weak his friend Culsu was that attacked me. Weak—all of them. He knew. Raum knew what was happening and he left me in the dark.

Tears burn the back of my eyes. I look away from Sebastian towards a swarm that moves off to my left. I don't want him to see me cry, or see how angry I am. I feel so stupid.

Sebastian tells me the demons showed change slowly. At first, their figures thinned and then their powers started to fade. Where one could teleport before, it was suddenly grounded. When they started to bleed, they ran. Within the first year of the bees returning, it was as easy to kill them as it was a mortal.

Sebastian tells me his group was larger before, a total of thirteen, but once they made it to Boise safely, they sent others out to see if it was the same anywhere else. That was six months ago and only two people returned only to be sent back out again.

He stops and touches my arm. "Let's go inside. They can sense your distress."

I blink and look up. The swarms have changed their pattern, moving into one massive black cloud. Their dance is more aggressive than before. I follow Sebastian to the room we were in previously. He closes the doors on either end so we won't be disturbed. Sebastian leans against a steel table while I pace the room like a caged animal.

Raum knew. He and Eblis and the others even talked about it in front of me. They hadn't meant the rise and fall of the mortal cities, they meant their own.

Mara had even mocked me for not knowing and I had been too stupid to see what he meant. My hands curl into fists. I want to hit something.

"You really had no idea?" Sebastian asks.

"No," I say a little too sharply. "Three years ago, I ran away from Marquette, Michigan to the mountains. Most everyone I knew died when Sin swept through. I lost my boyfriend in the Possession. I didn't want to be another pawn in my city, so I ran. No one could compromise my life and the demons couldn't take anyone else from me. They couldn't get me." Raum was right. I am a coward.

"And all this time you never noticed the change in the cities?" Sebastian looks at me incredulously.

"I haven't been in a city since I left."

Sebastian runs a hand through his short hair and inhales deeply. When he lets it out, his body seems tenser. His shoulders draw together and he turns his head like his neck has become stiff. A series of cracks pops through the air.

"Food has been scarce. There are no fruits in the mountains and the animals are rare and thin," I tell him. "I survived mostly on roots, leaves, and meat when I was lucky."

Sebastian smirks, flashing his teeth. He shakes his head. "I don't know what to think of you," he says. He scans my face again and then his eyes drop to my neck. "It's no wonder you have that. The wilderness is crawling with demons. I have to ask, though, how did you escape?"

"And survive?" I finish.

I touch the mark. It's tender. Where the teeth pierced my skin are firm little scars from the tissue building beneath it. I want nothing more than to hurt Raum as bad as he has hurt me, yet I can't help but protect his memory. He abandoned me, I remind myself, among other things. Did he know we were close to humans? Did he do this as a mercy?

I look over Sebastian and try to read through his persona. I have the strong feeling to trust him, but I know I can't. Raum might not have given me his venom, but that doesn't make me any less dangerous if Sebastian feels I might be a threat to his community. If I tell him the truth, will he believe me?

I skip over the part of Culsu and tell him that Raum found me instead. I don't mention his name either, for whatever reason. "He kept me as a sort of pet, I guess." I wince at my choice of words, but it's true. Raum had only been affectionate when it suited him or when I was well-behaved. I mention coming across Eblis, Leyak, and Mara, but I leave out that Leyak was the one who stole James away from me. I don't mention that they attacked us or that Raum ate one of them. Suddenly, I remember Mara's bite and I reach back to feel for it.

"So, when we took you, you were in the demon's camp?" Sebastian asks, looking at me curiously.

"Yes," I say. I feel over where I remember the hunk of skin to be missing, but there's nothing there, just smooth flesh. Perhaps I only imagined him ripping the meat off. I could have sworn he did, though. I remember his teeth sliding against my bones. There had been so much commotion my mind could have been playing tricks on me.

"Do you think it will come looking for you?" Sebastian asks.

"No," I say quickly, his tone registering too slowly. I pull my hand away and look back at him. If Raum comes looking for me, it means I'm a threat to Sebastian and his family. "No," I say again, this time softer. "He left me. I believe if he wanted me back, he would have been here by now."

Sebastian's eyes go dark, his muscles flex across his shoulder tops. "Demons might not be as powerful as they once were, but that does not mean we don't take precautions. We use sulfur to hide our smell."

That makes sense, and it explains why I wasn't sure what they were when they initially caught me. "I think if he decides he wants to search for me, he will look for the group we were with a few nights ago. They attacked us, so he will have to assume they came back to finish the job."

"Why did they attack you?"

"I think some questions are better left unanswered," I say curtly. I say this to keep the memory not only from him but myself. If I can wash that night away completely, I can keep my sanity.

Sebastian smirks. "Providing it does not endanger us, you can keep your secrets."

"Thank you," I say.

The entrance door opens and Devon pokes her head in. "Hey. How are you?" Her movements are careful, like she doesn't want to startle me. The gesture mildly annoys me, but I refrain from commenting on it. I'm upset, not a wounded animal.

"I'll be fine," I say.

She smiles softly and turns to Sebastian. "Everyone is asking questions."

"And answers we will give them," he says, not taking his eyes off me. Sebastian seems nice enough, kind though his dark eyes tell me he has seen and done bad things. I noticed his hands were raw earlier, worn with experience. I suppose if he wanted to, he could hurt me with the same hands that extend to help me to my feet. As I take his offer, and turn to Devon, I catch a look in his eye.

Sebastian doesn't trust me. Through his smile, I see suspicion. Though I've escaped Raum's grasp, I can't help but feel there is a wolf at my back as I follow Devon out.

There are five other people in the group: Anna, Chris, Anthony, Sarah, and Michael—who goes by Mike. Liam continues to look at me with a sneer. I give him a wary once-over. I have no idea what he has told them, but I can't imagine it's anything complimentary.

Anna is the one who calls Sebastian by his pet name, Sabby. She's short and stocky with green eyes. She tries to ask Sebastian how he is and what happened that caused them to be gone for so long. She is overrun by Chris and Mike who want to know about me.

"Three years?" Mike asks. "That's amazing. Especially you being a woman." He catches himself. "Not that you being a woman means you can't, but you know—I think it would be more difficult."

I'm not offended by his words. He's not wrong. It had been difficult, especially when my period came once a month. Mike's face reddens whenever I smirk at him. "It has been difficult, but not impossible," I say.

The men are more curious about how I've managed to stay alive, while the women scrutinize me with hard glares. I don't mind that either. I rather like it compared to Devon's sympathy.

"I mean… how did you do it? You must have had help. Three years is a long time to be alone," Mike says. He's skeptical, but I don't blame him. Chris interrupts him to ask me where I had been last. What cities had I been through? What did they look like?

I do my best to answer their questions. I hate how disappointed everyone looks when I can give them no answers, further revealing I'm in fact a coward.

"So, where is the demon whose camp you were in?" Liam breaks in. It's not a question I wish to answer, but I can't deny the fire rising within me.

"You tell me," I say coolly. "You carried me off before realizing the camp was not my own."

Liam's gaze darkens and he crosses his arm below his chest. "How do we know she isn't a spy? It could have been a trap. She could have a real bite somewhere else." Behind him, the man named Anthony nods in agreement. Mentally, I put him on the same list as Liam.

I do not like Liam. I don't know where Raum is and, even if I did, I have no reason to protect him. A part of me brushes that thought aside. He kept me alive, so I could help him remain the same. If he met his end some other way, then that is out of my hands, but I'll not give any information about him to an arrogant boy.

"Would you like to check?" I ask him directly. "Perhaps I'll even give you a little show."

"*I* will check," Devon says, cutting Liam off before he can respond. She throws him a sharp look. "The audacity."

Sebastian wipes a smirk from his mouth.

Liam's face reddens. I don't know what drives me, but I want to egg him on, push him over so he will snap.

"I'm sure you want a shower anyway," Devon says.

I smile. "Yes, thank you."

"Yes, Liam, you're so rude," Anna says, placing a hand on Sebastian's thigh. I'm still looking at Liam, but I can feel her eyes on me. I laugh silently to myself. Poor girl must be a weak soul. She can't be too weak if she has survived this long, but still, she's fragile. I have more important things on my mind than stealing Sebastian away from her. The only thing I want of Sebastian is for him to stop looking at me with those cutting brown eyes.

XI

Devon checks me over thoroughly, but she can't find any suspicious marks. There are a few bruises that mar my skin but nothing that waves a red flag. She apologizes profusely whenever she touches me or turns me in a certain direction. She blushes when she inspects the bruises on my thighs. A crimson stain of my own colors my skin.

She clears her throat and steps away. "I think you're good."

Devon passes me a set of folded clothes. She makes another quick sweep of my legs as I step into the pants she gives me. She frowns. Yes, Devon, this was only one of the terrible things he did to me, I want to tell her.

"What do the marks look like?" I ask to break the tension. I'm thankful she doesn't ask me about the more intimate marks on my body. I'm sure she is smart enough to put two and two together.

"Similar to the one on your neck. Instead of fading, the mark darkens." She hands me a little handheld mirror.

"I never actually saw this one," I say and twist the glass until I can see it. It certainly looks as nasty as it felt when he gave it to me. The circle is about six inches across. Triangular black abrasions line the out-side, impressions of Raum's fangs. I run a finger around the dark mark.

"Can I ask you something?" Devon asks. I nod, setting the mirror down. "How were you bitten without being poisoned? Are you immune or something?" She laughs a little, her smile twisting into a frown as she realizes there's nothing funny about her questions.

"He never gave it to me. I don't know why. He did a lot of terrible things, but binding me to him wasn't one of them." I look away distantly. I'll never stop asking myself that question. "Why do you think we are immune to Sin?"

She folds her arms as she leans her back against the tiled wall. "I don't know. Maybe this whole thing has been a test?"

"A test," I say bitterly. I smooth the cotton t-shirt down, savoring the way the clean threads feel against my skin.

"What do you think?"

I shrug. "I think it's a curse. Mankind was destroy-ing the world long before the demons. I don't know if this is God's doing or not, but if it is, I'm not sure that I blame Him."

Devon smiles softly. "You don't believe in God?"

"I don't know what I believe in. I never thought to care before, and then I started praying. Now?" I look down at the damp floor. "I don't know."

Devon shows me to my room, four stone walls with no windows. I understand that we are under-ground, but I hate not having a window. It feels like the space is closing in on me. I may have to tell them I can't stay here. Should anything happen, I can't be confined.

I ask Devon for a map of the facility, but she tells me it isn't big enough to draw one. I suspect, though she has been the nicest to me, that she doesn't trust me to know everything about them yet.

We all eat together in the common area, where I first came in. Anna and Chris fix everyone's plates. They might have bees and grow their own food, but the group sticks to strict portions. I take a spot on one of the couches and curl my knees to my chest. I'm grateful for the food. I eat slower than everyone else, savoring every bite. They steal glances from time to time, but someone must have said something because they no longer bombard me with questions. I silently thank whoever did.

Meanwhile, Liam and Anthony sit at the table by themselves, their heads bent together like they're conspiring. They're probably just talking. Who am I to jump to conclusions? I'm being ridiculous and entirely ungrateful for their hospitality.

During my assessment of everyone, my eyes come to Sebastian. He is laughing at something Anna has said. I was right; he does have a nice smile. It's charming and makes him look younger than I perceive him to be. They make a cute couple, though she is much younger. Their skin tones and wide smiles make them look striking. Sebastian does have an accent, but I've noticed it only comes in on the tail end of words. It sounds foreign, but it could be something he picked up from family. I like it.

All this company makes me uncomfortable. I turn to Devon who has been protectively at my side. She pops a green leaf into her mouth. "I think I'm going to head to bed," I say quietly.

"Mm, I bet you're tired. Do you want me to come with you?" She brushes her fingers together and sets her plate on the coffee table in front of us.

"No, I think I remember the way." I stand before she can protest.

"I'll escort you," Liam offers. The legs of his chair make an obnoxious scrape against the floor as he backs away.

I look at Liam coolly. He is all smiles.

"Thank you," I say. Sebastian gives Liam a stern once-over as we leave the room.

"I think we got off on the wrong foot," Liam says. I'm all too aware of how close he moves beside me. His shoulder bumps into mine as he slows to keep pace.

"You can save face. It's just us."

Liam smirks and gives me a sideways glance. "I'm sorry," he says. "For the way I treated you. And for kicking you," he adds quickly.

I figured it had been him who kicked me. Sebastian doesn't look like he would be cruel for the sport of it. "I can't blame you," I say. He tries to make small talk. I oblige only to be polite and try to get a better feel for him. I catch his eye several times on our walk; each one is different than the last. Sometimes he looks angry, other times curious or hungry. There's something off about him.

When he follows me into my room, a chill runs down my spine. Cornered. I clear my throat and smile at him. "Thank you for walking me back."

He scopes the room until his eyes settle on me. Now they are cold. "If you need anything, my room is next door."

"I think a woman might be better to assist me if I need it." I won't be going to Liam for anything.

Liam flashes his teeth with a dark look. "Devon's room is across from mine." He points over his shoulder to the right. "But she tends to be a heavy sleeper. I, on the other hand, am always awake."

I can't tell if he is trying to threaten me or make some offhand suggestion. "I'll keep that in mind," I say.

"Goodnight." His footsteps fade down the hallway. I assume he is heading back to the main room. I wait a few heartbeats before closing the door. There is no lock on the inside.

I try to sleep, but when I hear Liam's door open and him shuffling around inside his room, I grow paranoid. Devon checks on me once and I tell her I'm alright, but only because I don't want her to worry. She is too overprotective for my nerves. I wonder if she used to have a child with the way she dotes on me.

Hours tick by and still I can't sleep. Aside from worrying about Liam, I wonder if Raum *is* looking for me. I'm convinced he left me, but he seemed so adamant about keeping me close. My being here could be putting these people in danger.

I open my door and sit at the foot of my bed, my back against the mattress, and stare. Everyone has gone to bed. The hallway is heavily shadowed, though a white light tries to break them apart. If anyone or anything tries to sneak into my room, I'll see them long before they do me.

Footsteps come from the end of the hall, drawing louder the closer they get to my door, and I hold my breath. A shadow slides across the stone floor and comes to rest as it pools across my threshold.

Sebastian ducks his head. "I thought you would be asleep." He scans my door frame, like something about it has become particularly interesting.

"I'm not used to sleeping," I say, slowly letting out the breath I had been holding.

Sebastian pulls my knife out and extends it to me. I stand and take it from him. Before I can pull it away, his grip hardens. I had stripped off the pants Devon gave me. His eyes are fixated on the various love bites decorating my legs.

I blush. I hadn't thought about covering myself before approaching him. It wasn't necessary with Raum. Not only that, I realize the marks might give Sebastian more cause to worry.

I clear my throat and pull the knife free. "Thank you," I say. I grab the door, but Sebastian puts his palm up before I can close it.

"You're safe here, Leah," he says softly. His eyes reflect the sadness in his voice.

I don't feel safe. His doubts have needled their way into my brain and all I can think about is Raum tearing this place apart to look for me. I think about Liam sleeping a few feet away, about being underground and the lack of windows and sunlight.

I nod. I close the door before he can say anything else. I can't stand the way his judgmental eyes have weakened by seeing the marks on my legs. I don't want anyone's pity. I don't need it.

A few minutes tick by before I hear him move away from my door and go through another, the one directly across from mine.

XII

Sebastian leads a scout the next morning to check the perimeter. I have no doubt this is a usual run for everyone else, but for Sebastian this is because of me. He is harsh with his commands. His eyes cut to me from time to time, like he blames me for something I have no control over. I truly believe he would have left me behind had he known the camp didn't belong to me.

"Leah, a word," he says.

Anthony and Liam exchange glances. When Liam catches my eye, he winks. His sudden shift in attitude makes my nose curl. I follow Sebastian. I try to ignore the way everyone watches me. Their stares crawl across my skin, making me feel vulnerable.

"What should I be looking for?" he asks me quietly.

I take a deep breath. "Nothing." I pause, looking between his eyes. "But if something happened to catch your eye," I say, lowering my voice so no one else will hear, "taller than you, long hair." I cut my hand across my collarbone. "The same skin color as you, maybe a little darker, and big. He isn't sick like the ones you drove out of here."

"How strong?"

I imagine the fight and how he fended off Eblis while tearing into Leyak. I remember Mara screaming and fighting as Raum's mouth fit over his head. Raum was unscathed save for the tears in his shirt.

"I don't think he can bleed," I say. If blood is a sign of their weakness and mortality, Raum has none.

Sebastian's eyes harden as he looks me over. He shakes his head. *What has he gotten himself into?* The question flits across his eyes before he turns away from me. "Stay with Devon," he says. "She'll find work for you to do."

The three men leave with their guns. They're going to need a lot more than a few bullets to protect them. But, I remind myself, they have survived this long. I'm sure they will be fine.

I help Devon and Chris tend to the gardens. We pass through the hives to another chamber closer to ground level. UV lights dangle from the ceiling like tacky chandeliers. We dig through the dirt, harvesting various greens and vegetables.

"Where do you get your power source?" I ask, nodding to the lights.

Chris looks up. At eighteen, he is one of the youngest of the group. Mike would be the next, who can be no older than his early twenties. It's hard to imagine Chris is still a teenager. He has a coarse beard and a hard look in his haunting gray eyes I would expect from someone twice his age.

"There's a river a couple miles out. Man-made— or demon-made," he says quickly. "We built a wheel to turn the water, strung up a couple of lines." He points to a cord that disappears to another level of the compound. "The water generates electricity."

I smile. "That's smart."

"It was Sebastian and Robin's idea." Chris glances at Devon as soon as he says it and ducks his head.

"Who is Robin?" I ask, looking at Devon.

Devon moves stiffly. She brushes the dirt from her knees before setting her basket between mine and Chris'. "She was my sister," she says softly. "She was one of the two who came back from our first scout. I begged her not to go again, but she was too stubborn. She said I worried too much. I practically raised that girl," she says, looking past us. By the hollow look in her eye, Devon hasn't talked about, much less thought about, her sister in a long time.

"I'm sorry," I finally say.

Devon flippantly tosses a cloth over the baskets. "It's not your fault," she says. "I just hope she is somewhere dead. Better that than possessed." Devon's blue eyes snap to mine, making me jump. "Let's go up to the surface. Chris?" She turns before either of us can say anything.

Chris sticks close to my side. "Don't take it personal."

I nod.

"Devon doesn't look it, but she's near forty. I don't know the whole story, but she took to raising Robin when she was ten. It doesn't get easier."

"I don't imagine it would." How hard it must have been to look after someone so long only to lose them so quickly.

Chris keeps his gun raised as we climb a ladder to an alcove of trees. He looks for any signs of life that might give him reason to pull the trigger his finger dances over. I glance at the black metal briefly. I wish I knew how to shoot. That is one thing I never got the opportunity to try out.

Between the maples and junipers are apple trees. Not all are in bloom, but it's still an incredible sight when I see bits of red peeking through. I watch Devon pick the biggest ones, leaving the smaller ones to grow. There aren't many that meet her requirements.

"What is it?" Chris asks, giving me an odd look.

"Don't you think it's strange there are only apple trees?"

"Because it's the forbidden fruit?" he teases.

"No one knows if it was really an apple," Devon mumbles.

"Maybe," I say. "Apples are more delicate than, let's say, a pear. Even if the plagues hadn't killed them, they'd likely die in the winter. These have been here for a while." There is no way they planted these trees. And why are they in bloom when the maple leaves still cling to their color-faded trees?

Devon hesitantly puts the last apple in a bag. "I think we should take the blessing for what it is," she says.

"Is this the only fruit?" I ask as we walk back towards the barracks.

"Yes," she says stiffly.

How strange. I don't say anything else. I can see that my questions have bothered Devon. The prior mention of her sister probably doesn't help the situation. I'm sure there is no rhyme or reason to the apples blooming, much like the bees' return, but I can't help but wonder.

It's well after dark by the time the men return. I'm playing cards with Devon, Anna, and Mike when they trod in. They look tired and haggard, but untouched otherwise. I meet Sebastian's gaze and he shakes his head. I let out a sigh of relief. Raum has left me for good. I know it.

I bite the inside of my lip and look back down at my cards. A smile threatens to reveal itself.

"Hey! What've you got there?" Mike asks. His breath smells like peppermint. His lanky form teeters on the edge of his seat as he leans over to look at my hand.

"Back off!" I fold them against my chest. Anna leans over to peek at Mike's hand as he tries to look at mine.

"Mhm, then why are you smirking?" He sits back in his seat, taking a long hard look at the black and red suits. When he notices Anna, he scowls at her and swats her away. "Cheater."

A surge of sadness runs through my body. I have no reason to be upset, but the idea of Raum being completely gone does something to me. I fold my hand. This is asinine. He tortured and used me. I know the feeling is irrational, but I can't stop as it comes in full force. I don't know if I necessarily miss him, but the idea of being free of him feels foreign.

"Let me see," Mike says and lifts my cards. "Why the hell did you fold? That's a good hand!"

"I'm not really feeling the game," I say.

"Pfft, you haven't drunk enough," he says, sliding away from the table.

"I haven't drunk anything," I call.

"Exactly!" Mike's voice rings from around the corner.

"Now you've done it," Devon laughs.

"Done what?" I look between her and Anna. Mike comes back and slams two cases of beer on the table, in the middle of our pile of cards.

I laugh. "In a post-apocalyptic world there is beer?"

"Hell yeah! There is tons of it!" Mike passes something with a pink pony on the label.

It doesn't take me long to put down three ambers before I have a little buzz. Sarah laughs at something Anthony says and covers her mouth with her hand. Her eyes squint and her body shakes. Anthony grins and says something else that makes her snort with laughter. Her amber hair falls over her face as she leans forward, slamming her bottle on the table between them.

Mike, Devon, and Anna still play cards. Anna is clever, but Mike is right; she is a cheat. She's just very good at not getting caught. I catch her a few times slipping her fingers into the deck between them when she thinks no one is looking. When she catches my eye, she winks.

Mike slams his hand down and points across at Anna. "Got ya!"

Anna lays down her hand with a smirk.

"Oh, for fuck's sake!" Mike slides his hand across the cards, spilling them into Anna's lap.

They're an interesting family. They're all completely different, but they work well together. I'm sitting on one of the couches watching them. They haven't made me feel unwelcome, but I don't want to impose either. I feel so out of place, lonely even. I'd give anything to have the connection these people share with each other. I find myself smiling at Anna and Mike despite myself.

This will take some getting used to.

"You look like you're settling in," Sebastian says, sitting beside me. The couch is big enough for four people, but he has sat closer to me than necessary. I take it as a sign that he trusts me. At least a little bit.

"It's the booze," I say with a sigh. I bring my bottle up for another taste and savor the ale as it spreads across my tongue. It surprises me that demons continued to process this stuff before they fled.

He turns the bottle around, circling the base through the air. "So, tell me about yourself."

"Well, you already know—"

"I mean before," he waves his hand through the air, "all of this."

"Oh, well. I don't think any of that really matters." I tuck my feet under my body and turn to him. I don't want to talk about my past life, but I give him my full attention anyway.

"Of course it does. It's who we are," he says matter-of-factly.

My mouth twists. "I'm not who I was."

"Humor me." His brows arch. He brings his thumb up to his mouth while he waits for me to respond, pressing the nail against his lower lip.

I tell him I was going to college for a degree in marine biology when the plagues started. I don't want to talk or think about losing anyone all over again, so I don't mention what happened after that. Just before. I tell him I had a German Shepherd named Cash, after the man himself. Sebastian smiles from behind his beer and says I have good taste. In passing, I mention I used to journal. I love to write even though I have no real creativity.

In turn, he tells me he is from the west coast. He used to be in the Coast Guard and was taking a year off before he decided if he wanted to work as a contractor for the government. During his free time, he liked to surf.

"What made you come here?" I ask.

"My grandmother, ah, that woman was a saint! She used to read the *Bible* to me when I was little. I never really believed in any of the stories she read me, but I always listened." His speech is faster, moving smoother now that he has a steady stream of alcohol running through him. "I remembered she said that God's people always fled to the wilderness, to the mountains. It seemed like the safest place to go." He pauses and looks across my face. "You?"

"I knew the mountains would be safe," I agree.

"Smart choice," Anna says.

I didn't realize we had drawn everyone else's attention. Anna, Liam, and Anthony have found seats close to us. How long have they been there? More importantly, how much have they heard? Not that it's sensitive information. I'd just prefer not to open myself to them, Liam in particular, who is currently smirking at me.

"What about you?" I nod to Anna.

"Anthony and I are from Portland." She throws her thumb back at him.

I look back at Liam. "A little place called Burns. It's in Oregon, and how I met these two." He nods back to Anna and Anthony.

Everyone else joins our group, but it's much the same. They all came from relatively close places. It seems I'm the one who ran the farthest. Liam sits forward so he can look directly into my eyes. There's a twisted gleam in his eye that reminds me of Raum.

"You must have been scared," he says.

"Yes," I say evenly. "Weren't you?"

The glow coils back behind the soft brown of his eyes. Liam shrugs. "Not really."

"You little liar," Anna scoffs. Her lips twist into an amused expression as she looks back at me. "You should have seen him when we found him. He was crying like a baby."

A dark look flickers over Liam's eye that passes as soon as his face splits into a grin. "Those were tears of joy."

Anna rolls her eyes in response. Anthony chuckles and leans forward to tousle Liam's mop of brown hair. They throw fake punches and, while they are distracted, Anna gets up from her seat to whisper something in Sebastian's ear. Devon sits on the arm next to me and stretches her legs over Liam's knees.

"Where did you learn everything?" Chris asks. "You seem to know a lot."

I smile. This isn't the first time Chris has asked me about my survival skills. I know he is only asking because of my questions about the apples. Devon must realize it too because she stiffens.

I focus on Chris' gray eyes when everyone else turns theirs toward me. "A demon held me prisoner in the first year of the Possession. He would send me to the library to collect documents whenever I wasn't at his side. I started bringing more books than he requested, kept them hidden and took notes. I wrote down every edible plant from Michigan to northern California. I sketched photos so I would remember what they looked like. I knew a lot about hunting animals from my boyfriend. I used to go with him on hunting trips."

"What happened to him?" The question comes from Anna. I tense at the question. I said too much when I revealed it to Raum. I feel like I'm making the same mistake when I answer her.

"He was possessed by the demon who kept me in Michigan," I say.

Anna rests her hand across Sebastian's shoulder. I look at her protective touch. I envy them. I can see by the way she looks at Sebastian that she would do anything for him. I wish I had that back then.

Sebastian is looking at me with the same intensive stare Anna gives him. It makes me uncomfortable, but I try not to let it get to me as I look away from him. I'm sure every leader feels the need to protect those beneath them.

"You left him?" Sarah asks, her tone condescending. It strikes a fire in my chest that must reflect through my eyes because she jumps when I look at her.

"Sarah," Devon hisses.

"Have you ever been able to extract a demon from a host?" I ask coolly.

Her face reddens as she looks down.

It's Liam who speaks. His arrogance is gone. "No," he says. "But that doesn't stop us from trying."

Liam would make an excellent host. He is everything Raum was without the supernatural abilities. If a demon ever managed to slip inside of him, they would have a field day. The bloodlust that fills his eyes tells me everything I need to know about the torment he and the others might have inflicted. He runs his tongue over his teeth the same way I imagine him sliding a blade over soft flesh.

I turn back to Sarah. "To answer your question," I say, my voice still taut with venom, "I left him only after he stopped coming to the surface. That is how the demon culled me. When my boyfriend disappeared, so did I."

Sarah clears her throat. "I'm sorry," she mumbles, still not meeting my eyes.

"Why don't we talk about something lighter?" Devon offers.

"Oh, things are just getting good," Liam says. He squeezes one of her feet and gives it a playful shake.

"I think we should play another round of cards," Mike says. He slaps his thighs and stands up.

"Do you want to lose again?" Anna teases. She jumps up, making her way to the table with Mike hot on her heels. Sarah follows them without meeting anyone's gaze. It's only me and Devon who stay with the rest of the men who start their own debate of scouting farther outside the city.

"We need one more!" Anna calls. She points to Sebastian then to Anthony, who rolls his eyes and reluctantly gets up.

I lean against Devon's hip. She slides her fingers through my hair. The tension coursing through me runs dry beneath her touch. I smile and mouth "thank you". I respect Devon more after learning about what happened to her sister. There's wisdom in her bright eyes. I close my eyes and enjoy her caress. When was the last time someone touched me with kindness? Her nails scrape the front of my scalp and down the back of my head, spreading through the ends of my hair I have started to leave down again.

I must fall asleep because the next thing I know I'm being lifted. "I've got her," someone says. I float through the air. I should wake up. I don't need to be carried. But it feels so good to be held.

An overwhelming need to be close washes over me. Close to *someone*. I pull the front of his shirt as he lays me down in bed. I know it's a man by the strength of his arms and his masculine scent that smells like pine needles and tobacco. My eyes flutter, but it's hard to make out the details of their face as they lay me in bed. It's too dark. It could be Sebastian or Liam, they're built alike. It must be Sebastian because Liam wouldn't dare touch me. Not with the way he sneers at me. And Sebastian is kind, even if he is distrusting.

He leans over me when he lays me down. I don't know what comes over me, but if I'm not close to him I will surely die. As soon as I feel his face bent over mine, I kiss him. At first, he resists. His fingers harden on my shoulders as he pushes me back. I pull him down by the back of the neck and press my lips back to his. His mouth presses firmly into mine. He releases me only to grab the back of my head and my back, pulling me closer.

Touching Sebastian is like coming home, and yet it's not enough. I feel complete and still I want more. The heat already coursing through my body flames, making my skin tingle. My head swims. I open my mouth and his tongue slips through eagerly. The bed

sinks farther as he lies over me. He tastes good. I wonder if the rest of him is just as delicious.

There is something erotic about not being able to
see each other. It makes everything more sinful. We
can't strip our clothes fast enough. I'm halfway done
pulling my shirt off when he enters me. My back
arches, his arm encircles me and lifts me up. His moans
of pleasure match my own.

He is rough; his hands threaten to bruise me
though I know he does not have the strength. Not the
way Raum did. He bites and sucks my neck and chest
without drawing blood. Raum would have left me tender and broken.

"Harder," I moan.

Sebastian pins me down. As much as I try to dis-
suade the thought, it's only Raum I think of. Raum's
hands on me. Raum filling me. Raum's lips skimming
over the mark on my neck.

XIII

I have been here two days and already I have made a mess of things. I sit up with my face in my hands to fight against the sick knots forming in my stomach. I've taken Sebastian from Anna. It might only be a one-time thing, but it's enough to break anyone's heart. Memories and visions of Raum float into my mind. I pull my hands away and stare across the room in horror.

Even apart from Raum, I can't escape him. I must be damned if I can lust after him still.

It's no surprise that I'm alone in bed. Despite the turmoil raging inside, I'm relieved I don't have to face Sebastian just yet. I feel terrible about the whole thing.

Time evades me. I can't sit still long enough to contemplate anything and dress quickly. I only pause when I catch a glimpse of myself in the mirror as I shrug a shirt over my torso. I pull the collar down.

There are bruises on my breasts. Hickies. It's warm, but I slip a jacket on anyways, like it will give me extra protection. Not that I need protecting as I was the one who instigated it all. At the very least, it will hide me from further embarrassing myself.

I have to get out of this room. I fling the door open and burst into the hallway, straight into a wall. The wall catches me, steadying me when I stumble.

"In a hurry?" Sebastian asks.

My face warms as I meet his eyes. My mouth opens but no words come out. I lick my lips instead.

"Is everything alright?" he asks seriously. His voice deepens, his brows furrow.

We can't avoid talking about what happened, as much as I'd like to. His hands are still on my arms. I imagine them touching me the way they did last night. His eyes scan my face. My face must have darkened because I can practically see the blush in the reflection of his eyes.

"I think we should talk about last night. I don't know what happened. I don't have any excuse for it." I lick my lips again, nervously.

He cocks his head. "What are you talking about?"

I open my mouth to tell him but stop. Is he playing stupid to spare my feelings? The only other reason he would ask such a question is if it hadn't been him. Had Raum found me? I had been consumed with thoughts of him. Perhaps he had crept in and ravaged me after all. But no. The person I was with was too human. The way they moved and felt, even smelled, had been human.

Raum or human, the thought chills me.

"You didn't come into my room last night?" I ask slowly.

"No. Why? What happened?" His grip has hardened, a simple flex of the fingers. A protective hold.

I feign a smile. "N-nothing. I'm sorry. I've been having crazy dreams and you must have been in this one." I touch his arm to pry myself away. I'm too afraid to ask who carried me to bed.

"You dreamed of me?" His voice takes on a curious tone.

I laugh nervously. "Apparently. I'm sorry, I need to go. I told Devon I'd help her with some chores, and I think I've overslept." I slide past him, aware that he turns with me, his eyes enveloping me.

"You'll have to tell me of this dream later."

Not even if my life depends on it.

I work mindless chores with Devon. I clean vegetables out of a box she hands me and cut away any bad spots. I only half-heartedly listen to her. I can't get the dream or reality out of my mind. I felt wide awake when it happened. I was very aware, very in charge. I remember leading the sinful dance.

"Look who finally decided to wake up," Liam says.

I break away from my thoughts only to scowl at him. "I'm not used to a routine." I cut into a potato, working away at the eyes.

I don't hear Liam come up behind me over the running water, though I should have. He is too big to be soundless. His chest presses against my back as he reaches over my head for a glass. His free hand, meant to steady me, slides a touch under the hem of my shirt.

The sharp edge of the knife slides over the skin of the potato to the edge of my nail. He pulls away once the glass is in his hand and pushes it under the water, moving aside as if to say the touch was nothing more than casual. I suppose it would be if it was anyone else. But I know, as soon as I felt his hand on my skin, that it was Liam who took me to bed last night.

"You should be more careful," he says, nodding to my hands. The look he gives me is condescending. He must have been drunk last night. Maybe we both were. My head felt so clear, though. Stupid! Stupid!

"When you're done with that, why don't you scout with us?" He tosses the glass back to finish the water. "I'm sure you can talk Sebastian into giving you a gun."

"I don't need a gun." I toss the potato into a bowl. "I'm much better with a knife."

Liam smirks, and a laugh hisses through his lips as he shakes his head. "I bet you are."

I can't stop the blush that rises to my face.

"Leave her alone, Liam," Devon scowls. She throws a skin at him to make her point.

"What are you going to do about it?" Liam looks back at her coolly.

Devon blinks. "She's not going with you."

"What's this?" Sebastian's voice startles me. I glance over my shoulder, all too aware that Liam brushes past me. His arm against mine sends flames to my face. Sebastian is standing on the other side of the table. There's a bag over his shoulder and two others in his hand.

"She's bored," Liam says to Devon, waving a hand at me. To Sebastian, he says, "Let's put her in the field."

"I thought you didn't trust her," Sebastian says.

The blush thickens. I hope no one notices. I can practically feel the stain creeping down my neck.

Liam chuckles. "I don't and neither do you. Any of you," he adds pointedly to Devon.

A long silence stretches between the three of them. Devon puts her knife down and she shakes her head. "I don't like it. I'm sorry, Leah, it's not that I don't trust you." She cuts a cold look to Liam. "I just think there are some things you should get accustomed to before going out with them."

The men look at me. I keep my head down. I don't want to quarrel with anyone, so I say nothing. My silence seems to do most of the talking for me because Sebastian tosses me one of the packs. I fumble to catch it, the strap slipping over my fingers.

"Get ready," he says.

A look of annoyance flashes across Devon's face, but she doesn't say anything. If I had to describe her look, I'd say she is almost dejected. I frown. I like Devon, but I *am* bored, and if there is a chance for me to get outside, I'll take it. This time I'll be able to take in our surroundings and, when the right time comes a-calling— No, stop. I have no reason to run anymore. Especially when they have food, water, and electricity. Weapons.

Our scout consists of me, Sebastian, Liam, and Anthony. Anthony is an interesting character. He's a mean-looking SOB, with thick-hooded brows that have a natural furrow and sunken cheekbones. When he smiles, he looks like a boy, flashing a row of pearly whites that stand out against his dark skin. He is quiet, more reserved than any of the others, so when he has a gun lifted in front of his face, scoping the area, it makes me nervous. He looks like the kind of person who would shoot first and ask questions later.

I'm glad he was not part of the entourage that kidnapped me.

Sebastian hands me a small pistol. It's nothing compared to their bigger guns, AK something. They tell me they collected them from an old military base not far from here, along with several other weapons and explosives. I haven't seen where they keep these accessories, but I suppose it's in another part of the compound they've yet to show me.

I take the gun, but I keep the safety on and my finger away from the trigger. I smirk. They must trust me a little bit if they're giving me a firearm. I never felt comfortable with guns. I always let James do the shooting.

The air is cold, skies shrouded with thick storm clouds. A puff of fog comes out of my mouth as I exhale. It had been warm yesterday. The sudden shift in the weather doesn't make me too nervous. I'm used to it, but something about how heavy the air feels makes me uneasy.

I stick to the back of the group. We are too many people to be considered a scout. Only one or two should go at a time, but four seems like a ridiculous number. If anything happens, I have every intention to split off.

We scour most of the city with no sign of life. Not even the bees fly this far. It's spooky to be in such a large place and for it to be completely abandoned. It makes me wonder how many people were killed or possessed to leave it so desolate. I look at the backs of the men before me. How is it that so few of us have survived and that these are the only people to live here? How many of us are left?

I get the feeling we are being watched. Behind every black, glass window, I feel someone or something peering down on us. It makes my skin crawl. My fingers tighten around the grip of the gun. I glance at each man individually. Can't they feel it? There is a profound darkness in the air.

I find myself drawing closer to the buildings, pressing myself against them so nothing can see me. I don't realize I've shortened my pace until Sebastian slows down next to me. Liam looks back and Sebastian waves him on.

"Leah," Sebastian says softly.

I know he says my name, but I don't pay him any mind. I'm staring at our reflections across the street of an abandoned zoo. Something draws me to it, but my feet are rooted to the ground.

"What happened in there?" I ask. I know something did. I can feel it.

Sebastian touches my shoulder when I step forward. "Don't," he says.

I should listen to him. I should, but a darker part of me wants to appease the calling inside of me. I'm only vaguely aware that Anthony and Liam have stopped. Sebastian waves them on again, but neither of them moves. Liam's gaze is fixated on me as I push through the red gate of the zoo's entrance.

Stuffed animals and old candy are scattered outside the shops. On the left is an exhibit for the snow leopards. The glass is covered in dark grime. I run my hand over it to clear a patch. I can't see anything on the other side except for tall weeds and algae-filled water.

"Let her," I hear Liam say.

I glance back at him as I run my hand farther down to see more of the exhibit. His hand is extended over the front of Sebastian's chest. Sebastian gives a short shake of his head that tells me not to. I turn back and clear the glass quicker. What doesn't he want me to see?

There's something— What is that? Oh God.

There are two humans, their bodies preserved well enough that their faces are still twisted in anguish. Around their necks are collars with spikes pointed inwards. One is missing her lower jaw. The other reaches toward the glass without hands. Their naked bodies are covered in lacerations, exposing them to the bones. Their skin is broken apart by the boils of Sin.

"We haven't had a chance to clear this part of the city yet," Sebastian says, but I'm not listening.

My vision blurs as I look away. I turn toward the path that leads to more exhibits and I run. I tear through them. Every exhibit is the same, full of mutilated humans on chains. I run past a broken carousel with bodies strapped to the saddles. I stop when I get to the giraffes.

Bodies upon bodies are strung in the trees. Men, women, and children sway in the breeze. The faint smell of their rot hits my nose. I cover my mouth. Why couldn't I smell them before? My stomach clenches. I cover my eyes and turn away as the bile rises in my throat.

Oh God.

A sob escapes me as I look back at the trees. I want to scream, but no sound comes from my throat. What sort of sound do you make when witnessing such a horror? The hanging images blur together. I wipe my shaking fingers over my face.

"Amazing, isn't it?" Liam moves beside me. He folds his arms over his gun and smiles.

I give him a dumbfounded look through my tears. "How can you say that?"

He shrugs. "Their power was something extraordinary and this is all they have left to show of it."

Liam's smile twitches. It's a closed upturn of his lips spun in satisfaction. His shoulders are set comfortably. He looks relaxed, at ease to be standing before the horror.

A chill runs down my spine.

"Liam," I say softly. The question is on my tongue, but as he looks at me, I can't bring myself to ask it. His eyes are dark and dangerous. Sebastian comes up behind us and I silently thank him for the interruption. "Let's get out of here," I say instead.

We hastily leave the zoo. I keep my eyes down for the most part. Anthony walks ahead while Liam brings up the rear. Sebastian doesn't say anything as he sticks close to my side. We make our way to a grocery store to gather canned supplies. When I see old blood spattered across the tiles, I decide to wait at the entrance. I don't want to stumble on anything like I saw at the zoo.

Sebastian stays with me, letting the other men stuff their bags. I stare out the open window, listening to the clang of cans fall against each other. Surprisingly, there seems to be a decent amount of food left.

"I don't feel safe here," I finally say. I didn't before, but now that I've seen the extent of the horrors that befell Boise, I can't deny the urge to flee. If the men weren't keeping such a close eye on me, I'd have run already. Since the zoo, not even Anthony lets me too far from his gaze.

Sebastian looks out the window. "We'll head back to the compound soon," he says.

I shake my head. "I mean in general. Don't you feel exposed?" I look up into his narrowed eyes when I feel him studying me. "How can you feel safe when those bodies—"

"The city is harmless," he says.

I don't know about that. I lean forward to look into the windows across the street. Can he not feel all the eyes on us? "You'll have to forgive me," I say, letting out a breath.

"There was nothing like this in your city?"

I shake my head. "It was bad, but *nothing* like that." I close my eyes. Flashes of the bodies move across my eyelids. "This will take some getting used to."

Sebastian touches his hand to the back of my elbow. "I know. In the meantime, try to trust us, to trust me, when I say that you are safe. I meant it when I said it. No one is going to hurt you ever again. Hm?" He looks at me seriously. I want to believe him. "You don't have to see anything like that again."

"It's alright," I say. "I needed to know."

"Look what I found," Liam says. He tosses something to Sebastian that glints through the air. Sebastian catches it out. It's a necklace. On the end of the chain is a little gold cross. He runs his thumb over the four points.

The image had once been a symbol of hope. Once the world started to disintegrate, turning to ash and flames, it meant nothing. I feel sorry for the people who believed a little cross could save them from Hell. And yet, seeing it does give flame to a sliver of hope inside of me. Just like the bees, it's a glint of fresh air.

Sebastian flicks it out over his fingers so the cross dangles at the bottom.

"Take it." I refuse, and at the same time I hold out my palm to accept it. It's not practical to wear a necklace. Jewelry gets caught on things all the time, slowing you down or leaving a trace.

I slip the thin ribbon of chain over my head and touch the end gently. I don't wear it for the belief it stands for, the salvation God's children were promised. I take it to satisfy Sebastian and whoever it belonged to. I say a little prayer, a wish for the life it was so viciously stolen from.

I let out a strained sigh of relief as we make it back to the compound. I miss the smell and heat of a fire. I want to burn one, but there is no place indoors for one, and burning outside would be suicide. I never thought I'd come to miss the fires Raum started for me. Knowing what I do about the demons being in hiding, I smile. Raum had been afraid of the cabin, nervous about trekking through where he believed humans might be, but starting a fire had never been a concern. I wonder if the flames offer power to the demons.

I seek heat in the showers, turning the water high until my skin turns red. It's not hot enough, though it steams the bathroom with a humid white mist. I turn it all the way up, but the scalding water does nothing to appease me. I shut it off quickly and throw a towel around my body.

Liam catches me as I dart out of the bathroom. I would have slipped right past him and tripped if he hadn't caught me. I wrench my arm from his grasp as an image of him grabbing my hips from the night before flashes across my mind.

"Easy there, tiger," he teases. I'm not in the mood for his jokes or cold cynicism. I push against his bare chest. He leans into my touch, forcing himself closer than I'd like. "Always in such a hurry."

"I have become accustomed to not wasting time," I say.

Liam's brow furrows and he sucks his teeth. "You need to lighten up."

"Get out of my way," I say, pushing against him again. This time he does move, sliding out of my reach with ease. He mutters something crude that makes me feel even more dirty than I already did for being with him.

I can't get away from him quick enough and slam the door to my room. I fall face first across the mattress and groan. Someone knocks on my door and I jump forward, pulling the towel and sheets around me.

"Yes?" I brush a stray piece of hair from my face. Did he follow me?

Devon opens the door. "Oh, I'm sorry." I wave her off and she smiles. "I'm going to check on the bees. Do you want to come?"

My face must light up because her smile broadens. I tell her yes, but I need a moment. As soon as she leaves, I slip on a pair of jeans and a baggy long-sleeved shirt. Seeing the bees again both excites and upsets me. I have to see them, though.

I take Devon's hand as I follow her down to the hives. The steady hum overwhelms me, bringing tears to my eyes. Absentmindedly, I touch the cross I'm wearing under my shirt. I wonder if this is what the Christians felt when they touched the symbol of their Lord's passion. Surrounded by the bees, I finally feel safe. I let out a gentle breath.

"Do you mind if I just sit here?" I ask Devon.

"Of course not," she says. "I'll be across the field if you need me."

I sit within the folds of the tall grass and close my eyes. Every pair of wings is the tune to a song, coming together as one giant symphony. I hum along with them, the sound vibrating through my chest.

"What's that song?" Devon asks. Her voice is curious, but there is something in her eyes that frightens me. I didn't even notice that the song I hummed was the one Raum gave to me.

"I don't know," I tell her.

"It's very beautiful." She looks up at the bees and frowns. "I don't think they like it, though."

The swarm moves as a giant cloud to the left and then to the right. We watch them carefully, unsure if we should retreat to safer ground. Of course, the bees don't like it. I sing the song of the devil and they are our salvation.

XIV

I turn in early that night. Devon asked where we went and I couldn't bring myself to stay in the room when someone answered. For once, Liam hadn't sneered at me as I stalked out. His eyes only held a wide look of curiosity while Sebastian and Anthony seemed to pity me.

I've been trying to sleep for the last few hours, but every time I close my eyes, I see the atrocity. Leyak tortured people in our time, but not to the extent of what I saw today. He got bored quickly so those who fell under his wrath were disposed of just as timely. Those people in the zoo were tortured much longer before meeting their end.

I laugh to myself. It's all so twisted. Leyak enjoyed the pleasure of persecuting humans. Outside of his special interest in me, he would instruct the demons below him to dismember their victims. When he made a show of his power, he would have it cleaned immediately thereafter. Even Leyak could not stand the smell of decay for long. The humans were either eaten or burned.

I guess I *was* lucky.

I laugh again and rub my hands over my face. There is nothing lucky about this life. There is nothing fortunate in my survival and what it took for me to get this far.

A quiet knock stirs me from my thoughts. I sit up, half imagining I dreamed the sound until it comes again. Another reason I miss being above ground is I always knew the time of day. I wish I had a clock. My body says it's well into the night, too late for anyone to be knocking.

I grab a pair of pants and slip them on before answering the door. My stomach twists as the light-haired man meets my gaze. The hallway behind him is dimly lit; everyone's doors are closed.

"Yes?" I ask.

"Anthony and I are going hunting. Do you want to come?" I lean forward, peering past Liam to see Anthony standing at the end of the hallway. A bag is strapped over his shoulders and a gun slants across his chest. I slowly look back to Liam.

"I don't know if I feel comfortable going out after today," I admit. Neither do I want to be alone with them.

"I promise you won't see anything like that. Come on, Leah," he says.

The dark look in his eyes makes me uneasy as well as curious. I hate the way I feel towards Liam. He scares me, but I'm drawn to him. I throw another look at Anthony. He tilts his head back, looking bored.

"Just us?" I ask. I bite the inside of my lip.

He nods.

Something doesn't feel right. This could be a trick, a way to discard me. I stop myself. If Liam wanted to hurt me, he could have. Instead, he took me to bed, by my own encouragement of course, but still. He could have done something horrible then—unless he has been waiting for an opportunity like tonight. I swallow.

"Alright," I say hesitantly. "Let me change." If this is a way to dispose of me, it's also an opportunity for me to run.

Liam's eyes sweep over me before he turns away. I dress quickly. Out of everyone in our group, Liam and Anthony are the most dangerous. Maybe that's why I want to go. I miss the thrill of being with Raum. I cringe as the thought enters my mind.

I've been harshly judging the two men. I belt my knife to the back of my waist. Better safe than sorry.

I don't question anything about our hunt until we are well away from the compound. What is there to stalk in an abandoned city? I hold on tight to the gun Liam has given me.

It turns out there are rodents. The men have several traps placed throughout the city where we uncover mostly rats but a few small rabbits. Liam flips over a stone that has collapsed to reveal a cat. It's a sad sight, but I smile with Liam when he picks it up. It's been a long time since I've seen so many animals in one place.

"We've been lucky some of them stuck around," he says.

"That's a lot more than some." I pause as I watch Anthony disappear behind an old gas station. "Why did you bring me out here?" I ask.

Liam ties the cat on a line across his backpack. "I figured you couldn't sleep," he says.

I nod. How could anyone after seeing what I did? I'm sure he is used to it by now. I'm sure they all are. They have to be.

"I want to show you something," he says. He motions towards a dark-faced building.

I pause, looking for our other companion. "Where is Anthony?"

Liam looks around. "He'll catch up."

I stand a few heartbeats before following Liam. I stop short when I rush into the black behind him. The darkness is not just a void of color, it's a feeling. An overwhelming sense of evil washes over me. Liam's name is on my tongue when someone grabs my hand.

I let out a startled sound and they shush me.

"Don't do that," I say, letting out a breath.

I lace my fingers with Liam's as he leads me over what looks to be an overturned desk and across scattered papers. We walk up ten flights of stairs to a rooftop. It's not the highest point in the city, but it's tall enough to give me a better view. The disaster goes on as far as the eye can see. Like I noticed before, most of the buildings are collapsing in on themselves, roads are broken and overgrown. To the right, in the direction of the zoo, are stacks of bodies. They must be planning to burn them soon. There are so many bodies.

I'm glad I took my chances in the wilderness.

"This is where we saw your fire," Liam says. He points to a mountain pass in the distance.

I frown. Raum must have known we were close to people. Perhaps he *had* been merciful. He took my bag because he knew I wouldn't need it anymore. Why would he suddenly feel compassionate? After everything he did to me, it still doesn't make sense. I feel I should know the answer by now, but it continues to evade me.

I lean forward on the edge of the rooftop. A sharp pain makes me jerk back. Under the pale light of the moon, a shard of glass sticks out of my hand. I curse under my breath. It's not bad, but small enough that I have to squint to see it.

Liam grabs my wrist before I can pull the sliver from my flesh. He turns my hand to take it out. His fingers are hard, but it's not unpleasant as he grips me. What makes me uncomfortable is the dark look in his eyes. A slow breath of air sucks through his lips as they part.

"You really should be more careful," he says.

He brings my palm up to his face.

"Liam," I say hesitantly. I'm almost too afraid to ask the question I couldn't before. He looks up. "Were you ever bitten?"

He sneers. "Why would you ask that?"

I suddenly wish I hadn't. I take a step away from him. His grip hardens around my wrist. Something tells me that if I remotely struggle, he will hurt me.

"Don't get shy on me now," he says. My face flames. When I still don't say anything, he lets me go. "Why do you want to know?"

I lick my lips, a nervous reflex he doesn't miss. His eyes flick to my mouth then back to my eyes. "You remind me of someone," I say softly.

A dark laugh escapes him. "Is it the one that bit you?" he asks.

Chills run across my skin. I glance at the edge of the building. Liam has a crazed look in his eyes. I take a step back, suddenly afraid he will toss me over the edge.

"Can you keep a secret?" he whispers.

I nod. Liam steps closer, tightening the space between us again.

"One did bite me," he says. "I killed it before it could take hold of me though."

"How?" I blink. I've never heard of such a thing.

"It was injecting its venom when I did it. The process was never complete."

"But it still marked you," I say. The chills on my body tighten; my voice is barely an audible whisper. Liam might not be bound to anyone, but it doesn't eradicate the fact he has demon's venom in his veins. It explains his behavior, his dark allure that reminds me so much of Raum.

"Where?" I ask.

Liam presses his finger to his lips. I watch as he rolls up his sleeve to reveal a brand in the shape of a horseshoe. A line slashes across the center. It's dark and heavily raised like it has been touched up more than once.

"No one would have believed that I wasn't marked, so I covered it up," he says. People will do anything when they're desperate to survive. Liam burned himself to hide the evidence. He rolls his sleeve back down.

"I'm still human," he says, as if he means to comfort me.

I meet his eyes. I don't think that's true. Whatever Liam is now is entirely brand new. I don't know how it's possible he survived his demon's death. I'm not entirely sure how the bonding works, only that they use their venom to do it. Did a part of the demon slip inside Liam somehow? No, if that were the case, his eyes would betray the invasion.

"How?" I ask again.

Liam shrugs. "I don't know. I'm the same except, from time to time, I have urges." He steps in front of me, forcing me back to the ledge. My heart slams against my chest.

"What kind of urges?" I whisper.

"To do bad things." He brings my hand to his face. A red line from the cut glistens vertically along my palm. "To taste this."

Every muscle in my body is as taut as a hairpin trigger. I reach back with my free hand, slowly reaching for the hilt of my knife. Liam's mouth hovers over the wound and then he drops my hand.

"I deny it, but every day it becomes harder," he says.

I let the knife go. My release of breath is not as subtle and Liam smirks.

"Maybe that's why I'm drawn to you. We're the same," he says. "I get a sense about you that I don't from anyone else."

My throat feels swollen when I swallow. I am lightheaded. "He never gave me his venom." Liam's countenance hardens like I've offended him. "He did this to protect me from other demons." I delicately touch what is left of the false mark. The abrasions are nearly gone.

Liam flashes his teeth. "He did something to you, Leah. I can feel it."

"No," I say.

Liam leans forward. I throw my cut hand up in his face before he can kiss me. A red smear appears across his mouth when I jerk away. An apology sticks in my throat, but the look on his face stills me. I only wanted to stop him.

Liam flinches, like he's just been struck by an electric shock. A haze covers his eyes that he slowly blinks away. He looks down at me. My blood stands out against his soft skin; it curves up over his lips with its own twisted smile.

He leans forward and kisses me. Against any will of my own, my lips part under his. He is gentle. His tongue flicks across mine for a quick taste before he closes our mouths by pressing harder into me.

Panic shoots through me. I'm terrified of what he might do to me. He could excite the same power over me that Raum had and that is the last thing I need. I'm scared of my desire. Liam's words have needled their way into the back of my head, but I think I can feel the connection between us he mentioned. It's not real. I press my fingers against his collarbone.

The urge to follow him sweeps over me as he leans away, but I deny it. I lick my lips clean, repulsed by my own metallic taste. We just stand there, looking at each other without saying anything. My heart feels like it is being ripped apart; my stomach is so twisted it aches.

"You can feel it too," he says.

I shake my head even though I can feel a darkness inside of me that was not there before Raum.

Soft footsteps draw my attention away from Liam. Anthony climbs out of the stairwell and looks around. He nods towards the mountain range. "Anything?" he asks.

Liam moves away from me. "No. You?"

Anthony sucks the back of his teeth. "Nothing." His eyes narrow when he looks at me. I touch my lips tentatively. Is there blood on them? It's still on Liam's face. "What happened?"

Liam knocks their shoulders together when he passes him. "Just helping Leah get over her fears." He turns to wink at me.

Anthony spins on his heel as Liam heads for the stairs before turning to me. I wipe my hand over my mouth and stalk after him. I don't meet Anthony's gaze even when he tries to get me to look at him. I'm too embarrassed.

Liam is waiting for me with an extended hand. I take it reluctantly and follow him through the dark. It's not until Anthony turns on a light over his scope that I realize Liam's senses are heightened with an ability he should not have. My eyes have grown accustomed to the dark, but even I have trouble navigating through the heavy shadows. This is bad.

Everyone has been concerned that I'm a danger, but have they even considered what downfall Liam might bring? Do they even know? I want to ask him, but Anthony has caught up with us and I don't want him to hear.

For the most part, our trek back to the compound is quiet. The men walk ahead. They laugh at some inside joke. It's nice to hear human laughter, even if I am uncomfortable. I smile despite myself.

They drop their voices.

"Dude, what are you doing?" Anthony whispers.

"What?" Liam asks.

Anthony gives him a pointed look to which Liam clicks his tongue.

"We don't know anything about her," Anthony says. I lengthen my stride to hear a little better.

"What better way to learn about her?" Liam quips.

"Just think about what you're doing. If you're looking for someone, try it with one of the other girls. Not her." Anthony looks over his shoulder.

I turn away before he can see me, glancing down the street we pass. The road is strewn with various cars, some more sporty than others with butterfly doors. The old paint, still vibrant and unscathed. Demons clearly have expensive tastes.

I take Anthony's words as a sign that he doesn't know Liam and I have already been together. At least Liam is not one to brag about his conquests. Still, I don't like anything about Liam's interest in me. I don't care what he says; we are not the same.

"Look at her. She's harmless," Liam says.

I do look at them now. There's a dark look in Liam's eye to match his twisted mouth. I might be harmless, but he is not. The venom within his veins has made him unpredictable and dangerous.

Tonight is my last scout. I decide it as we slip back into the compound. It doesn't matter who will escort and protect me, I will not go out again. I decide to stay well out of Liam's company. It will be hard to do with him living next door to me.

I glance at him before he slips into his room. His eyes are shadowed and wicked.

"Goodnight, Leah," he says.

The sound of his door closing is like a nail into a coffin.

XV

Two weeks later, I finally feel like I can breathe again. Every day that a scout returns with a report that the city is clear, I'm filled with solace. I naturally fall into the chores. Devon and I have become fast friends. Though there isn't much gossip to exchange, we find things to talk about. We share memories of when times were better and any complaints we had about the world were trivial.

We are not often apart. I'm still getting used to having a constant companion, but I don't mind it. It's fun being a girl again. Devon likes to play with my hair. She loves to find new braids and twists to put it in. During one of our girls' nights, she pulled out a clear bag of cosmetics. I laughed.

I've gotten to know everyone a little bit better. Anna has warmed up to me. At the least, she pretends as much by occasionally joining Devon and me in our fantasy world of powder and perfumes. When she is not trailing Sebastian, she is often with Sarah or Chris.

During the day, I can keep my mind busy with everyone. I watch them closely. I'm attentive to my chores that involve gardening and beekeeping. It's at night that I'm tormented and constantly think of running.

I still think of Raum. I no longer fear he will find me. It's much worse. I think about our time together and ache for his touch. The thought of him should repulse me. Instead, I find myself fantasizing about his harsh bites and painful affections. There is no liking attached to his memory. Just white-hot need.

"I thought I heard you get up." Liam's voice comes from behind me. I lean away from the fridge and look over my shoulder. His palms rest on either side of the doorframe. Save for a pair of shorts, he doesn't wear anything.

Inked across his chest is a snarling wolf and on its head is the skin of a ram. It's all black work, save for the red saliva that drips from the wolf's open mouth. Chills run down my spine as I glance at his face, the look in his eyes baring the same as the vicious tattoo. A wolf in sheep's clothing, there isn't a better piece that would fit him.

None of what we have done has slipped my mind. The more space I sought to put between us, the more Liam sets himself in my way. He reminds me so much of Raum that I don't trust myself to be around him. His kiss only irritated the unholy desires tormenting me.

"I was thirsty," I say, waving a bottle of water at him.

Liam cocks his head to the side. The laugh lines around his eyes thin, his brown eyes darken. He parts his lips to say something then bites the bottom one as if thinking it's better not to say anything at all. I clear my throat. I don't particularly like the man, but with the way I've been feeling, my body is trying to reason with me that he must have some redeemable quality.

Dangerous, my conscious whispers.

"Well, goodnight," I say. I step closer to him in hopes he will move out of my way. He leans back and moves just enough so I have to squeeze past him.

"Is this about the other night?" he asks, turning. "Are you afraid of me now?"

Of course I'm afraid of him and yet....

"It's not what you think," I start. I bite the inside of my lip. "Do you make me nervous? Yes. But it's more than that. The night when we… when you took me to bed—" I don't even know where to begin. My face feels hot. I fidget with the bottle, tossing it between my hands. I should have brought it up sooner, before he told me about being bitten.

Liam looks at me with eyes that seem darker than their chocolate and amber color. The looks I've caught him stealing remind me of Raum. I sort of like it. That, in itself, washes me with guilt.

"Was I not good enough for you?" he asks, his tone mocking.

"I didn't even know it was you. I thought you were Sebastian." I flinch as soon as his name leaves my mouth. I look down at my feet, biting the inside of my cheek.

Liam looks at me darkly then runs a hand over his mouth, cupping his chin. He shakes his head and laughs. "Wow," he says quietly.

"I thought you hated me."

He makes a move towards me, pauses, then turns away. I grab his arm. I don't know why I stop him. I guess I'm just tired of being alone. I'm tired of fighting. He looks angry, maybe even a little hurt. His face is in an unusual scowl with a broad crease between his brows. The tick in his jaw jumps like an elastic chord.

"Liam." Just saying his name speaks volumes. My conscience screams at me to let him go and I squeeze tighter. I think he is right about me, about Raum doing something to me.

Liam is ill-suited for me, for anyone, but I can't deny he had been a pleasure. He made me feel good in a way only a human can. There is another side to him, though, the one that still reminds me of Raum, that draws me in. I don't need much. Just a little taste to be rid of the demon's shadow. Out of the corner of my eye the wolf licks its lips.

Liam isn't stupid. He stands firm, letting me come to him. I lean up to kiss him, my hand sliding up his chest, just beneath his collarbone. Tension leaves his body, like a curtain being drawn away, and he wraps his arms around me. I trail my eyes along his body slowly, noting for the first time that Liam is attractive. He has hard lines in his abdomen, tanned from working long hours in the sun.

He pulls back to look at me. The malicious glint has been replaced by raw lust that could make anyone weak in the knees. Wild heat courses through me like lava. If Liam keeps holding onto me, he might burn up.

The fire spreads beyond our lips, igniting the tension between us like gunpowder. He snakes his arm around my waist, pushing me back until my legs hit the kitchen table, scraping it against the ground. In one fluid motion, he picks me up and sets me on top, his lips hardly leaving mine. He kisses me passionately, so hard that I have to lean my head back to catch my breath.

Before I know it, he is inside of me. He continues to kiss me as he flexes his hips. It's delicious. I wrap around him, pressing myself as close as possible. I break away only to bite into his shoulder to stifle a moan. He strokes me deeper, slower than before to draw out the sound in the back of my throat.

We shouldn't be doing this, but I can't stop. Every touch pushes me closer to the edge.

Over his shoulder, movement catches my eye. I look up in my daze to see Sebastian walk into the connecting room. Our eyes meet and a ripple of white-hot fire runs through me, sending me over the edge.

"You feel so fucking good," Liam growls. I press my face into his shoulder as I grip him. I can't see Sebastian anymore, but I can feel him watching us. I can't help but think that perhaps Sin has tainted more than the air we breathe.

I stay in Liam's room once we're finished. I can't describe what it's like to be held by someone who means you no harm. His hands are rough when he grips me, but I know he doesn't have the strength to hurt me, nor the desire. I no longer fear Liam; I accept him. I accept what has become of me.

Being with Liam is not the same as it was with James, but it's the closet feeling of being complete I have experienced since his possession. I feel safe. It's the first time I fall asleep without nightmares. It's the first time I think of James instead of Raum.

Two days pass before what we have done finally gets the best of me. I stand nervously outside Sebastian's room, my hand hovering over the flat trying to decide if I should knock or not. Tension becomes an iron weight in my chest. I have no reason to discuss what he saw, but some unbearable need to do so taunts me.

His looks have become unbearable, like he accuses me of some wrongdoing. If I didn't know any better, I'd think Sebastian was jealous.

I knock on the door.

No answer.

Again.

I drum my fingers over my thigh and turn. Perhaps he left. I've been sleeping better, but I have a keen sense of when anyone near my room comes and goes. Living in the wilderness does that. You wake to even the slightest scratching sound or the shuffle of feet.

"Have you seen Sebastian?" I lean over the back of the couch where Mike lounges, flipping through an old magazine about cars. He stops on a spread about a custom R32.

"Yes," he says, throwing his head back to look at me. "He was looking for you, actually."

That's strange. He didn't knock on my door. Maybe he assumed I was with Liam. My face flushes and I clear my throat.

As far as I know, no one else has any idea what is going on between us. In fact, since Liam and I agreed to hook up, he has been more hostile in front of everyone. Something I was only too willing to take the bait for, lashing out to defend myself whenever he nitpicked me. It just made us more aggressive when we were alone, but Liam was never strong enough to hurt me.

"Where is he?" I ask.

Mike takes his lip between his teeth, chewing on it. He opens his mouth to say something then points. I look over my shoulder and see Sebastian standing behind us, his mouth quirked into an amused line.

"Oh," I say, straightening.

"Do you have a moment?" Sebastian asks.

I nod and follow him down to his room. He veers off to the side and I take the moment to look around. The room is bare compared to everyone else's. There is a small desk with a few trinkets. On the wall next to his bed is a dreamcatcher with black and brown feathers.

I nod to it. "Shouldn't that be over the bed?"

He smirks. "I guess, but it gave me nightmares until I moved it." I give him a funny look and he smiles. He holds a book out to me. "I thought you might like to write again."

The book is hardback; it could easily be mistaken for a classic novel. It's full of blank pages begging for fresh ink. He hands me a pen. I close the journal against my chest.

"I don't know what to say." I've missed writing. My book had been my only friend. Though this is an entirely new assortment of pages, it feels like I'm being reunited. "Thank you."

I open it back up and run my fingers through the pages. I'd only mentioned journaling once and he remembered. A twinge of guilt runs through me. I cringe inwardly.

"About the other night..."

"Another dream?" he teases. Before I can say anything, he stops me with a shake of his head. "I don't care what you or Liam do, but I have to ask... why him?" He pauses and the remaining two words come out sharp.

"I don't know," I say. "The first time I thought it was you."

I quickly tell him what happened before he can jump to the conclusion that Liam might have forced himself on me. I know that must have been his first thought because the look in his eyes startles me. There is a flash of red, a streak of anger.

"I just hope you know what you're doing," he says. He touches my face and runs his thumb down the back of my jaw, a generous caress. "He is a cold man. I don't want to see you get hurt when you finally have the opportunity to be free."

Does he know about Liam's bite? I want to ask him what he means, but words fail me. He is looking at my mouth. My heart skips a beat as he leans forward. "Anna," her name is a whisper on my tongue. He shakes his head and kisses me on the side of the face.

"Leah!"

My name is a vicious roar. It breaks us apart like cold water. The voice comes from above ground, booming through the thick walls and dirt. It's too strong to be human. Chills sweep along my skin. I grab Sebastian's arm.

"Leah!"

I spin away and Sebastian pulls me back. "Let me go!"

I try to pull my arm free. I can feel it now, the dark power that only a demon carries in the wake of its shadow. I can feel it seeping into the ground, falling on top of my shoulders like a cloak.

"Leah—" Sebastian starts.

"If I don't go, we are going to die," I plead.

Can't he feel it? I can smell it. Hatred as putrid as rotting flesh.

Raum has found me.

XVI

Sebastian is hot on my heels as I make a dash for my room. I belt my knife, slip on my jacket, and pocket my pistol. Sebastian grabs me by the arm, spinning me back against the dresser. He wrenches the gun from me.

"You have to leave me with something!" I protest.

"You're not going out there," he growls.

Anna comes to a skidding stop in the hallway. She glances between us, but if she suspects anything nearly happened between us, she says nothing.

"Leah," he calls after me as I dart past Anna.

"If she wants to go, let her," Anna says. She grabs Sebastian by the shirt but he shrugs her off as he tries to keep up with me.

Everyone else stands in the living room. They are like deer caught in headlights, their eyes wide and white-rimmed. Their fear is almost as potent as the smell of death. Chris and Mike, who I rarely see with guns, are armed and patiently waiting for a command.

"We should do something," Mike says.

"For fuck's sake! No one is going outside!" Devon tries her best to get everyone under control. They've clearly been arguing about this longer than I have. Her ivory skin is red and her forehead is dotted with sweat.

She must have been outside when Raum started calling for me.

I glance at the entry way. Did he see her? Will he know how to get in? Raum is clever; it won't take him long to figure it out even if Devon managed to slip past him.

Panic spreads through our small group like wildfire. They're trying to figure out if everyone should hole up with the bees or take their chances in another part of the compound. When I put in my two cents, they ignore me.

Liam pushes through and passes a gun to Sebastian. I intercept, taking a firm hold of it before Sebastian's fingers can touch it. Liam's grip hardens and his face twists into a sneer.

"Think you can handle it?"

"If I don't go, he is going to come in here," I snap.

That gets their attention. Even Liam's dark look changes to one that considers my words. As my name rips through the air again, he lets the gun drop in my hands. "I'm not sticking my neck out for her," he spits. "If one of those things wants her, let them have her."

"You'll always be my favorite," I say. Though we have been cold to each other for appearances, I expected he might feel a little remorse for sending me to my demise.

"I'm coming with you," Devon says.

"No," Sebastian and I say at once.

Everyone argues that no one should go except me, but Sebastian, for whatever reason, is adamant that he comes with me. I don't want anyone getting hurt on my account when I can probably convince Raum to leave them alone. If I go willingly, there is a chance I can spare their lives. Maybe.

There is no breeze above ground, just stark heat. Stinging drops of sweat run into my eyes. My fingers are glued to the barrel of the gun. If I let it go, for even a second, it might be too late.

My name runs like lightning through my veins as it's called out again. We scan the grounds, jogging between buildings and down dark alleyways. I shouldn't approach Raum with a gun. He'd been so angry when I tried to grab one before.

A small park surrounded by broken stones and statues lies ahead. Sebastian holds his fist up to stop as the demon comes into view.

A sense of relief floods me. It's not Raum. I recognize Eblis' long braids as he noses through the untrimmed field. Movement just behind him brings my attention to Leyak. White scarring covers his neck and chest.

Leyak stumbles behind Eblis. His steps are miscalculated, and he falls against his companion, leaning heavily against the broad-shouldered man. I tighten my grip on the gun and Eblis' head snaps in my direction. Leyak lifts his head into the wind as it wraps around me and carries my scent towards them. He pushes away from Eblis, forcing the demon away from him.

My finger slips on the trigger and I shoot Leyak in the chest as soon as his eyes find me. He stumbles back, then forward, and catches himself with one hand before falling to the ground completely.

"Oh, Leah, Leah, Leah. You're in big trouble this time," he growls. He turns his attention behind me, and

I stiffen. Sebastian walks slowly to my side, not once taking his eyes or weapon from the monsters in front of us.

"What are you doing here?" I train my sight over Leyak's head. "How did you find me?"

Eblis growls and snaps his teeth together so hard I imagine it's rattled his skull. "Raum is at our backs."

Fuck.

"You shouldn't have attacked us. Now he suspects you for what's happened."

"Suspects what?" Leyak hisses.

Eblis walks carefully. His chin lifts as he looks between me and Sebastian with a sneer. "I was defending my men," Eblis hisses. "He attacked Leyak and killed Mara."

"He did so because I belong to him." I might hate Raum, but I thank whatever god is in charge that he was there to protect me that night. "Leyak shouldn't have touched me."

"You belong to me! He had no right to you," Leyak spits. "You have been mine from the beginning."

Leyak, you jealous child! I don't have time to bicker with him. If Raum has been chasing them, that means they have led him right to me. How he hadn't discovered me on his own is a mystery. Why did he really leave me?

It hits me.

"When did you know I wasn't with him?" I shift my grip on the gun.

"Two days after we *fled*," Eblis says bitterly. "What a surprise it was to smell you ahead of him." Eblis eyes our guns, his lids lowering to gauge our stance. "You are coming with us."

Raum hadn't abandoned me. Neither had he shown me mercy. He'd left me to kill Eblis and Leyak. Unease settles in the pit of my stomach. There is the slight possibility that Raum might not know I left. Of course, it's a wild conclusion.

Raum isn't chasing them because he thinks the demons have me. He is after them to protect me.

Eblis surges forward and a loud crack rings next to my ear. His body jerks, but his momentum carries him too far forward. He lands on Sebastian with a vicious snarl. His mouth stretches, revealing sharpened fangs that he sinks into the side of Sebastian's neck.

"No!"

Eblis' back splits apart as bullets sink into his gut. I don't think about it; I press my gun to his head and fire. The body slumps forward, covering Sebastian entirely. Oh God, I've killed them both.

Leyak leans into his hands, sitting up with a wicked grin to get a better look. He sniffs and his smile falters. Eblis' body lifts then falls with a grunt as Sebastian pushes from underneath.

"Oh God." I roll Eblis to the side.

The side of Sebastian's neck is dark, but there is neither blood nor mark. It looks like Eblis sought to burn him instead. His hands shake as he raises his gun past me, fixating it over Leyak.

Leyak's hollow gaze has drifted to his companion. His breaths become shallow, his body tightens. When his eyes snap up to meet mine, it feels like I've been slapped.

"Don't," I whisper to Sebastian, touching him softly. I slip my arm around his waist to help him to his feet. Not once do I take my eyes off Leyak.

Leyak is shaking with rage. If anyone is going to kill him, it's going to be me. My finger brushes the trigger of my gun, but I can't shoot him as easily as I did Eblis. The familiar crinkles beside his eyes that once belonged to James make me hesitate.

"I'll give Raum something to be angry about. I'm going to rip your throat out," Leyak snarls. His nails elongate into talons, his teeth sharpen as he lurches to his feet. I've only seen Leyak this angry once. I had been one of the few to survive the bloodbath. I will survive him again. I curl my finger over the trigger and pull.

Leyak falls to his knees and touches over the red hole in his chest. A ripple runs across his shoulders as he laughs. The mechanical sound is almost musical as it swells.

"Oh, come on, Leah!" Leyak laughs. The blood in his mouth gargles as he tips his head back. "Is that the best you've got? After all I did to you? After all I'm going to do to you," he says darkly. The ground blackens beneath his shadow as his anger swells.

"Leyak, I'm willing to grant you mercy—"

"Leah," Sebastian whispers hoarsely. I glance back at him, then to Eblis, before turning back to Leyak. Letting Leyak go might buy us more time if Raum truly is hunting him.

"You let me run once so I'll do the same for you, if you leave now. If you choose to stay, I will kill you," I say.

"Ah, but if I leave then I'm running into Raum's teeth. Besides, you can't kill me. You don't have the strength for it." Leyak's already pale skin has become ashen. The shadows beneath his eyes sag, darkening into bold lines beneath his lids. The decay does not move out of his shadow; he is not strong enough to burn us, even from here.

"Leave, Leyak!"

"I would like to stay. I can find James. Would you like that? For the three of us to be together again," he sneers. "What do you think, James?" His laugh is mechanical and forced as his countenance changes. The bones in his face break apart. They become more rounded, his cheeks filling out and the height of his forehead shrinks. The heavy hood over his eyes pulls back, drawing the dark shadows away. Even his throat and shoulders expand, breaking apart like little platelets. His muscles smooth across protruding ribs.

Leyak falls forward on both hands and when he looks up his eyes are charcoal.

"Leah?" The voice rasps, unparalleled to Leyak's, so full of pain and sweet human mortality.

Oh my God.

"No," I say.

"Oh, God—Leah. Please, kill me," he begs. "Don't leave me again. Just kill me."

And that's when I know it's him. It's not a trick. It's James. Leyak would not mock me so; he would not give in so easily. All this time I imagined James had disappeared into some void or been consumed from the inside by his tormentor. I had abandoned the only person I loved and all this while he has been a prisoner inside a body that no longer belongs to him.

"I'm sorry—"

A look of agony washes over his face and the skin and bones shift again as Leyak bursts forth with laughter. Blood spatters across his chin and tears, whether from James' pain or Leyak's amusement, run down his face. I pray James can't feel the bullet as it pierces through Leyak's forehead, but only the sweet release he deserves.

I shoot him. The first bullet skims past his ear, but the second strikes true.

Leyak falls to the ground with a smile on his face. He doesn't die quickly like Eblis. He mocks me by fighting for air. I sling my gun around and pull the demon against my chest.

"Give him to me!"

Leyak's laugh hisses through his teeth. I search his black eyes for any sign of color. Where is the sweet green I remember? I clench his face between my hands and will the bones to shift. "Let him go, Leyak!"

The demon is much stronger than I imagined. His face blurs through my tears, distorting the crooked smile of sharp teeth. It's Leyak's body I cling to, not James'. I press my face against his and sob. It's not until Sebastian touches me that I realize Leyak is dead.

The sun burns the top of my shoulders, drying the wet blood into my clothes. I turn my face up into the light as a cool breeze moves through the park. It stirs the smell of rot and pollute from the demons' blood, making me gag. I find my feet quickly before I can be sick and lean against Sebastian as he helps me up.

"I thought he was dead," I say.

"Who was James?" he asks softly.

"He was my boyfriend," I choke.

"And Raum?"

The name jars me awake and I reach for Sebastian. James had been a distraction. How long before Raum would be here? How long before he came to kill us?

"We stole you from him," Sebastian says, putting the pieces together. His full lips press so tight they disappear. He is a strong man, but he feeds off my fear and he glances around the area, his finger hovering over the trigger.

"I have to run," I tell him. He grabs me before I can do just that.

"No," he says firmly. He starts telling me all the reasons why I can't. I'm desperate. I know exactly what is going to happen if I don't. I'll be lucky if Raum doesn't kill me. If I'm spared, he will not show the same kindness to everyone else. Especially if he is hungry. Gooseflesh sprouts along my arms and I hug Sebastian, looking erratically over his shoulder for any signs of my tormentor.

Get it together, I scold myself.

Sebastian wraps his arms around me. I cry. Call it cowardice or fear, but I can't hold back anymore. The dam bursts forth with a vengeance, and I sob. We stay like that for what feels like hours. Me clinging to him, he holding onto me like our lives depend on it.

I savor what I can of Sebastian once my head clears. The smell of sweat on his skin, the way his clothes feel against my face, how safe I feel wrapped in his arms. We have already wasted too much time.

"We need to burn their bodies," Sebastian says, as if reading my thoughts.

"We'll have to mix them with other debris. We can't burn the bodies on their own." It's the best shot we have at covering the demons' smell.

We gather what we can, moving quicker than the average man. By the time we have dragged the bodies and scattered wood together, we are drenched in sweat.

It's freezing out. Perspiration rolls down my face while fog puffs out from our mouths.

"You're not going anywhere," he says once we head back to the compound. We circle to the back entrance, through the orchard.

"Raum is after them to protect me. He is attached to me. Don't you get it?" I tell Sebastian everything. I tell him exactly what happened the night the demons attacked us. I tell him about Mara. "When I woke up and he wasn't there, I thought he abandoned me. I thought he was being merciful after you found me. He went after them," I say, waving my hand behind me. "There is a small chance he doesn't know that I'm missing. But now?" I laugh. My eyes burn. No, I mustn't start crying again. "He will smell me just like they did. He will take me back or he will kill me. Either way—" I stop myself.

"I'm not letting you go," he says.

"What do you think is going to happen when he finds I'm with you? He will kill everyone! I have to leave." Why does no one ever listen to me? I want to scream, but my voice might bring Raum faster.

"We are capable of defending ourselves, Leah. He is not stronger than anything else we have defeated. Come here," he says, reaching for me. I surge past him through the grove, all too aware I sound as noisy as a horse trudging through the forest. Sebastian frowns and runs a hand through his hair. "We will fight for you."

"*We*? At least half of your people won't fight for me, and I'm not willing to sacrifice any of you for *my* life." The only people who might protect me are Sebastian and Devon. Maybe Liam and Mike. But the others? I shake my head. Hell, they could all turn against me. One life is not worth eight.

"Then I'll fight for you," he says with frustration. His hands flex as he throws them up in the air.

"You don't even know me!" My despondency is quickly turning into anger. I want to shake him!

"I want to! I can't do that if you're gone!" His words surprise me, stopping a new flow of my own before they can cross my tongue. "You survived for three years and now you want to give up? Dammit!" His anger stirs the bees as we descend into their alcove. We pause and look at them hesitantly before creeping around the outer edge of the field.

The grass seems higher than before. It reaches up to my fingertips, tickles my nailbeds as I come to a halt. Sebastian takes my hand and brings it to his lips. Who is this man and how can he care for me so much and not even know me?

XVII

We agree not to tell anyone about Raum. Sebastian doesn't want to start a riot when there is still a chance that Raum might not find me. As he recounts what happened, leaving out major details, Devon sits beside me and drapes an arm across my shoulders. For once, I can find no comfort in her presence. I bite at my nails until one finally bleeds. I suck it off quickly. The metallic flavor sits heavy on my tongue.

Anna asks Sebastian about the mark on his neck, but he passes it off as the burn it is. We make it very clear that the demons who attacked us are dead. She looks worried, but she doesn't question further.

We are missing some people, Liam and Anthony. I scan the room thinking I've overlooked them, but no, they are absent. My heart patters. I sit up straighter, sliding Devon's arm off me.

Laughter trickles down one of the corridors.

I turn around to see both men striding in from another room. Liam's eyes brighten when he sees me, but the dark shadows that have clung to the brown hues of his eyes still linger. What we have is purely physical, but I thought he might show some concern for my safety. At the very least be excited to see I came back.

There is nothing more than amused surprise of my being here.

"You made it back," he says to Sebastian. When he turns back toward me, he flashes his best smile. "I'm surprised you're still alive."

Unbridled anger ripples through me. I'm across the room, as if I've teleported, in the blink of an eye. I slap him so hard that his face snaps to the side. Anthony moves out of my way before I can shove past him. The room fills with a silence so loud I can still hear the echo of my hand snapping against Liam's face.

It's only after I slam my door shut that Liam's anger erupts. He yells profanities at me. Let him spew. I'm already putting a pack together, cursing him and anyone else who might take his side. I can deal with Liam's callousness, but not when it concerns something as precious as a life. I throw the bag into the corner. He is like Raum. He's used me just as he did. He will have nothing to yell about once I'm gone. They can all get back to their happy little lives soon enough.

Hours tick by. I lay in my bed, fully clothed waiting on everyone else to go to sleep. Devon is the first to check on me, Mike the next, and of course Sebastian. The knight in shining armor. I turn them all away. I don't want them to know my intentions. They will all thank me later.

It's well into the night when my door opens. I sit up quickly, hand flying to the hilt of my knife on impulse. Liam closes the door and leans against it.

I inhale to get a good breath for lashing out at him. He puts up his hand. "Leah," he says softly. I can hear him swallow. He shuffles forward and sits on the end of the bed, noticing that my hand is still behind my back. "Can we talk?"

"I have nothing to say to you." I withdraw my grip, resting my palm on my thigh.

"What the fuck, Leah? Are you serious?" His lips curl in disgust, or pain. I can't tell which and, quite honestly, I don't give a damn.

"I know all we do is *fuck,* but you didn't even care if I came back or not. Whatever happens to me is on you. *You!* You stole me and you can't even own up to it." I lose control. My anger has a mind of its own. My vision turns a murky crimson, clouding the rest of my senses. "You don't care about anyone but yourself. We are nothing alike."

He turns his head, stretching his neck and rolling his shoulders. Moving to relieve the tension building inside without taking it out on me. Sebastian is right, Liam is a cold man. "I do care about you. Leah, I'm sorry."

"Please don't lie to me, Liam." I can't take it.

"I promise I do. Don't hate me because I don't know how to show you or tell you."

"You wouldn't have bat an eye if Sebastian came back alone," I accuse.

"Maybe not, but that doesn't mean I wouldn't have been upset," he says.

His hand rests on my knee. I look down, not quite sure what to do with it. When nothing comes of it, Liam slides it up as he leans forward. He kisses me. At first, I don't respond. I sit stiffly, even purse my lips together. But I can't resist him. I kiss him back. This might be the last time I ever see another human. His taste is bittersweet, painfully sweet.

I forgive him. I slide my fingers through the edge of his hair and kiss him back. Good gosh, do I kiss him! I don't have time to hate myself for it. I just savor him.

We fall together, trading our clothes for bare flesh. Something draws me to him. It's a dark energy that pulls back the sheets and lies out my naked body before him. I press against him, run my hands down his chest and stomach and lower, caressing him sweetly until his kisses turn to bites.

"Yes," I say, the word nearly coming out as a hiss.

He moves inside of me with urgency I've never felt from him before and I moan. For the first time, I don't care who hears. I grab his ass and pull him into me. He presses his cheek to mine as he fucks me, grinding his hips in slow circles.

My stomach coils as an icy dread fills my body. It surrounds me, filling up the room so there is no clean air to breathe. It's the sort of fear that only animals can smell. My eyes snap open.

"Liam, get off of me!" He grabs my wrists as I try to push him away. "Liam," I hiss. "Stop, you're hurting me." I bend under his fingers, afraid he will snap my wrists. Can't he feel it? The air is polluted with darkness, toxic power. Where did his strength come from?

Liam fucks me harder, as if the presence of evil excites him. He lets go of my wrists only to grab my hips. His nails cut so deep that I cry out. He is like a man possessed. The more I struggle, the harder he uses me. His thrusts become erratic and painful. A lustful gleam fills his eyes before he tips his head back in his release.

Long talons sweep across Liam's neck. They slice the flesh like it's made of paper. The two pieces break apart and let out a flow of crimson water onto my chest

and face. I don't know if it's more horrific that he is
bleeding over me or that he has started to come inside
of me. A scream lodges in my throat, but suddenly I
can't breathe. My heart slams against my chest and I
clutch the sheets. I can't breathe!

A shadow behind Liam surges up and throws him
to the side. His skull cracks against the stone floor with
a loud snap.

The shadow climbs on top of me and a face appears, dark and menacing as I remember. Raum's
tongue flicks out of his mouth. He licks the blood running down my sides and his hands smear the red stain
into my breasts and stomach.

A surge of air rushes into my lungs, but before I
can scream, he clamps a bloody hand over my mouth.
"Don't make a sound," he hisses. Tears flow down my
face as I let the sound erupt behind his palm. "This is
what you replace me with?" His grip becomes ironclad
across my face and I whimper. I try to shake my head,
tightening his hold further still.

"I told you if you ever ran from me, I would bring
you back screaming." He shoves his fingers inside of
me, long spurs that tear my sensitive flesh. His eyes
gleam wickedly as I scream again into his hand. I
writhe beneath him. There is no escape. While he as-
saults me, he laps at the blood on my body hungrily.
His tongue is long and reptilian. It snakes across my
skin, not wasting any drop of the glittering rubies.

Suddenly his claws retract, and his fingers soften
inside me to a delicate stroke. He nuzzles my neck and
slides his hand from my mouth over the top of my collarbone. "I have use for you still, or I would kill you
now for betraying me."

"I didn't," I cry. My voice is hoarse. "I didn't run. They kidnapped me. I thought you left me."

"How could I ever part from something as sweet as you, Leah?" As if to make his point, he bites me, sharp teeth penetrating the vein in my neck. At first it burns, but like the first time it becomes hot and luscious. His tongue coaxes the blood out and his lips suck greedily. My pain becomes pleasure and I hold his head to me.

He pulls away. "But if it is so, how could you allow this boy inside of you? You forget that you are mine."

My blood glistens on his mouth; the color fascinates me. I lick my lips. He still strokes me gently, his nails sharpening once more, his fingers curving upward, lifting my hips.

"I thought only of you," I gasp. Pain or pleasure, I *had* thought of Raum. Every single time and I wanted them both. I wanted the desire he gave me and the torture along with it.

"I have been kind to you, Leah." His words send a chill down my spine, as if what he is about to do will show me how completely wicked he really is. He withdraws his fingers that are coated with what is left of Liam and my blood. He wipes the mess across my face.

"I can come in whenever I want. I will rip their throats out one by one and make a show of feasting on them in front of you." He tears the crucifix from my neck and tosses it across the room. His anger is maddening. It sends a sharp pain through my body. I've never known a feeling to be so overwhelming and torturous. Already, I'm shaking beneath him, my hands jittering.

"I will come for you in the morning. Convince them that you must go. I will not have them chasing you. You are mine," he hisses. "You do not belong to them. You never did and you never will."

Sharp pinpricks needle their way into my skin as his power strengthens. I twist beneath him to shimmy out from under them. If anything, the movement makes it worse. I whimper. God help me. Anyone help me.

Raum leans forward and the pain suddenly ceases. He presses his forehead to mine. He inhales, breathing me in, and lets it out slowly. "I left my path to Babel to protect you. I heeded your words about Leyak. I meant to kill him for you." He inhales again. "What a surprise it was to smell you all over him. The fire you started was not so hot to hide you away."

His tongue runs over the smear on my face. He takes my lower lip between his and sucks, biting on it gently. A sharp ringing pierces my ears. Like an addict, I succumb to him. It's the worst thing I can do yet I can't stop myself. I kiss him. Fighting back doesn't make sense.

Raum's mouth moves over every inch of my body. His tongue wraps around me, lifts me up so he can get every nook and cranny. It's rough, rubbing my skin raw, and yet I adore it. This is what I've missed, the sweet pain of his touch.

When he is finished cleaning me, he presses his forehead to mine again. He breathes in quietly, the sound of air sounding like water against the shore. "Go to sleep, and in the morning you will come to me."

I nod. I watch him slip onto the floor over Liam's body. I had forgotten about him. It all seems so hazy now. I run my hand over my chest but the blood is gone, as if from a faraway nightmare.

"What are you going to do?" I ask, turning on my side to watch him.

"Sleep, Leah."

My body becomes numb and darkness envelopes me. I think there is a sound of breakage, the soft rustle of leaves or the sound of a campfire. The snapping of bones is like a blaze. How sweet the heat of the flames are against my face.

XVIII

The compound is abnormally quiet. I'm up earlier than usual, but I can't be the only morning bird. I have half a mind to check the rooms to be sure everyone is still alive. I know something terrible has happened to Liam, but for the life of me I can't remember what. There is only the urgency to get to Raum before something worse happens, a cold fear that holds me tight around the throat like a collar.

I haul myself up the chain, gliding up easily like a snake. I crouch down once I'm at the top and listen. The only sound is the soft clink of the links as the chain sways back and forth from my climb.

Overhead, the stars shine brightly, flashing in the dark sky. On the horizon, peeking behind the mountaintops, I can see the first trace of light. Midnight blue fading into the inky blackness above.

A malevolent wind moves across my skin as I delve deeper into the city. I take the fear building in my chest and convince myself that it's only strength I feel. The darkness is stifling; it warms the chills on my body the closer I draw to it. It's like there is a tether within my soul that constricts with every step I take.

Raum slips into the road, melds right out of the shadows as if he was a part of them. There is something like relief that passes across his face. Then he smiles at me. The smile falters and he hisses.

"Hold it," someone says.

I spin around so quickly dust spews up beneath my boots. They're all behind me with guns, save for Anna and Chris. They're insane. I look between them and Raum, then back again. They are all wearing something of mine. A bandanna or torn shirt is wrapped around the men's wrists and forearms. Sarah and Devon wear one of my shirts. Raum couldn't smell them because there was only me. How did they know I was leaving? My eyes cut to Sebastian.

I don't know how Raum didn't hear them. When I look back at him, he flashes his teeth, his lips curling to reveal inflamed gums. "You better think twice before you pull your triggers," he hisses, the inhale of his breath sounding the same. "If you really care about Leah."

"That's why we're here," Devon snaps. For someone so sweet, she is a fierce woman behind the barrel. "You can't have her."

Raum laughs; it's a beautiful sound, full of sweet hatred. "She already belongs to me."

Someone shoots. The bullet sinks into Raum's knee. He doesn't show an inch of pain, but he does smile. It twists wide into a Cheshire grin. I want to go to him, but I'm too afraid of getting caught in the crossfire if anyone else decides to take a shot.

"If you kill me, Leah will die," he says.

"She doesn't have your mark," Devon says.

"Checked everywhere, did you? Perhaps you weren't thorough enough."

A dreadful cold falls over me and I sway under his oily stare. The demon smirks as his lids lower as he makes a trail down my body and stops where he means. He snaps his gaze up to me and I tremble.

"You didn't—"

"I did," he interrupts. "Don't you remember how sweet it felt?"

I look between Raum and the humans. "It's not true," I tell them. The only opportunity he had was when we were at the cabin. He asked me what I wanted, and I said him. I said his name again and again. Suddenly, I remember the sweet ecstasy not flowing out of me but into my bloodstream as he bit between my thighs.

"Tell them whatever you want, but *we* know the truth. We know that you screamed my name and tightened your hold on me. We know—"

"That's enough," I say thinly. I shake. My ears ring. The ground tilts beneath me.

"I don't think so. Come here, Leah, and let me take another bite," he says, snapping his teeth together.

I step forward. Someone grabs my arm and hauls me back. I look down at the hand holding me, Sebastian's hand, then back to Raum. Inwardly, I crumple. How much of our time together had been real and the rest of it controlled by his will? There is no struggle of whether I should cling to Sebastian or run to Raum. I want to go to him. I want to throw my arms around his neck and press close to my oppressor.

"Let her go," Sebastian growls.

Raum chuckles and my sudden desire for him evaporates. In that moment, someone else fires. Anthony, I believe. A dark stain spreads across the front of Raum's shirt, unfolding like flower petals.

"Don't!" Sebastian yells.

"He's lying," Anthony says.

Raum's attention slides smoothly to Anthony, the twisted sneer falling from his face. The force of his power washes over all of us and I fall to the ground screaming. My knee and chest are on fire. I can feel the blood running from the hole in Raum's chest like a river.

"Do you believe her screams?" he growls.

Devon drops down beside me. She presses a compress against my chest, but there is nothing for her to stop. I'm not the one who has been shot. "Do something!" she screeches. She turns her shining blue eyes to Raum when no one else moves. "Stop this, please!"

Raum cocks his head. He peers at her for a few slow heartbeats. The pain slowly recedes and I feel like I can breathe again. "Your bullets cannot kill me, but if I allow it, Leah will feel them. Any torture you inflict upon me will become her own. I can withstand anything. Do you think she can? She lives as long as I allow it."

Devon gathers me, helping me to my feet. The tears I'd been crying cease as I lean against her. My chest and knee throb with warm pain, but at least I can breathe again. I can stand.

"Let her go," Anthony says as he turns towards us. "She isn't worth it."

"We should just kill them both," Sarah whispers.

"Enough," Sebastian says. "We aren't killing anyone." If I could applaud Sebastian, I would. He looks

Raum in the eye with as much hatred as Raum presses upon us. "They're coming with us."

A trembling click ripples in the back of Raum's throat.

"There has to be a way to break their bond." Sebastian looks down at me with a frown. "We are too few. We can't afford to lose another life."

"She is already lost!" Sarah scoffs.

"Listen to the girl," Raum says. "Leah is mine. It would be within your best interest that you release her."

"No," Sebastian says again. "You're coming with us."

"You cannot remove my mark." His eyes drop from Sebastian's face and he smirks. "You of all people should know that," Raum growls. His muscles are bunched, poised, and ready to strike.

"We don't want any harm to come to Leah, so none will come to you. Providing you do not try to hurt us," Sebastian says. Now he does look nervous. Something about Raum's words have frightened him.

"This is insane," Mike whispers.

"You trust me not to kill you where you stand?" Raum approaches us, slow and cautious.

"Let me go," I say. Finally, my voice comes to me. I look at each of them in turn, coming to rest on Raum. "Let me go with him. It's not worth it."

Raum continues to approach and all but Sebastian and Devon disperse. Mike moves out of the way, slightly behind Raum. Anthony and Sarah are off at his other side. The demon is bold to trust them with his back.

"If you try to kill us, we will have no choice but to react. Leah means as much to you as she does to us,"

Sebastian says firmly. Someone mutters "bullshit" under their breath. Raum swings his head toward Sebastian and sneers. Sebastian lowers his gun as a sign of good will. His hands are shaking.

"I will kill you before you can get another bullet in me," Raum hisses.

There is a blur behind Raum's back. Before I can warn him, Mike raises the butt of his gun and slams it into the side of Raum's head. The world goes dark and we fall to the ground.

Noise; there is so much of it. Raised voices beyond recognition fill my head. I groan as I sit up, my head swimming. I feel like I'm going to vomit. The sickness rushes to my throat and I lean to the side, relieving my stomach. I groan again.

Everyone turns abruptly. Devon rushes to my side, snatching a random towel. She wipes my lips.

"Release them, or kill them, those are our only options," Anthony hisses, ticking off one finger then the other. "The way I see it, the only reasonable option is to kill them."

Sebastian leans against the wall, his forearm extended to hold his weight. His other hand covers his face. "There has to be another way," he says softly.

"Why do you care about her so much?" Anna accuses. "Is she worth more than all of us? Me?" Her cheeks are bright red, her brows knitted close together. Her small body is taut, like she wants to hit something. Hit him.

"She's right, you know," Chris says. When he catches my eye, he looks away quickly, wincing.

"The human race is few and far between. Even though she's marked, how can you not understand how vital she is?" Sebastian throws his hand out as his voice rises. He curses under his breath.

I remove Devon's hands from me. "Where is Raum?" I can feel the tie between us. I close my eyes, follow it through the compound until I find him. It's in a room I've never been before. I don't recognize it, but through him I know how to get there. Somehow. I stand. Devon grabs my hand as I sway.

My head feels heavy, my face swollen. I touch it, but there are no marks. I feel like I'm going to throw up again.

"Sit her down," someone says.

"Where is he?" I ask again.

"He's fine," Sebastian says quickly.

No, something is wrong. I grab Devon's arm to steady myself, and grip the furniture as I pass, following the thread that binds Raum and me.

"No! Just let her go!" Anthony yells. "It's not like anything worse can happen!" He curses. Something shatters, followed by a loud bang. Everyone's voices raise, fading into the background as I hurry down a darkened hallway. Devon stays close, hovering like a mother bird.

A black door separates Raum and me. It swings out with a groan as I pull it open. Behind narrow bars is Raum, wrapped in chains. He turns his face towards the door, into the light. The bruises are already healing, but whatever they did to him must have been awful. I touch my face, feel his swollen jaw in my own.

I rush to the gate and pull. It's locked.

"Why did you let them take you?" My voice falters.

Raum's expression softens, his lips part to let through a whisper of air. "Men become irrational when they are afraid. You would have died had I not done so."

I don't know whether to thank him or not. I hold onto the bars to steady myself. They're sturdy. I give them a shake, but they don't move. Raum could break them. I know he is strong enough.

"Why have you not come out?" I test them again. The more I shake, the more tired I become. I run my hands over the corners, testing for weak spots. He smiles at me as he watches me work.

"They have given me something that has taken my strength." As he says this, his eyes darken. He looks over my shoulder to Devon. If looks could kill, she'd be dead by now. She backs away, her feet scuffing the floor.

"What?" I come back to the gate. "What is it?"

"It was sweet," he says softly.

"What did you give him?" I turn to Devon.

She twists her hands together and looks down. "Honey," she answers. She looks up slowly, her blue eyes full of tears. "It won't kill him."

"It's done something!"

"It takes their strength— their powers. You have to understand that we are taking a huge risk by bringing him here." She shakes her head, bites her lip, then reaches for me.

I slap her.

Devon jumps back, startled. She blinks quickly and takes a couple of steps away from me. A red welt in the shape of my hand flames across her cheek.

"How dare you," I hiss.

Her gaze whips past me. Her eyes harden and she snatches her hand away from her face. "He is doing this to you," she says, pointing.

Raum laughs at her accusation. It's sinfully sweet. So much that I actually turn and smile at him. "I can do a lot of things, little girl. There is more to be afraid of than a slap to the face."

Devon's eyes narrow then widen. She lunges for me. I throw a punch that she deflects. She twists me around and shoves me forward. My knife! I grab for it as she slides it out of the sheath. It slices across my fingers and I pull back with a hiss.

I watch my blood fall from my blade and laugh. It trickles forward like silver bells. Mixed with Raum's deep rumble, it's music that could make the whole choir of Heaven fall in envy.

XIX

"I'm not going to wait around for you to figure out what the hell we are going to do!" Anthony's voice echoes down the hallway. "Have you even asked yourself where Liam is?" he asks as he draws closer. I move to the center of the room, ready to face him. "Where is he?"

Anthony storms in. Devon steps in front of him, but he shoves her out of the way. She catches the corner of a chair with her hip and lets out a painful gasp before falling to the ground.

"Anthony!" someone yells.

I smile. Anthony rounds on me as soon as I do. He grabs me by the throat and shoves me against the bars. I choke in a breath when he slams my head back.

"You take him to bed then suddenly, on the day you try to run, he goes missing. What have you done?" he growls.

My smile falters. I pull at his fingers as his grip constricts. My vision narrows, faces and colors blend together in one giant meld.

Sebastian and Mike rush forward and pull him off me. Anthony swings, striking Sebastian in the face. His head snaps back with a crunch. One of the women screams.

"Anthony! Stop!"

"What are you doing?"

Mike and Anthony tussle until Chris jumps in to
split them up. Sebastian reaches behind his back and
aims towards them. Anthony immediately straightens.
He raises his hands. His lips curl back, flashing his
blunt teeth.

"Oh, so you're the only one who is allowed a gun?"
Chris growls.

Sebastian trains the weapon on Anthony.

"See what fear does, Leah," Raum says. His head
is cocked to the side, his eyes trained on Anthony.
"This is what I wanted to protect you from," he croons.

"Ask her what happened to him," Anthony growls.
He eyes Sebastian's hand, the distance between them.
I've always thought Anthony looked mean, but I con-
firm it as his eyes narrow and his arms flex. He's just as
capable of being wicked as Raum is. I can see it burning in his eyes. I can feel it in the impressions he's left
in my neck.

Sebastian doesn't take his eyes off Anthony when
he questions me. "Where is he?"

I look between him and Sebastian. I take a step
closer to the cage. Sebastian waves the barrel at me and
back to Anthony, signaling to someone to pull me
away. Mike grabs my shoulder, dragging me to the
other side of the room. Across from us, Devon gives
him a simple shake of his head. I think Raum even
whispers for him to be careful.

"Where is he?" Sebastian asks again.

"He's dead," I whisper. It feels so strange saying it.
There is no emotion attached to his memory. I remember how I used to feel about him, but now there is noth-

ing. Nothing at all. The only thing I remember is how Raum made me feel after he killed Liam and that I liked it. The thought feels foreign but right.

"How?" Ah, Sebastian, such a simple man.

I look at Raum. "It doesn't matter. He isn't coming back."

Sebastian looks at me for a brief moment. It's the opportunity Anthony needs. He grabs Sebastian's wrist, twisting the gun free in a motion so fast it's hard to see when the gun transfers from Sebastian's hand to his.

"Give me the key," he snaps. "Now!"

"Think about what you're doing," Sebastian says.

"Just give it to him," Anna whispers. She makes a motion to step forward then stops, her hands coming to her lips.

I glance at the cage. The bars are too narrow to shoot through. It would be easy to miss, and a stray bullet could do worse than not. Anthony needs an unobstructed shot. I smirk.

Sebastian remains still, his jaw tightening. I want to go to Raum, but I'm afraid Anthony will turn on me as soon as I move. He turns the barrel toward me anyway. "Give it to me or I'll shoot her."

"What are you doing? Drop the gun!" Mike says, stepping in front of me.

"Who do you think did it? Which one killed Liam? Him or her?" He waves the gun between me and Raum, swinging it back towards me. "My money is on Leah." My fingers slide over Mike's back, but he doesn't budge. "I told you, there are only two options!"

Sebastian reaches into his pocket. Anthony's grip tightens. He reaches his free hand beneath his arm and holds out his palm. The key drops soundlessly. Anthony looks between us then walks over to the cage to unlock the bolt, his weapon still fixed on me.

Once the gate swings open, he steps inside, pointing the gun to his new target.

"Raum!" I try to rush for him, but Mike grabs me. *Click.*

Anthony pulls the trigger again. An empty chamber. I can't see his face, but by the look on Raum's, Anthony is furious. Raum sneers at him. Anthony swings the gun down against the demon's face. The blow sends my head reeling. Again and again, he pounds Raum's face. I call out his name as I fall to the ground.

"Release your hold!" Sebastian yells at the demon.

A new wave of strength flows through me and I find my feet. I rush to the gate. Sebastian scoops me up by the waist while Mike hauls me back by the shirt. At the first sign of blood streaking down Raum's face, something breaks inside of me. His cheek splits open, a red line snapping apart by the blunt force of the grip. I jerk my arm free and throw my elbow into Sebastian's already broken nose. He lets me go with a yell. I spin around, throwing my fist at Mike who releases my shirt before I can strike him. My momentum sends me crashing into the bars.

I feel like I'm going to pass out. Everything blurs together as Anthony continues to assault Raum. Every blow feels like it's cracking my skull apart. I turn into the cage and shove Anthony forward.

Raum's mouth clamps over the first bit of flesh he can find. I've thrown Anthony off balance so Raum misses his neck, sinking his razor-like fangs over his ear and jaw instead. I fall at their feet. Raum's skull must be broken. It feels like my head and face are going to explode.

Anthony cries out. Chris and Mike rush in and try to pull him away from Raum, but the demon's bite is too strong. They only manage to pull him free when Raum decides to release him. Blood drips down his chin as he grins. He spits a spray of it at the men, misting it across their faces.

Someone must have grabbed the key. I hear the gate slam, then lock. I roll onto my back and cry out, pressing my hands to the side of my head. Devon is the one with the key now. Behind her, they carry Anthony away. Anna is trying to assess Sebastian's face. He shoves her away and leaves the room abruptly, following the rest of the men.

"Do you think that's a good idea? Leaving her in there with him." Sarah nods to Devon as she comes to stand next to her.

Devon shoves the key in her pocket. "She doesn't know what she's doing," she says softly. It's so quiet I almost don't hear her. That and her voice breaks. Her blue eyes shine more than usual. She's crying. "If we let her out, he will use her against us."

"Monster," Sarah whispers.

"Says the girl who watched me being beaten with a smile on her face," Raum hisses. "I came for Leah peacefully and in turn you capture and torture me. You knew what would happen if harm came to me. Look at what you've done. Look at her!" His voice booms, making the women jump.

"We didn't mean for any of this to happen," Devon says. "Not like this." She brushes a tear from her face.

"That is just it with you humans. You never think. You react on impulse, relying on your own stupidity like you do your god!" Raum's anger doesn't mix well with the pain consuming me. The room grows dark. I moan and curl against his feet. I touch his ankle. It's the only way I can beg him to stop, to cool his temper. God, just make it stop.

I blink lazily as I come around again. I must have passed out. I reach up, pulling myself across Raum's knee. The room sways and I duck my head, leaning heavily against him.

"Slow down, Leah," he says softly.

"My head," I start.

"I have tried to suppress what I can from you, but I am not strong enough to take it all. Not yet. I gave you my strength." He stretches his hand forward beneath the chains and touches the top of my head. I sigh painfully.

"What's happened?" I mumble.

"Your new family has abandoned you." His fingers stretch, stroking the side of my face.

I groan. "They're not my family." It's not like I ever really gave them a chance.

Someone clears their throat. I turn my cheek to the other side, wincing. Devon's arms are folded across her chest. She looks over her shoulder then steps a little closer to the gate before crouching down. She pulls out red meat and a shining apple to match.

"You should know better than to eat those," Raum scolds as Devon passes me the fruit.

She glances up at him before sliding the food across the floor. The smell of fresh meat makes my stomach growl. I fall off his lap and eat it greedily while Devon watches with a disgusted look. When I'm done, I lean back against Raum's legs, tilting my head over his kneecap.

"Thank you," I whisper.

"You're my friend. I can't let you starve." She glances over her shoulder again. So, the others don't want to feed me. Poor Devon and her soft heart. It's going to get the best of her one day.

"Am I? You cut me with my blade." I turn my fingers out, but the slash has already healed. I chuckle softly. Raum can heal me, but he can't heal himself. Something about it amuses me. I press my shoulder against his knee. That explains why I couldn't find Mara's bite either. Raum had already marked me, cleansed my skin of everything except for marks left by him.

"You would have used it on me," she says thinly. "He was manipulating you and you didn't even know it."

"I knew exactly what I was doing." I close my eyes. She doesn't know what she is talking about. The ringing in my ears has become a constant wave of music. I press my fingers against my temples. I wish it would stop. Even if it does sound nice, I can't think clearly.

"He isn't good for you," Devon says.

Raum growls. She moves a few feet away from the cell. "I am the only thing that *is* good for her. I have done nothing but protect her. When I bit her, she became my responsibility."

"You knew she was your ticket to staying alive. Your time is over, and you know it. You knew it when you bit her," Devon snaps.

"Who is to say I didn't do it out of love? There is nothing more selfless than giving a part of one's life to another." He touches my head affectionately to make his point.

"You poisoned her! That is not love!"

"She seems to think so." I lean my head back so I can see his smile. Anthony's blood has dried black across his face. The blemish doesn't daunt how beautiful he is.

"Because you have infected her mind! She no longer thinks for herself!"

That catches my attention. I swing my head down, the room spins less. I glare at her. "You think I'm incapable of my own thoughts? I haven't lost my will. Be careful, Devon. If you keep raising your voice, someone is going to hear you. You don't want them to throw you in with us."

"Are you even listening? To either of you? He doesn't deny it!" Devon paces the floor. She waves her hands wildly in the air. When they come down, she throws them against the bars.

"Bond or no, I would still be here protecting him from *you*," I say defiantly.

Devon's lip trembles as she turns her head down. "No, you wouldn't."

I fall forward with my head in my hands. I cry. All my emotions flow out in choked sobs and sniffles. "I would. You don't know what it's like to be alone for so long. When Raum found me, it was the best thing that could have happened to me until you did. I can't turn my back on him just because he isn't human. If he wanted, he could jump from this body into yours, or somebody else." I reach back to touch his other leg. I grip his knee. "You know it. You know even though you've poisoned him he could be free if he really wanted to be. But he doesn't do it." I look back at him for reassurance, but his cold eyes are fixated on Devon. I turn back to her.

Devon takes her lower lip between her teeth. She knows I'm right.

"Let me out," I say.

Devon shakes her head, her fingers tightening on the bars.

"Let me out."

"Let *us* out," we say. Our voices whisper to her. Caress her delicately, draw her to us. She blinks slowly. Her eyes become heavy. Devon sways forward until her face is pressed between the bars. She sighs and reaches out to me. I crawl forward and reach for her hand.

"Devon!" Her name breaks her from the trance. She snatches her hand away before I can grab it.

Mike grabs her by the armpits and hauls her back to her feet. "What do you think you're doing?"

She looks at me pitifully, her eyes deglazing. "How could you do that?"

"How could you lock us up?" I snarl. I shake the bars so hard that dust falls from the ceiling.

"Get out of here. Now," Mike says and gives her a push. Devon turns away, but not fast enough. I see the tears running down her face before she can hide.

Mike looks at me for a couple of heartbeats. He shakes his head, his mouth twisting with disgust. My heart softens and I sit back. What is wrong with me? I feel like I'm going crazy, like I'm not myself. I know this is me, though. These are my actions, my thoughts, and yet I feel out of control. I blink again and suddenly I'm angry that Mike still stares at me. My hands curl into fists.

"We're going to figure this out," he says. He gives a passing look over Raum before turning on his heel, slamming the door behind him. I hear something slide on the other side. A lock or blockade.

"Leah, will you give me your blood?" Raum's voice caresses me.

I crawl onto his lap and pull my hair away. I could give him my wrist, something easier, but I know it's my throat he wants. I press it to his lips. I feel his teeth sharpen against my skin as they slide beneath the surface. It's a light pressure that gives way to the flow of blood. I cradle his head, running my fingers through his hair while he drinks. We grow stronger the more he takes.

XX

Raum's cool gaze slides over me, roving. Red flames flicker across the abyss of his black orbs, threatening, promising deadly relief. He holds my eyes as his muscles flex, stretching the chains link by link. His toxic heat overwhelms me, making me sweat as he struggles to break his bonds.

"Do you need more?" I'm already pulling the collar of my shirt back.

"I cannot take anymore from you. If I do, even with my strength, you will not be able to survive for long." He jerks his wrist up, snapping the chains taut. They clack as he tilts his head back to rest.

Raum has cut me off from his influence. For now. I think that's what he has been doing, at least. I can't really tell when he is in control. Moments ago, I could feel the chains as if it were my body they were wrapped around. Now there is only the sensation of the stale air against my skin. My head feels clear, the room less suppressing even though his rage has risen in volume. The ringing has stopped.

"You said you wouldn't mark me," I say. Knowing the truth and saying it are two very different things. I worry my hand over my chest, but nothing alleviates the pain that digs at me.

"I lied," Raum says simply. His upper lip tugs up to flash his fangs that have yet to retract. Rows of sharp teeth glint in the dim light. I touch my neck tentatively. The bite has already healed, the only remnants of it are a few drops of crusted blood.

"Monster."

He hums. "Small, weak little Leah. It was only a matter of time before you killed me." The air around us suddenly goes cold, though the heat coming off Raum intensifies. The look in his eye shifts the same way, looking deadly then hungry. Has he always been so wicked and I've been too blind to see it?

"I hate you," I say.

A sound emits from the back of his throat like stones grinding together. "Hatred and love are so easily confused," he says. Something like a caress reaches towards me through our bond.

I move in front of him, squaring off. "You might have control over me now, but you will never trick me into believing that I love you."

"I don't have to," he says, leaning as far forward as the chains will allow. The touch retracts, leaving my body feeling cool and empty. "Now get me out of here," he says softly.

I want my freedom as much as he does. I press against the bars. Perhaps they have a weakness from this side. Were the circumstances different, I might be happy that the honey has weakened Raum. Being what they are, it frightens me. I don't know how the humans will react, if they will change their minds and kill us. Has Sebastian turned against me? Surely Devon has.

"They have bound the boy that I bit," Raum says with a hiss.

I shove my shoulder into the gate before facing him. "Anthony?" I scan the wall behind his head. Why would they bind him? "You marked him?" An absurd rise of jealousy touches my chest. I scan the top of the cage and try to refocus my attention. There is nothing for me to be jealous of.

"I'd like to have done more," Raum says bitterly. "I have called him to me, but he is being held against his will."

Against his will. I scoff. "He was our only hope of getting out of here then. I'm going to test the top," I say, stepping up on his arms before he can answer. Raum says something about the view. I *accidently* knee him in the face as I push the top of the cage. It moves. Raum twists his body to accommodate my weight so I can lean against him as I push up again. The bars pop up then slam back with a loud bang.

"I'm not strong enough to lift it," I say, shoving against it again. "Not this way, at least. I need better leverage."

"Call one of them to let us out," Raum says.

"That worked so well the last time," I say irritably. I know I should feel guilty about what I did to Devon. Instead, I'm angry it didn't work. Perhaps another one of Raum's influences.

"They cannot all be restrained," he says matter-of-factly.

I grab the top of the cage, leaning back to look at him. "What are you talking about?"

"They eat from temptation." He gives me a dark look. The corner of his lip curls up as understanding sets in. "By me you are irresistible."

"The apples," I say. Raum hisses in response. They're the only fruit to grow because the demons planted them. I curse. I'd been eating them too, although I don't suppose it matters much with Raum's venom inside of me.

"Get us out of here," Raum says.

It takes only a moment for him to sway me. I step up onto his shoulders, hunching forward and pressing up, shoving the top of the cage over my back and shoulders. I surge up and the top pops open enough for me to slip through. I jump down as it slams shut behind me.

The door is still firmly locked, or blocked. I throw my shoulder against it anyway, my feet sliding across the floor. My back and shoulders ache. Sweat blurs my vision as I wipe it from my brow. "Does honey really make you so weak?" I groan.

"So it would seem," he growls, a steady tick coming from his throat. The chains knock together as he flexes once more to try and free himself. He has started to sweat with exertion. I can't remember ever seeing Raum sweat. First the bullet in his chest and now this. If Raum is weakened to the point of mortality, we are both dead. Keeping him alive is my only salvation.

"Help me!" I bang against the door with my fists.

"Good girl," Raum whispers.

"Please, help me!" I cry. I let my voice rise until my throat feels raw. One of my knuckles splits open as I strike the door again. I hit it twice as hard in frustration. My head falls forward, pressing into the cold steel. I try to tap into whatever influence Raum believes I have over the humans.

I lean away when I hear someone on the other side. Something slides across the door before it swings open.

The nose of a gun is the first to come through and I pull myself against the wall. Mike cautiously eases in. He holds the gun toward the cage. He jerks it towards me when he realizes I'm not inside.

"Oh, thank God," I sniff, reaching for him.

Mike thrusts the gun at me. "Don't move, Leah."

"What are you doing?" I look from the barrel to him and hold his eyes. Keep looking at me.

"How did you get out?" He looks at Raum when he asks the question, like he already knows.

"I climbed out the top. Stop pointing that at me, you're scaring me." I back away nervously. I could possibly disarm him, but he might shoot me first. I like Mike. I want him to trust me. I also don't want to hurt him, but there is only one way we're getting out of here. I can't be sure if Raum is influencing me as I move closer to him.

"He's asleep," I say. I take a chance in touching Mike's arm. He looks over my shoulder with me.

"His eyes are open."

"That's how they sleep," I say. I wind my fingers around his arm, stroking softly to pull his attention back around.

"Is it really you?" he asks, turning slowly.

"Yes," I say tearfully. "It is."

Mike holds my gaze a few moments before lowering the gun. I fling myself against his chest. He wraps his free arm around my shoulder and rests his chin on the top of my head. He murmurs something into my hair with a quick kiss.

"I never thought I'd get out of there," I say, pressing my face into him. "Hurry, let's go before he wakes up."

Mike runs his hand down my arm, gripping it softly as he leans away. "I can't let you out. He's marked Anthony. It's been hard enough trying to keep him in control." His eyes sweep over me and he frowns. "I'm sorry. We can't take any chances."

"You can't leave me here!" I dig my fingers into his shirt, twisting.

"I can't let you out." He grabs my hand in an attempt to pry mine off. "Leah, let go."

"You can't leave me here, Mike. You don't know all the terrible things he has done to me. Oh God! What he is going to do!" I pull him forward with both hands. Mike continues fighting me. He tries to point the gun back at me, but I'm too close. My body is shoved up against his, forcing him back against the wall.

Just a little closer.

There is a mound jutting out of the concrete wall. If I can edge him closer, I can slam his head against it. I know I can knock him out. He is afraid of me, his fear almost palpable. His terror is my strength. I abruptly shove him back.

Mike stumbles, but he is quicker than I expected. He brings his gun up and fires as his head smacks against the wall. A bullet drives through the top of my shoulder, grazing the side of my neck. I clench my jaw and shove him again. Another loud smack runs through the air and he slumps to the ground.

I kick the gun away from him.

"I'm sorry," I say half-heartedly. I don't feel sorry, but I know that I should. We had been friends of sorts, after all. I grab him by the front of his hair and slam his head down again for good measure.

I rummage through his pockets until I find the key to the gate. It's just the one. I double check again to be sure I haven't missed something. There is no key to release Raum from his chains. Mike blinks up at me lazily. He slurs as he tries to say something.

I unlock the gate, flinging it open. I hurry back to Mike as it slams against the cage. He groans as I drag him across the floor. "You're smart, Mike, but you're too slow. You shouldn't have opened the door. You shouldn't have trusted me."

"D-don't," he mumbles. He reaches for me, his hand barely coming off the ground.

"It's already done, don't you get it?" I heave him up onto Raum's lap. He lets out sounds of pain, moaning and groaning like an animal. "You can bleed to death or you can help us." I touch Mike's face softly and smile. "Don't you want to help us?"

He stares at me before giving me a long blink.

"That's right. Now close your eyes." I lift his arm up to Raum's mouth. The demon fastens his teeth over the soft flesh. Mike moans, but it's a sound of pain. Tears run down his face. Poor thing, he keeps his eyes shut.

Raum flexes.

Pop! Pop! Pop! Pop!

He falls forward onto the ground, on top of Mike, and tears into his neck. Mike, too weak to fight, tries anyway. He pushes against the demon's face, whimpering. The horror of what is happening doesn't hit me the way it should. I watch Raum with new fascination. Perhaps even adoration as he rips the man apart. I can see the strength flowing back through his body, rippling in every muscle. He doesn't waste a drop of blood. He sucks every bit of it out of Mike before crushing the man between his fists.

I pick the gun off the ground and step through the doorway. Raum is no doubt about to consume Mike's body. I move slowly, stopping every now and then to listen. Somewhere, Anthony is screaming. I can hear his muffled voice coming from some distant hallway. If I get to him first, I can release him, send him directly into Raum's teeth. It would give me time to find the others.

Anthony is not as heavily guarded as Raum and I were. Idiots. Did they really think we wouldn't get out? I go to push his bedroom door open, then stop. It could be a trap. Getting to him is almost too easy. Unguarded in his own bedroom? I step off to the side and turn the handle, pushing it open.

Nothing.

The screams have also stopped.

I push the door open a little farther and step in, keeping my eye down the sight of the gun. Sarah is at his bedside. She stands up quickly, bringing up a weapon. I shoot her first. She drops to the ground. I look up, blinking. Gore slides down the wall where she had been standing.

Anthony cranes his head down as she falls. I turn Sarah on her side. Half of her face is missing, leaving her completely unrecognizable. My aim has significantly improved.

A thick hilt sticks out at her side and I smile. Raum must have had it hidden on him somewhere. I unsnap the sheath that holds my kukuri and fit it onto my belt, but not before pulling the knife free. The familiar weight of the blade steadies my racing heart.

Anthony's bonds fall free with a single pull of iron against rope. The foreign strength sends a tingle down my spine that makes me tighten my hold on the knife. I step back when Anthony sits up, yanking the ropes from his wrists.

"I guess you weren't as much of a threat as us," I mumble, sawing the ties away.

Raum's bite has the same shape as a shark attack on the side of Anthony's face. The black imprint stands out dramatically against his dark skin. It's a hell of a bite. Each fang mark is a divot where Raum tried to rip his face off. Covering the mark is a faint haze of black where Anthony's skin has been burned.

"They used all the chains on Raum," Anthony says, standing. He touches the side of his face absent-mindedly and looks behind me. "Where is he?"

"Waiting on us," I say, hauling him to his feet. The urge to send Anthony to Raum suddenly becomes less pressing. "Where are the others?"

"I don't know. I overheard Sebastian talking with Mike earlier about leaving, but they're worried about the bees. They don't want to leave them." He bends down, stepping in the glistening pool of blood gathered at Sarah's face to retrieve her gun. I slip the kukuri back into its sheath, leaving it undone in case I need to pull it quickly.

A flash of heat runs through me. They were going to leave us here. How dare they leave us caged and tied to rot.

"What now?" he asks.

"We find them. Buy Raum time to escape. He'll come back for us." We creep down the hallway, listening, ready for anything. No doubt everyone is in the hives, doing what they can to protect their sliver of salvation.

"Are you sure?" Anthony whispers.

When Raum does come for us, it will be for me and me alone. I'm the one he wants. He will take Anthony too, but not in the way the man hopes. Even now his eyes are wistful, glazed over like some love-struck puppy. Raum will torture him, but only after he has run the man dry. Raum will kill him.

I smile at Anthony. "Absolutely."

XXI

The compound is too quiet. I figured with the shots that have spoiled the air that someone would have come running. Anthony walks ahead of me, his thick brows drawn together, making his sharp face more threatening. He holds up his hand suddenly to stop me. He turns and brings a finger to his lips. I heard it too, the slightest inhale of someone holding their breath.

I signal him to wait. There are four people left and my guess is that whoever we heard isn't alone. I'm trying to figure out if they're stupid enough to be clustered together. Whoever they are, they do not have our patience. A black gun pokes out. It shakes. Whoever holds it is as cautious to come out as we are to go in. At the first flash of skin, Anthony fires. They yell, dropping the gun.

Before I can stop him, Anthony rushes forward. Bullets fly from both sides of the doorway. Anthony stumbles back, pushes forward again, and sends off another three loud rounds. I rush after him. Chris is on his back, his hand ripped apart from the first bullet. A wet sound pops from his lips, a final breath.

Anna is a few feet away lying on her side. I push past Anthony and turn Anna over with a kick. She turns; dead weight.

"Two more," I mumble. Two more and then we will be free of this nightmare. I close my eyes briefly. I've grown accustomed to the smell of blood, but this is so much more pungent. The copper smell burns my nose, bites into the back of my brain. I can almost taste it.

Anthony groans and I look back at him. Blood stains the bottom edge of his shirt; another patch is spreading through the denim on his thigh. "Son of a bitch," he breathes and leans against the doorjamb.

"How are you holding up?" I ask.

He groans again. "Perfectly," he says through gritted teeth.

I tap my finger on the side of my gun. Anthony is going to bleed out unless Raum decides to help him. I assume the demon is already using his power, otherwise Anthony would be laying out with the other two bodies. I could kill him now, save everyone the time and trouble of hauling him around. No, better not. I might need to use him to take another round later.

I smirk. "Let's go then."

This time I lead us. We search for Devon and Sebastian as we make our way to the front exit. They're either well hidden or they've run. From what I can tell, the place is abandoned. Anthony points me in the direction of all the spaces they kept hidden from me, but every room and tunnel we come across is empty. The only life roaming through it is us, blood thirsty wolves. There are no sounds other than the ones we make.

I wave Anthony to a stop as we reach the end of the main tunnel. The opening to the compound is wide, the edges jagged. Pale light filters down. Dust specks dance in the warm glow, fading in and out of the shadows. What I don't see is a way out.

Anthony curses as I walk a little closer. They've taken the chains. I search the ground and inner rim, but they're gone. Even if I can find them, there's no way we can reattach them from here.

"We have to go out the back," he slurs.

Anthony leans over, the tip of his gun resting on the ground. He isn't going to make it. His dark skin is ashen and drenched with dying sweat. His eyes are bloodshot and heavy-lidded. Why is Raum still holding onto him? Blood drops line the path we've come, leading our enemies straight to us if, by chance, they are following us.

"Grab your gun," I say, leaning down to him. I should leave him, but instead I sling his arm over my shoulder. Anthony leans against me, sliding my foot out to the side as I try to accommodate his extra weight. I practically drag him down the hallway. The orange glow of the utility lights marks our path back to the inner circle of the compound.

The walls feel close, like they're pressing in around me. I run into the sitting room, straining to pull Anthony with me, before they can close in. For good measure, I look back to the hallway that hasn't changed a bit. I'm losing my mind. I've got to get out of here. This place feels like it's about to come down on our heads.

I shift my weight, throwing Anthony higher against my shoulders. I'm too busy fumbling with him that I almost miss the feeling. Power seeps into the room in the form of a sweeping shadow. I stand, letting

Anthony sway upright, and step forward as Raum approaches.

His black eyes envelope me as he comes into view, coming through the doorway where Chris and Anna had last been seen. He is larger than before. The change is so minor someone else might not notice, but I do. I'm all too familiar with his body. I recognize the new pounds of muscle, the length of his limbs, how the blood has revived the color in his face.

I reach up and run my thumb across his cheek. The cut has healed completely. A thin smile spreads and I lean up. Raum bends down to me and presses his forehead to mine.

"I thought you left me," I say.

His face lowers, his breath warming the side of my neck. "Never again," he says and kisses me. His teeth graze my neck, but he doesn't bite it. Everyone else has already filled him up.

"Let's go," Anthony growls.

Raum's head snaps up. His eyes flash, narrowing like he had forgotten Anthony was here. He pushes past me and grabs him by the neck. He squeezes. Anthony's face turns purple, his eyes bulge. Spittle covers his lips and his nails dig into the demon's hand.

What's that sound?

"Raum—"

Sebastian shoots before any of us have time to register the sound of their footsteps running into the hall. Devon comes up behind him, a gun in each hand. Bringing up the rear is Anna. She'd been faking it and I had been too distracted to check. There was so much blood I just assumed she was dead. I should have slit her throat.

Raum lets Anthony go and grabs my hand. Anthony falls forward and stumbles after us. He takes the brunt of the first shot. We sprint from the gunfire, from the people I started to love not too long ago. The first door on our right is locked, so is the next one, then the one on our left. We wind through the labyrinth of hallways, looking for any door that will give us shelter.

Hot, searing pain hits me. I cry out as a bullet sinks into my shoulder. It penetrates the bone. I pull my arm close and fall against Raum to hide from the burst of brass shells they rain down on us.

Raum moves like lightning, striking with the speed only a demon has. He turns quickly and kicks Anthony backward into the hail of bullets. Anthony's eyes widen. It's in that moment I realize Raum has released his hold over him. Anger, then fear, passes across his eyes before he seizes as the shots tear through his body. Raum grabs the door handle closest to us and shoves it open, pushing me inside. I know this door. It's the wrong door!

"Raum! No!" The door slams behind us, enveloping us in harsh white light.

A horrible sound of churning wings pierces my ears. Raum and I fall to the ground, our hands pressed firmly over our ears. Over the sound of the bees, I hear a bolt slide into place. I crawl over to the door to test the handle. It's locked.

The bees writhe through the air. Their music is nothing if not torturous. They dart back and forth through the ashen sky. I've always loved being surrounded by the bees and their humming. Now I'm terrified. Sweat sticks my shirt to my skin, dampening the back. I grab onto Raum's arm for reassurance, but it

only seems to make things worse. Wave after wave of
fear hits me. I duck behind him, hiding away from the
bees that move above us with their hideous colors of
black and gold.

Raum grabs my hand, pulling me roughly into the
field. He drops to the ground as soon as our feet meet
the grass and slips his fingers between the tall reeds. A
wave erupts through the air, like a sonic boom. Instantly, the ground beneath his touch blackens, smoke
tendrils rise, and behind those, flames. The fire spreads
swiftly, sweeping through the grass with a desperate
hunger. The hives go up in a blaze.

When the first one lights, a sense of relief runs
through me, followed by an overwhelming wave of hatred. I clench my teeth together as the feeling spreads,
urging the fire to move more swiftly.

Something inside me changes and I jerk my hand
from Raum's. Instead of fighting to get me back, he
turns his attention to the hives beyond us, in the fields
that lead to the orchard. By sheer sight or his power,
they too go up in flames.

I blink quickly, my eyes becoming clear when I
recognize Raum's attention is no longer focused on me.
I watch the boxes erupt into towers of red.

No!

The heat I couldn't feel before now scalds me. I
flinch away from the flames too close to my skin. The
bees' soft hum becomes desperate, violent, like they're
screaming. I turn around desperately. There must be
some way to save them!

I scream. My tears evaporate before I can shed
them. I grab one of the hives that hasn't caught fire and
pull it down. The top breaks apart, releasing a black

cloud of insects into the sky, into the thick smoke that clots the sunlight.

Everything is black now. I can't find Raum. I can't see anything through the thick smoke. I spin around again. I'm going to die with this last shred of hope. What have I done? I scream. This time, it's to save myself. To truly save the last piece of humanity I have.

"Help me!"

I pull my shirt over my face. Flames are everywhere. I can't even drop to the ground to get clear of the smoke without being engulfed by them. Already, they're circling me, eating up the grass like it's their last meal. I close my eyes when the smoke becomes too much. The heat weakens even though the fire has spread to a mere two feet from me.

Someone grabs me, scoops me up in their arms and pushes my head down into their chest. I recognize Raum's strength and hold onto him as he crushes me to him. A whoosh of air takes hold, whipping around us like a storm. It's breathtaking. The air is sucked out of my lungs and my head snaps back. It feels like a force is trying to rip us apart. The front of his shirt slips through my fingers. My head slams into him as the world around us flashes: red, black and then blue as the sky opens.

The sensation and bursts of colors end abruptly. I gasp, panting for the fresh air that envelopes us. The world outside spins around like a kaleidoscope and I wretch. Where is the fire? The hives?

Raum sets me down on shaking legs and takes my face between his hands. I get the vague sense we are somewhere outside of the orchards, but I can't see past Raum. I've never seen him so afraid before, so completely and utterly human. His brows furrow as he looks from one side of my face to the other.

I notice the hole in his shirt. It wasn't me they shot, it was him. I poke my finger through it. The flesh is mended, unmarked by any stain the humans tried to leave on him. I pull my hand back and meet his eyes. He used me against them.

Nausea coils in the pit of my stomach. Raum's influence must not have withdrawn from me entirely because I am faster than I should be. I shove him away from me, pull the kukuri free, and slash it towards him before he can blink. Raum grabs the blade, letting it slice into the palm of his hand instead of his midsection that I was aiming for. He jerks the knife from me and grabs me by the shoulder with his free hand.

"What have you done?" I'm overwhelmed by the fear still hounding him, our anger and my own despair. The bees are burning and we left everyone else to die. We killed all those people. *I* killed those people. "Let go of me!" I scream when I feel a desire to be close to him. "Fucking let go of me!" I clamp my hands on the side of my head and bend over, sobbing.

Raum slides his touch up to the back of my head. His fingers thread through my hair and he pulls me up to face him. "After all this time, you still hate me." Surely, that isn't sadness I hear in his voice.

"Let me feel what is real," I beg, my voice cracking.

"*This* is real," he hisses and hardens his grip. He gives my head a rough shake. "*I* am real. What you have *done* is real." He grabs me with both hands now, pulling my face up as he bends down to me. His blood singes the side of my face. "You saved me because it was your will."

I lean forward, my head pressing into his chest. "I would have let you die," I whisper. My forehead rubs against his shirt as I slowly look up at him. My body burns, inside and out. I don't want to look at him, but I must.

"That is not true," he says, running his thumbs down my cheeks. The touch smudges the tears into the soot on my face.

"I'd run back into the fire if it meant those people lived and you died," I say through gritted teeth.

Raum's glare is hollow, cold. The frigid glint sends chills across my skin. It holds my spine rigid and stops my breath. It's the kind of cold that scares you stiff. He is warm, but I am ice cold beneath him, frozen.

"I think you've had enough free time," he hisses, his throat swelling as the sound escapes him. He tilts the blade between his hand and my face.

I grab his wrist, taking an iron hold. "Don't." I look between his fiery eyes. "Don't take my humanity."

"Give me one good reason," he growls. He takes a rough hold on my chin and squeezes.

"I won't fight you." I should let him take hold of me, wipe the guilt from my conscious. Good sense won't let me, though. "I'll stay at your side. Just, please, get me away from the fire."

XXII

There is no way anyone is getting out of the compound. There were only two exits, one of which was on fire, the other completely unattainable. Raum assures me the fire will spread. The steel door won't be able to hold back his flames; it will finish what we started. No one will survive.

To be sure, Raum checks the perimeter I line out for him. He goes past the invisible map I draw, sniffing to be sure neither of us has missed anything. I don't know how he can smell anything over the smoke.

He doesn't clean the kukuri before shoving it into the sheath at my hip. Neither does he say anything as he pushes the snaps into place. For whatever reason, he chooses to dismiss my attack on him. Maybe he pities me.

We pass through the city, working our way through residential neighborhoods. I leave what is left of my gun in the road. It has melted from the flames. Raum walks behind me. He might have let me keep a weapon, but it's clear he doesn't trust me enough to be at his back.

I torture myself, reliving every moment of our escape. Every shot fired, life lost, all the way up until Raum pulled me out of the flames. That part of my memory hurts the most. Physically, at least. There is still a carnal ache in my bones. Everything else feels like a broken heart that will never be mended.

"How did we escape the fire?" I ask.

"I pulled us out."

"But how?" I look over my shoulder and slow down.

Raum's lids lower as I fall at his side. We both know he can flip the switch inside my head at any moment. I swallow, waiting patiently for him to answer. I try not to think about his death. I don't know if he can read my mind, but I don't want to take any chances.

He snaps his fingers. "Like that."

"Like teleportation or something?" I look at him and along the road we walk on. "Why are we walking? Why can't you just," I snap my fingers, "us to Babel?" I assume that is where we are still going. Raum isn't anything if not dedicated.

"You ask too many questions," he says irritably.

I turn, stepping in front of him to block his path. Raum comes to a stop, his dark eyes narrowing when he looks down at me. "What's really going on?"

We stand like that, not saying anything. He doesn't blink. I cross my arms over my chest and widen my stance. We aren't going anywhere until I have answers.

"Babel is in Syria. My power is not what it used to be, and it is your friends I have to thank for that. If I were to attempt to take us there now, we would most likely end up in the ocean, or some part of Asia." His jaw is clenched; a thick vein stands out in his neck.

Does the effect of the honey still have a hold over him? What if they did something else to him? I run my tongue over the underside of my teeth.

"What difference will a few more miles make? If that is the farthest we can go with your power, won't we end up in Asia anyway?" I dig my nails into the base of my arm. I don't want to feel that pain again. The transition had only lasted a few seconds. Crossing the sea would take hours, days even.

"I would rather know for certain we will land in Asia instead of taking chances. Wouldn't you?"

I don't want to go. Period. My next question weighs heavily, though. It's one that has always been in the back of my mind, but I'd never gotten around to asking it. "What happens when we get there?"

A sinister light sparks behind his eyes when he says, "I become a god."

Raum, a god? I can't wrap my head around the logistics. What I do know is it can't happen. I can't even begin to imagine the horrors he would inflict on the rest of the world. Does that mean he is keeping me as a sacrifice? Isn't that what you have to do to gain that sort of power?

"Why do you really need me?" I ask quietly.

Raum steps forward, draping his long arm across my shoulders as we start walking again. His fingers play across my shoulder then move down until they reach the back of my neck. "What does any demon want with a human? Be content that I find pleasure in keeping your company."

There is no comfort in his words. I appreciate that he was candid in telling me about his power, but he is lying. I know he is. There are a few fine details he is intentionally keeping from me. I wish our bond worked both ways. I wish I could influence him to tell me the truth.

We walk for a little over three hours, if I had to guess, passing through a town called Meridian. It's dry here—barren. There are big holes in the ground where lakes might have been, but the only water is collected in a small pool at the very bottom. We look around until we find two discarded water bottles. Raum climbs below while I play scout.

The sky is hazy with the smoke from the compound. It follows us like a dark cloud, spreading farther than any normal blaze would allow. Maybe the fire spread to the forest. It'd be a good thing if it burned the orchards. Then again, they survived stranger elements before.

I convince Raum to let us rest inside a cottage on the other side of the town. He might not want to admit it, but we need the rest. I'm exhausted. The last thing I want is for him to carry me, although we'd probably cover more ground that way.

"You need to rest. Let your... food digest." The words stick in my mouth. "Just for a few hours, then we can start again." I touch his arm affectionately to try and reassure him. With a heavy sigh, he succumbs and follows me over the threshold. Old blood stains the floorboards. Nail marks scratch across the floor. Whoever used to live here went away painfully.

We pull the curtains shut, make sure every entrance is locked and secure. We can't be too careful. Raum tells me we will have to be vigilant. We can't risk any demons or humans finding us.

I should never have stayed with those people. I could have left in the middle of the night and no one would have been the wiser. I continue to hound myself over every "what if" as I strip a bed and shake the sheets free from dust. There is no running water here, so we will have to sleep in the grime.

Raum stretches across my lap. He hooks one hand beneath my thigh. I sit up in a nest of pillows I've made myself, leaning against the headboard. As soon as he is settled, he lets out a sigh of relief. I frown. This is wrong. Even as I think it, I run my fingers through his hair, combing back every dark tendril. I touch along the extension of his feathers.

The quiet hum of his song vibrates through his chest into my legs. Tears well in my eyes. It's such a beautiful song, but it's full of hatred I never noticed before. Death. I can feel it now. Still, I run my fingers along his feathers, delicately stroking each one.

It doesn't take him long to fall asleep. I continue to run my nails along his scalp, staring straight at the wall. I replay their deaths. The only one I can't recall is Liam's. I know he is dead, though I can't understand why. Why does Raum keep it from me? It bothers me, yet I feel nothing for Liam and whatever it is we lost.

I go over each life until I come to the meaning of our journey to Babel. Raum intends to become a god. When I think of God, I think of the Christian God. When I think of those lesser, I think of the half-animal, half-human beings in Egypt or perhaps even Greek myth who ruled over the elements, emotions, and war. What balance does Raum offer if he reigns? I can only envision catastrophe.

There are so few humans left. Then again, for all I know there could be hundreds, possibly thousands in hiding, though it seems unlikely. If there are more bees or signs to protect us from the demons and their power, surely Raum will eradicate them. I never thought our world could be worse off than it is.

I know whatever Raum has planned will not be for the better of humanity. What is going to happen? I must stop him, but I have no idea how. He'll suspect if I try to kill him long before I have the chance to execute anything. I run my hand through my hair.

Raum sleeps until my legs lose feeling. I ease out from under him. I can't stay here, but neither can I run. I search the house until I find a piece of paper, yellow with age. It takes a bit longer to find a pen, but when I do, I use it to write a note. I tell Raum I'm going to find supplies for myself but that I'll return. It's risky business, but a tale he will hopefully believe. Now that I'm aware of his influence, he will be right to assume I will return to him, whether I want to or not.

I slip a butcher knife from the kitchen into my belt. I still have the kukuri, but it's better to be over prepared. I wait a few minutes longer than I'd like, but I want to make sure Raum is truly wrapped up in a world of dreams. After waiting nearly thirty of said minutes to tick by, I leave.

There must be a store somewhere nearby. Meridian isn't as big as Boise, so I wander through pretty quickly. I find a couple more water bottles, some twine, and a new bag to put everything in. I'm still pissed Raum discarded my belongings so carelessly. He is cunning enough, but the act was no more than childish. At least he kept one of my blades.

It's nearly dark by the time I head back to the cottage. There are no traces of Raum's presence or his influence, so I can only assume he is still asleep. I'm about a thirty-minute walk out, so there's more than

enough time to get back to him before he notices anything. Hopefully.

There is one house on this block I haven't checked.
It's one of the few that still flies an American flag. I bite
my lip. It won't hurt to make one last stop. I ease
through the cracked door and listen. The hardwood
floors are covered in dust. When I can find no tracks or
evidence of anyone else, I walk in, heading straight for
the kitchen.

There are two cans of beans and a loaf of molded
bread. I take the beans and scour the house for anything
that might make a useful weapon. I'm digging through
a dresser drawer when I hear it.

A trickle of a sound comes from outside. I stiffen,
pressing myself against the closest wall. I can't hear
anything now, but there was definitely something. I
move to the front of the house, stepping quietly while
desperately hoping none of the floorboards creak. I
peek out the curtain in the living room. I cover my
mouth before a sob can escape me.

Walking, nearly stumbling down the road, are Sebastian, Devon, and Anna. How are they alive? Their
skin and clothes are black with soot. Devon practically
carries Anna. Her feet slip and slide down the dusted
path. Sebastian walks ahead of them, his gun stuck out,
ready for anything. His forearm has been burned.

I wait until they are nearly out of sight before
creeping out of the house. Please, don't let Raum wake
up. I don't want him to hear them before I've had a
chance to say my peace.

I follow them for a good ten minutes before making myself known. I purposefully scuff my foot, sending a trail of pebbles rolling their way.

Sebastian is the first to turn around. His finger flinches over the trigger. He is going to shoot me before I even have a chance to speak! I fall to my knees. I press one of my fingers to my lips before raising both hands to the sky.

The women turn around quickly. Devon looks between us, her eyes wide. She protectively wraps her arm around Anna. I lick my lips.

"Raum doesn't know I'm here." I hope that he doesn't. "I wanted to say that I'm sorry. I tried to warn you." I make it a point to look at Sebastian directly when I say the last part. He won't meet my eyes. His mouth twists. I feel sorry for digging the knife deeper. It's obvious he has been blaming himself.

"Sorry?" Devon chokes. "That's all you can say? That was a massacre—"

"Let her finish," Sebastian says quietly.

They look at me with red-rimmed eyes, swollen from the smoke. I need them to listen to me. For one second, I need them to not hate me.

I nod. "Raum is leading us to Babel. He has every intention to cut through the desert until we reach the coast. I can't stop him. I've convinced him to release his control over me, but I don't know how long it will last. If I try anything, he'll flip the switch." I look at them pleadingly. "He doesn't know you're alive."

"There was another exit," Sebastian says. "One we never told you about."

"I'm glad," I say.

Sebastian looks at the women. Anna slumps over. Devon carefully helps her to the ground. Her face is glistening with sweat. Her tan skin is ashen, bloodless. I feel guilty for ever thinking she was weak. She's tougher than bullets. I know Anthony got a few rounds in her. Looking at her now, maybe she hadn't been entirely faking when I rolled her over.

"Sebastian," I start, but he cuts me off.

"How do we know Raum isn't coming now to finish us off?" He looks past me, scouting the homes and broken roadways.

"Because *you* know," I say. A black bandanna is tied snugly around his neck. It stands out because he's never worn anything like it. The only thing he would have to hide is Eblis' bite which should have faded away by now. It was a burn. "It's not gone, is it?"

Sebastian tightens his hold on the barrel as his eyes drift back to me. The slight shake of his head tells me not to press it. I'm right. And by the look on his face, no one else knows.

"Is what gone?" Devon asks. She looks between us.

For the time being, I ignore her. Sebastian was and has always been their leader. He is the one I need to convince. "I think you know that I'm telling the truth. Liam could, you know? He knew I was marked before I did," I say to him.

"What are you talking about?" Sebastian's brows pull together to form one dark line. The corner of his jaw ticks as he clenches his jaw.

I glance at Devon and her trigger finger. She could very well turn on both of us once she knows the truth, but I can't afford anymore lies. None of us can. Devon stands, letting Anna lean against the side of her leg.

"Liam was bitten once, but he killed the demon before the mark was complete. He had a brand on his arm to hide it," I say.

"What does Liam have to do with this?" Devon asks. She too scopes the area for any signs of Raum. I need her to believe this isn't a trap.

"He wasn't right in the head. You saw the way he treated me, you all did, and yet we were drawn to each other. It didn't make sense. I didn't understand it at the time because I didn't know I was marked. Liam knew things about me because we both had venom in our blood." Did they ever notice Liam was different than the rest of them? They must have. You'd have to be blind to miss it. How long would it be before Sebastian started to go mad?

Devon's nostrils flare, her eyes widen. "You're marked?" she hisses.

"No," we both answer.

"Not in the way you think. He's not bound," I say. Stay with me, Devon. Her finger slides closer to the trigger. "One of the demons we killed attacked him. The binding wasn't complete."

Sebastian pulls down the bandanna. The burnt flesh from Eblis' bite has healed, leaving a black half-moon mark imbedded in his skin. The crescent shape is much larger than the one that scarred Liam's arm.

"Are you fucking kidding me?" Devon screeches.

I press my finger over my lips. "Please, don't. Raum will hear you."

"Fuck Raum," she whispers. "Fuck you all."

"Liam was with us for months and nothing happened," Sebastian says, smoothing the fabric across his neck back in place.

"Liam was a psychopath and you know it. You were as afraid of him as the rest of us and that's why you never did anything about him." Devon glances down as Anna sits up.

Anna's eyes widen. In her anguish, she looks just as frightened as Devon does. This is my fault as much as everything else that has happened to them. If Sebastian hadn't gone out with me, he wouldn't have gotten hurt.

"You know me, Devon, Anna. This is just another curse I've managed to survive," Sebastian says.

"Listen to me, please. I don't know how much time we have." I do my best to interrupt their argument without raising my voice. Their paranoia feeds into mine, though, and even I start looking around to see if Raum will slink from the shadows.

"Leah is right. I don't get the sense she is lying to us," Sebastian says eventually.

Devon curses under her breath.

"Sabby?" Anna slurs. He ignores her, fixing his dark brown eyes on me.

Devon lets out a deep breath. She opens her mouth, closes it, and then opens it again. "I don't really have a choice, do I? You're half marked, whatever the hell that is, and you—you *are* bound." She thrusts her gun out to me. "What do you want, Leah? We're as good as dead anyway."

I force a stiff smile. "I want you to follow us. Carefully. The smoke is trailing us so it shouldn't be too hard to hide your scent." I give them a collective once-over before directing my attention back to Sebastian. "I'll do what I can to keep him distracted. At first chance of a clear shot, take it."

Devon helps Anna to her feet. The smaller woman grunts and leans against the blonde like when I first found them. I can see indecision weighing on Devon. I'm also not blind to the fact that she and Anna are probably mulling over killing me right now. Devon is probably trying to decide if she should kill Sebastian while she's at it. I don't think Anna has the guts to do it.

"If Raum makes it to Babel, he intends to become a god," I add for good measure.

"I'm sure half of the demons have the same plan," Sebastian says.

"They don't. They're in hiding like you said. When we came across the others, they were surprised by Raum. None of them want to make the journey. It's too risky," I say.

"Do you think he'll actually do it?" Devon whispers, half to us, half to herself.

"Do you?" I look at her pointedly. I know Raum will do whatever it takes to get there. Any demon who feels entitled to sit on a throne is bad news. But Raum? Bye, bye humanity. "I know you don't trust me, you have no reason to, but I'm begging for your help to kill him. Please."

Sebastian keeps his gun trained on me as he approaches. "You'll die."

"I know." I nod. "I would die a thousand times if it brought back your family." I don't know where it comes from. The words are out before I can stop them. It feels like I'm about to cry. I can't cry. I don't want them to think I'm manipulating them.

Sebastian holds out his hand to me. I look at it nervously. I've never deserved these people. I take his hand and he pulls me to my feet. "You are our family, Leah," he says hoarsely.

Devon runs her tongue across her teeth behind closed lips, but even she nods. There are not many of us left, she must know that. This is also an opportunity to get revenge on what I've done, as well as Raum, and potentially stop it from happening to anyone else.

I close my eyes to fight back tears. "Promise me you'll do it."

"I promise," Sebastian says. He smiles at me grimly, his mouth pulling into a tight line.

"One of us will," Devon snaps.

I nod. "Good." I take a few steps back. I need to get back to Raum before he wakes up. "Be careful. If you get ahead of us, he'll smell you." I turn to leave. The sound of a gun shifting makes me stiffen.

"Leah," Devon says quietly. I look back at her and how she has graciously lowered her weapon. She looks around as her voice carries on the wind, tensing. "We know it was Raum."

We know it wasn't you is what she means. No matter how true her words might be, it will never be enough to wash the blood away. It will never be enough for them to forgive me.

XXIII

I stand over Raum, watching him sleep. The way his back expands and recedes with each breath is almost therapeutic. He doesn't wake up until I crawl back into bed. He wraps his arm around my waist and pulls me against him by grabbing my opposite hip. I turn my face away when he nuzzles my neck. The bottom of my shirt slides up, embracing my stomach with cool air.

That's all he does. He touches me softly, caresses me. I don't know if he takes over, or if some sick part of me enjoys it, but I touch him back. I turn on my side and run my hands down his arms, over the curves of his muscles. My hand snakes back up to his face, through his hair, and I lean forward. He pushes me back and kisses me so hard our teeth gnash together.

Electric fire courses through my veins. I yank the back of his shirt up, my nails catching skin and pulling it apart. Raum arches away from me so I can relieve him of the cloth and swoops back as soon as he is free to kiss me. My lips, neck, shoulders, arms—his lips devour every bit of my skin.

"I feared I would never touch you again," he murmurs. "Never taste how sweet your skin is."

I lean my head back and arch into him. Sharp lines trail across my skin as his teeth lengthen and graze my flesh. A shudder runs through me, one I cannot restrain even if I wanted to.

I lean up, meeting him as his face comes to mine.

I look at him, really look at him. I'd like to imagine Raum was not always so evil. That maybe something drove him to be the way he is. There is no redemption for him, though. Not when his hot lips fall on my stomach as he pushes my shirt up. Nothing pure can feel so sinful.

I blame it on his power over me, but I know it's not true. I'm too *aware*. Raum doesn't deserve my kindness, he doesn't deserve me, yet I find myself giving into him. Not because I want it, or even that he wants it. But because he needs it. Maybe I need it a little bit myself. Sometime soon, we are going to die.

For the first time, Raum doesn't hurt me. His grip hardens, but he doesn't bruise me. His control only wavers before he enters me. He stops himself, pressing the side of his face against my leg he draped over his shoulder.

"I want to bite you," he says.

I smirk. "What's stopping you?"

"Will you let me?" He kisses my knee, looking at me from the corner of his eye.

I don't think. "Yes," I whisper.

He lowers my leg and leans forward. I wrap my legs around his waist as his mouth touches my neck. Lush fulfillment runs through me when he pierces me. From my neck all the way between my thighs, it feels like I'm on fire. I hold his head to me as he pushes inside of me. He takes a single swallow of my blood. His lips are bright red when he kisses me again and I, so wrapped up in him, stick my tongue out so I can taste it.

We sleep for a few more hours. I do, at least. I sit up and stretch only to find Raum sitting at the end of the bed watching me.

"What is it?" I pull the sheets up to my chest and nervously look around the room. If there was danger, he wouldn't look so forlorn.

He cocks his head to the side and smirks. "Nothing, Leah. Go back to sleep."

The hike we make is long and scorching. Two days go by and I wonder if Sebastian and the others have gone their own way. Maybe they are on a different path. If they are sticking with the plan, they are somewhere behind us. Raum is fast, though, and I worry they might have fallen behind. Anna is only going to slow them down. I didn't know her very well, but I hope she makes it.

The terrain swiftly changes. The ground becomes more clay red than the muddy brown. Raum carries the bag I found with a few water bottles we were able to collect. I drink sparingly. What we don't have is food. I stop short and stare out at what is quickly turning into a desert. Broken rocks and boulders line the ground. The mountains look like hills. The plants grow scarce. Even for this part of the desert, it's more barren than I anticipated.

"We should slow down," I say.

Raum looks down at me. "We need to speed up."

"How long do you think I can go without eating?" I wave my hand at the sky. "We can't keep walking under the sun. We should cut back through the mountains.

There is likely to be more resources there. There's nothing out here."

"There is *no one* here," he clarifies. I'm leaning forward when he looks me over. I stand up straight. I don't want to appear weak, but you'd have to be blind not to see I'm quickly fading. "If it comes down to it, you can eat from me. I'll heal quickly," he says.

I look at him in horror. "You mean eat *you*?" Saying it makes me want to throw up.

Raum shrugs. "Desperate times call for desperate measures."

"I'll starve first," I say, climbing over a rock. Raum chuckles. He looks back at me to flash his wide row of white teeth. "You're disgusting."

"I will sustain you as long as I can, but in the end, you have to eat. You will do what you must." He says it seriously, but there is still a hint of a smile on his face.

By nightfall, Raum is carrying me. Even under the moonlight and the cold air soothing my sunburn, I'm exhausted. I'm dehydrated and ravenous. Raum switches between slinging me over his shoulder and draping me in his arms. My jacket covers my face and upper body to prevent further blisters.

My head is on fire. I clench his back and heave. The pain is worse when there is nothing to vomit. I shudder, chills spreading across my skin at high noon.

Raum sets me down. I tug the jacket across my eyes and peer out from under the cover. I can barely make out his movements between all the colors that blur my vision. Bright iridescent dots spot over everything, making my head scream. There's a bright orange glow. I think he is making a fire, but I can't tell. I groan and roll onto my stomach.

"Raum," I moan. "Please."

I feel his presence over me, towering and dark as always.

"Take this from me. Please."

He rolls me over, tugging the jacket from my face. "If I do this, you will be influenced by everything I feel and do."

"You made me kill the only people I cared about," I slur. "Just do it."

Raum's lips press together. I think they do. Everything is blurring together. When will this fucking heat stop? I grab the side of my head and moan. I'm going to die in this bloody desert.

It feels like someone runs their fingers through my hair, threads them all the way to my neck, shoulders, over my breasts and down the rest of my body. Sweet relief. *Power.* I open my eyes and can see more clearly. The sun is harsh, but it doesn't burn like before. In fact, I welcome the heat.

I duck my head under his arm as he assists me in sitting up. I smirk. The flames of his fire are high, they demand attention. It's bold to be burning out in the open like this. But he is right. No one is around to see.

I know I was in pain moments ago, but I don't really remember it. It's a distant memory, a fog. Speaking of fog, gray smoke clouds still cling to the sky. They haven't stopped following us. How far is this damn fire going to chase us?

Raum pulls out a knife. My blade, Leyak's tracker knife to be exact. I look over his person but can't see where he has pulled it from. I never considered demons had the ability to wear glamour.

"Where are they?" I'm asking about my knives. It took a long time for me to collect them, all beautiful.

"This, the one at your hip and the karambit are the only ones that I kept. The others were useless." He nods towards me. "Close your eyes."

I look over his body again but can't find the other blade he mentioned. Instead, I let my gaze drift back to the tracker knife.

"What's that for?"

Raum slides the sharp end of the blade over his arm. He runs it along again, and again, until he has six strips of flesh and muscle in his palm. Something in the back of my mind shakes me, but I can't look away. I stare on in fascination. He holds his hand out over the flames to sear the meat, turning them between his fingers until they are good and roasted.

There is nothing better than the smell of cooked meat. My mouth waters, drenching the cotton on my tongue. I lean over as soon as he extends the first piece and bring it to my lips. It's salty. I take a bite and, much to my relief and disgust, it tastes good.

Raum smirks, the line spreading into a full-on grin until he is laughing at me. I slide my foot out, trying to scuff dust his way. "Stop laughing. I'm hungry."

"Mm, says the woman who *wanted* to starve before having a taste of me." He looks at me wickedly. In his ebon eyes, I can see all the terrible things he wants to do to me. I like it.

"Now, here we are," I say. I make a show of it, sticking my tongue out and putting the meat on my tongue. Something about it strikes a nerve in Raum and a flick of desire hits me.

By the time I'm done eating, Raum's arm has started to heal. "That must be nice," I say, motioning to him.

"Through me, you have the same power. You should have seen your back after Mara bit you." He says it lightly, but there's a trace of something in his voice I can't place.

"Oh yeah?" I lean against him, turning my head on his shoulder. He's so solid, full of hard, defined muscle. Dangerous, I remind myself, but the thought is fleeting. I have no reason to fear Raum. Not anymore.

"From your shoulder to your third rib down, he ripped you open." He looks down and smirks. "I could see everything."

I scrunch my nose and I lean away. "How can you make something so horrific so dirty? I still have night-mares about that night."

Raum shrugs. "I wish I could have done it myself."

I pause, considering his words. I have a vague memory of him looming over me with flesh between his teeth. "You did, though, didn't you?" The image becomes no clearer the more I reflect on it. "After you marked me, so I wouldn't notice."

A dark look falls across his countenance. "Yes," he says.

I lean farther as he moves to nuzzle the side of my neck. Is he going to take a bite out of me now? He chuckles and nips the lobe of my ear through my hair. I glance up at him nervously as he pulls away once more. I suppose Raum has decided to use his influence whenever it suits him. I wish I could tell the difference, when he is in control and when my actions are my own. This must be what it is to go crazy.

Raum laughs again, rich music that sings to me. "Come. We need to get going."

I touch his arm. "Will you tell me what else happened that night?"

The upturned line in Raum's mouth falters. "No," he says. "It cost me enough to take it from you. Do not ask me about it again."

We leave the fire unattended; it doesn't matter. The flames behind us will catch up and burn what is left of the sand and brittle grass.

The sun still burns my skin, but it no longer scorches me. I wear my jacket as a hood anyway. It's a habit and I'd rather be safe than sorry. Something in the back of my mind tells me to slow our pace, but Raum keeps us on a fast track. I can't help but feel we are running away from something.

Whenever I ask him to slow down, he quickens. He tells me there is not much time left. Time for what? The thought of what will become of me once we reach Babel sneaks into my mind. I mull over the possibilities, but the only outcome I can truly see is my death. Either Raum will sacrifice me or he will be rid of me by some other means. I think it's the first. He constantly talks about my purpose all the while keeping the details from me.

Who does he plan to present me to? I wish I had been braver when I was with Leyak. It was through him that I first learned about Babel. I don't know if it's a city or a great land, only that you can speak to whichever higher power is in charge. Leyak claimed his orders came directly from Babel, though he never said who decreed the laws he imposed. If I had been braver, I might have eavesdropped when he was discussing the matter with other demons behind closed doors. Instead, I hid from him, knowing full well he would always find me. I could have learned more.

I ask Raum once more what will happen to me when we get there. He answers me before I finish, like he knows what I've been thinking, and tells me it's a surprise. There is no hint of sympathy in his eyes as he says it.

"Why do you still lie to me?" I ask.

Raum is not clumsy, so when he falters, I notice. He scans the horizon before turning on his heels to walk backward. Miles ahead of us are red rolling hills; a canyon maybe, it's hard to tell. Before that, there is nothing but flat ground. I glance over his shoulder toward the mounds, hoping there will be some shelter or water.

Raum says nothing, just looks at me.

"I don't know what is real anymore. You have complete control over me yet you still keep things from me. Why?" I lengthen my stride until we are inches apart, forcing him to stop.

The dark look in his eyes I've come to know so well shifts. I've always known Raum was wicked, but never before have I seen such a sinister glow reflect in his eyes. A slow smile touches the right side of his mouth, flashing his teeth that remind me he is not some lap dog. Raum is a keen wolf biding his time. "I fear, Leah, that you are stronger than you appear."

I swallow. "Your mark has weakened me."

Raum hisses, his tongue making a sucking sound against the back of his teeth. "Perhaps, but your heart is still heavily guarded."

As elusive as always, he says nothing more about it and turns back on his heel, leaving me trailing behind him with more questions. Every word exchanged with Raum leaves me wanting more. It's a never-ending cycle.

The sun is low to the ground when we reach the tall crags of the desert. The terrain is harder on me. I require too much of Raum's assistance to crawl over boulders and jagged stones, so we stop as the sky turns lilac. It will do neither of us any good to continue once it's dark. It's too dangerous. I suppose Raum could manage it on his own, but he has me to look after. With his power, I'm more durable, but it does not make me invincible.

Black clouds move in from the west, rumbling thunder in its wake. We stand and watch as the storm draws closer. The dark shadow of rain slants to the side, heading right for us. A spike of fear shoots through me.

Raum chuckles and takes my hand, leading me through the labyrinth of the canyon. "Are you afraid of a little storm?"

"I'm afraid of getting struck by lightning," I confess. What if it rains enough to flood? I don't want to be stuck at the bottom of the canyon and find out.

Raum clicks his tongue at me. "We will be safe here."

We make shelter beneath an overhang that covers shriveled succulents. As soon as we press ourselves against the wall, the rain falls. It starts out in little droplets and then, in a matter of seconds, it pours. There will be no fire tonight.

I don't know how long it rains. I fall asleep only to wake and find that the storm still hounds angrily over-head. My clothes are damp from the wind blowing through our shelter. Raum presses me against the canyon wall, my back to his chest, to block what he can of the storm. His heat keeps the chill out of my bones.

It's rare that Raum touches me affectionately, so when his fingers trail down my arms I jump. It's a small start, but one that makes him pause. When I don't move, he picks up again, tracing the curve of my shoul-der down to the indention of my elbow. I stretch out my fingers as his creep closer. His nails graze the inside of my palm.

Being with Raum is like walking through a field of landmines. I never know when he will go off. I stay still, letting him explore the top of my skin. It's as if he is experiencing me for the first time. This is how it should have been between us. If he was not what he is, maybe it could have been.

The soft vibrations of his song hum through his chest, reverberating against my back. I close my eyes. The melodic music has always comforted me. It has been a haven in the darkness he shrouds me with. A creeping feeling wraps around my neck when I realize it's a different tune than before. It's hollow, devoid of the affection he shows me.

XXIV

I have no idea what time of day it is when we start out again. The sky is still dark from resistant rain clouds and smoke. I wonder if the humans managed to catch up with us, or if they were also forced to take shelter. If they had abandoned their quest altogether, I wouldn't put it past them. They have suffered enough and what I asked is too high a price to pay. Again, I think of Anna. They can't have been making the journey with her, but neither do I believe Sebastian or Devon would abandon her.

Another day passes. It seems that even Raum's powers have their limits. The sun's touch becomes a discomfort and he has slowed down, pausing every few miles to rest in what little shade we can find. We can't continue this madness.

"We will have to divert our path," I say, the voice of reason.

"No," he says. "Changing our path will not change anything." Raum stops suddenly. His head snaps to the side so quickly I hear the vertebrae pop. He sniffs.

"What is it?" I flank his right side and listen. We are still surrounded by deep red walls. The breeze that passes overhead is warm, but whatever it carries is indiscernible to me.

"There is water. It is still many miles away, but closer than it should be," he says.

"An old river, perhaps?" I offer. Maybe the rain caused a flood farther up.

Raum shakes his head. "No, there is salt in the air." His tongue rests on his lower lip.

"We're too far away for it to be the ocean," I say, considering. "It must be something else."

"If it is the ocean…" He doesn't finish. Raum's eyes dart back and forth.

Raum is much more careful, his head constantly turning one way and then another as he listens. I stick to his side until I have to use the bathroom. As usual, he grumbles about it but waves his hand towards me. He lets me backtrack until I'm well out of sight to relieve myself.

I button my pants once I'm done and walk a couple paces before leaning back against the stone wall. It seems so long ago that I was living in a cave in Montana. It had been a beautiful sanctuary. I press my wrist to the back of my forehead and sigh. There is no use dwelling on the past. There is nothing I could have done differently to prevent what has happened.

A dark flutter catches my attention. I look under the crest of my hand. My heartbeat quickens. Tucked at the base of a Joshua tree is Sebastian's bandanna. How long has it been there? More importantly, how did Raum and I miss it the first time we passed? If he can smell salt water, he can certainly pick up a human's scent.

A sick feeling coils in my stomach. They wouldn't have expected us to backtrack, which means they're ahead of us somewhere. How did they manage it? They must have pressed forward through the storm. Raum and I lost a day or two when we sought shelter. My heart slams into my chest. What if it's the humans Raum smells and not the ocean? It must be. It's why he is being so cautious.

I stuff the bandanna in my back pocket and head back. Whatever happens, I want a piece of them with me. I pray to whoever is listening that all of this will be over soon.

Raum paces like a caged animal. The hard lines of his arms soften when he lays his eyes on me. I want to tell him what I've done. The need is so strong that my lips part. His eyes trail down to my empty hands and I wonder if he can smell Sebastian on me. I shouldn't have touched it, let alone carried the piece of cloth back with me.

He knows. I should have placed the look in his eye the night at the cottage. Raum knew as soon as I returned. He knows it now. The slightest tilt of his chin sends chills down my spine and his nostrils flare as he sniffs.

I brace myself for the impact. Instead, Raum nods and turns on his heel, leading us closer to what is surely our demise. I'm too afraid to say anything, so I follow in his shadow, mulling over the possibilities of what he is going to do to me.

After another hour, Raum decides it would be best if we were back on stable ground. He lopes up a steep incline of the canyon effortlessly, his long legs carrying him with ease. I call it an incline, but it's much more like a ledge that juts out from the wall at an awkward angle. I'm not as graceful as I try to keep up. I end up straining to heave myself over the edge. Raum made it in four bounds. I'm on my belly, kicking myself forward. We are several feet from the bottom.

"Not much farther and we will be at the top," he says. He looks down at me.

The energy I've had the last few days suddenly vanishes. I dig my nails into the top of the ledge and kick wildly. The sun is so hot it feels like a thousand blisters spread across my face.

Raum cocks his head to the side. Is he doing this? After watching me for several more seconds, he finally bends down and offers me his hand. We clasp one another's wrist and with my other hand I press off the top of the ledge. His fingers dig into my skin and he shoves me back.

I scream.

"Raum!" I latch onto him with my free hand as I dangle mercilessly over the bottom. "What are you doing?"

His grip tightens.

I cry out as the bones in my wrist splinter. He is breaking my hand. God help me, but he is really going to do it. I reach up, digging my nails into his arm. If he sends me over, I'll take him with me. As steady as an anchor, he doesn't move as I try to climb him.

"You're hurting me," I say. I look up. "Raum," I whisper.

There is fire in his eyes as he squeezes tighter.

I feel every bone shatter in my hand; every fragment pierces the underside of my skin. I cry out. My voice dips and Raum squeezes again, sending another scream tearing from my throat into the air. I let go of him in a desperate attempt to get away from the pain.

Raum yanks me forward, pulling the bones in my hand apart and my arm nearly out of the socket. I fly past his feet and slam into the ground. A bestial sound fills the air. It's only when I catch my breath that I realize it's coming from me. I grit my teeth and stifle another agonizing yell.

I cradle my broken hand to my chest. "Why?" I cry.

Raum's eyes are narrow as blades. "I am no fool, Leah. I hoped you were no longer the stupid child you were when I found you. Be thankful that I did not toss you over the edge."

I roll to my side, pressing my forehead into the dusty ground. "Please fix it," I sob. Two of my fingers stick up like tree branches. I shut my eyes, but it doesn't change anything. The pain is overwhelming and, when I open them, my fingers are still broken. My whole hand has been destroyed.

Raum reaches behind me, snapping Sebastian's bandanna free from my pocket. He binds my hand cruelly despite my protests, knotting it at the top. "Your hand will remain as such until I forgive you," he hisses.

"I'm—sorry," I say through broken sobs. I can't describe the pain in my hand, only that it's one of the worst feelings Raum has ever inflicted on me. The physical pain is near unbearable, but then comes the fact he has shattered my dominant hand. What am I going to do?

"Get up," he barks.

I crawl to my knees, shaking. He could have let me fall; it would have been so easy. I glance towards the edge he had been holding me seconds ago. A low growl rips from his throat and snaps my attention to him. I stumble to my feet, shying away from him when he makes a move toward me.

"You knew the consequences," he says.

Through the pain and tears, I find the strength to curse him. It's the only spark of fight I have left. As soon as the words leave my tongue, the orange glow is snuffed out.

Raum laughs darkly. "You never fail to surprise me. I wonder how many lessons I will have to teach you before you finally learn."

We travel two more days, only stopping to rest on the second night. I imagine Raum wants to put as much distance between us and the humans as possible. I don't blame him. I'm foolish to think my plan could have worked. I'm destined to be at his side until he tires of me. God help me, but I'm already growing used to the pain in my hand.

Raum sets me on my own to collect various debris for us to burn. It's hard to carry things one handed. I stuff most of the twigs and brush into the crook of my arm. Raum starts a fire with a brush of his fingertips once I return.

Before I can sit down, he motions to me. "Come here," he says. He turns his hand out to me, sending chills down my spine. What more will he do to me?

I shake my head.

Raum growls.

I take the place at his side and give him my bad hand tentatively. "I'm sorry," I say.

Raum hums. He lifts my hand up for inspection, untying the knot none too gently. "I had to do it," he says. "I have been too lenient with you." He hovers over my twisted fingers and I whimper.

"Raum—"

"Shh."

My hand is swollen five times its normal size and black with bruising that climbs well past my wrist. There are distinct marks from his fingers. The same fingers that did this grip one of my bent fingers. Without so much as a warning, he snaps it back in place. Halfway through the scream rising in my throat, he resets the second one. I bite my lips so hard that I taste blood.

A stifled moan escapes me as I lean forward. I press my forehead against his chest, shaking.

Raum reties the bandanna. He runs his palms over both sides of my hand. "I am kind, am I not?"

I look up at Raum through tear-filled eyes. Already, the pain has stared to subside.

I no longer know the difference between kindness and cruelty. It's funny how one has become a stranger and the other a dear friend. I touch my broken hand to Raum's cheek. He smiles and turns his head to kiss it.

Our path grows more treacherous the farther we journey into the desert that I would require assistance to climb even if my hand wasn't broken. At least we are out of the canyon. I did not like the way I felt trapped down there. There is no danger of potentially falling to my death from where we're at now.

The sun is in the eastern part of the sky. I chew on a piece of jerky that Raum passed back to me not too long ago. I'm no longer bothered by the thought of eating from him. The idea is still revolting, but I find myself eager to eat whenever he feeds me. I can't let myself wither away. Already, despite Raum's best efforts,

I have lost weight. My face has thinned and my ribs stand out when I stretch, much more than when they were surrounded by a healthy amount of fat and muscle.

"What do you do for fun?" I ask. It's funny how I went three years in near silence and now I can't bear it.

Raum's brow shoots up when he looks back at me.

I wave my hand. The swelling has gone down, the pain a dull ache. "When you're not taking over the world."

His mouth thins as he tries to suppress a smile. "Before endearing you, I was a ruler."

Of course, he was. No wonder he is so adamant to get to Babel. I shift the makeshift hood of my jacket over my face so I can get a better look at him. He was a tyrant, no doubt.

"A *kind* ruler?" I ask mockingly.

Raum chuckles. "A fair one."

Raum eases down over a rock. He turns to me, extending his hand to help me down. When I extend my good hand, he shakes his head. I give him the other warily. Raum runs his palms on either side of it before pulling the bandanna free. My hand is smooth and unblemished. I wiggle my fingers slowly. It's completely healed. A strained smile pulls the corner of my mouth up.

Perhaps we are far enough from the humans that my punishment no longer matters.

"I didn't think you would ever forgive me," I say.

"Do you think so little of me?" he asks. "I have always been generous when it comes to you."

His rough palms slide along the underside of my forearms and hook behind my elbows. The color of his skin has darkened under the sun, appearing more bronze than gold. His shining black hair, more blue than before. He is undeniably beautiful.

I've heard demons are the angels that were cast out of Heaven. If it's true, how tragic it is that something so beautiful fell. I take his face in my hands, tracing the line of his jaw and his cheekbones. My once-broken hand cups the edge of his face as he turns into it. I wonder what he would have been like had he been an angel. Would he have been as kind, truly kind, as he is cruel?

I can't say for sure that I know what love really is. I like to imagine it's what it felt like being with James, innocent and beautiful. The purest feeling that only children can express yet, somehow, we managed it. How sweet it had been, loving a man like him. How pure it had been in the way that he loved me in return. I miss him so much.

I know I don't love Raum but, looking into his ebony eyes, I feel like I'm home. What a dark place it is, but it's a home nonetheless. One I have found solace in since he came into my life. It's wrong that I should feel drawn to him, but bond or no I can no longer deny it.

"Perhaps when all of this is over, I will show you my kingdom," Raum says.

I smile softly. "I don't think I would like it," I say.

"You have come to like me," he says.

How sinfully right he is. God or whoever forgive me, if a power higher than the demons exists, but he is right. It's not by fault of my own that I can't tell the truth from the deception he lays over my heart.

Raum leans forward and presses his forehead into my chest. I tangle my fingers in his hair and hold him there. I can feel my heartbeat now that he is touching me. How quickly it thrums for him.

"Leah," he whispers. My name is a prayer, an offering, on his tongue.

I lift my head and look out. A glint of light catches my eye, a silver flash. I tighten my fingers through Raum's hair, drawing him closer to me. They were ahead of us. I lengthen my touch through his hair, down to his feathers. Dying in the arms of my enemy and lover is a good place to be. I deserve no better than this.

I stroke my fingers down to Raum's face and hold fast. His hollow eyes are full of sadness when I look down at him. The burnt glow of his skin darkens. It blackens, stretching out like a low shadow across his face and down his neck. The darkness feathers out, coiling into the wind until his edges fade into smoke tendrils. His mouth widens and stretches into a curved snarl that looks like a beak.

A sound cracks through the air as Raum disappears in a flutter of wings. I reach for the bird that tears up into the sky the same moment a bullet sinks into my chest. The ground rises to meet me too quickly. It rips the air from my lungs as I fall.

"No!" Sebastian roars. The pound of his boots becomes clearer. How long had he waited only to fail?

A raven circles, flying higher and higher, a little black speck in the sky. It's not the only darkness, though. The sky is growing dark too, my vision thinning.

Sebastian skids to his knees beside me. He rips his gun and shirt off next. He tears the front of my shirt, pressing his over the hole in my chest. "Not like this," he says. The pressure only makes the bleeding worse.

He can't stop it. The bullet meant for Raum is in my heart.

I see the blue lakes of Michigan looking down at me as Devon comes to me too; tears splash onto my face. I have missed the waters of my home. They look so pretty streaking dirty trails down her face.

"Leah, please. Stay with us," she pleads.

Behind their desperate attempts, I watch the sky. Honey bees scatter through the air, running away from the smoke and flames that have followed us like a plague. They coil up into a wind that will lead them to be someone else's salvation. There is no music beneath their wings as they flee.

Darkness comes, swift and kindly. It picks me up and sets me down on big black wings.

***

Thanks for reading *After the Bees*.
Enjoy this sneak peek of *Through High Waters*.

Dying is one of the most horrific events I have ever experienced. It's hot, sharp, stifling, and dark. The only thing it isn't is lonely. I should have felt alone when the bullet struck me, but I am the exception to the rule. I'm bonded with a demon and even in death he could not let me go. I could feel Raum with me as he flew away, abandoning me but selfishly holding onto me simply because he could.

To learn more about *Through High Waters* and my other works, check out my website or follow me on social media.
www.authorallisonpaige.com
www.facebook.com/authorallisonpaige

Acknowledgments

There are so many people I am truly blessed by and would like to thank. Sean Locklear and Kaylee Roberts, without your encouragement I never would have put any of my stories to paper. Thanks to you, I have found my voice. Mom and Dad, for always supporting me, even if you don't always approve of the things I write about. Josh Davidson, for helping me break through my writer's block and staying up far too late to help me work through the scenes until they make sense. To my editor Amber Richberger, who has corrected all my errors and has been patient with me despite all my meticulous questions and missed deadlines. And last, but certainly not least, to those who read my work when it was rough and stayed hungry for more.

ABOUT THE AUTHOR

ALLISON PAIGE loves traveling with her camera, particularly in the Irish countryside, and has several ongoing projects that she writes out of her home in Charleston, South Carolina with her corgi. She fills her spare time working with animals of all types and is a fervent advocate of bee, ocean, and wildlife conservation.

Printed in Great Britain
by Amazon

54472506R00157